# THE JACKAL WHO CAME IN FROM THE COLD

# The Jackal Who Came In From The Cold

The Jackal Who Came In From The Cold edited by Darren Pulsford

Published by:
Fox Spirit Books
www.foxspirit.co.uk
adele@foxspirit.co.uk

# Contents

# Introduction

Twenty years ago, yours truly, a young kid from Denmark went to London to hang out with a bunch of people who wore homemade tails and ears, had animal style makeup and talked about things like "scritching". They did this all while making animal sounds at each other, and getting up to all kinds of different artistic endeavours, like painting, costume creation, and storytelling. Quite a few years later, now considerably older but still one of those furries, I have come to know the publishing outfit known as Fox Spirit, who after a while of publishing many different genres had realised that with a name like that, it was practically rude not to at least attempt to put together a collection of stories for the furry community. To make sure that the stories would be sufficiently furry, as a member of the skulk, I was asked to read through the stories submitted to them and comment on what made the story furry or not. It was, frankly, a delight, and I found myself with no envy for those who would have to select the stories which would have to be cut.

"Would you mind," the question came, then, offhandedly one day in an email, "writing an introduction?"

So for a house which until now has not published any furry literature, it seems reasonable to introduce that collection by describing what constitutes furriness in the eyes of one humble author. To set that out up front, I do not think that it is reasonable for me to try defining it much more tightly than an affinity for anthropomorphic animals. That is, animals which have been ascribed human characteristics in some way or another. This might be a community of rats living in our own, human world who have been given sufficient lucidity to create societies. It might be an entirely different world of animals who walk on their hind legs, wear clothes and visit coffee shops with other inexplicably animal-shaped bipeds. Or it might be a world of magic creatures, human shaped or otherwise, all interacting with each other simply as people.

If you ask me, the way that Fox Spirit did me during the production of this anthology, the stories found within these pages are all furry in nature. Some will disagree with me regarding some of them, and you might find it strange to learn that I do not think they are necessarily wrong in that. The foremost idea that you should take from this is that what constitutes furriness is vastly different from person to person. Some will be more strict in their choices than others, and as such, as I was the one to be asked in this instance, I have tried to embrace the concept, and allow there to be stories which even the most strongly opinionated persons would consider furry, even when those persons might disagree with each other.

A number of terms will be used to describe certain particular types of furriness that are encountered in stories. Some are classic terms, such as fable, which suggests that one might describe specific human characteristics by employing a certain animal's stereotypical nature. A fox might be a trickster. A pig might be a politician. A snake might be an evil master of convincing arguments. An eagle might be a person of honour, if perhaps slightly aloof. A hare might be a slightly skittish middle child of a hundred siblings. All exaggerations, even caricatures, but all grounded in some particular trait or another found in human nature, and rightly or not assigned to some species of animal.

Others will be more specific to the furry fandom itself. An example of this would be the term zipperback, which is supposed to describe a story in which the animal nature of the characters in a story is not used for anything other than, effectively, another pronoun. Where the author has simply decided that a character should be some specific bipedal animal, just because they like the idea, rather than trying to ascribe meaning to the choice.

Somewhere between those, you might encounter the concept of funny animals. This is what was originally used to describe the nature of the characters in such stories as Bugs Bunny, where the animal nature is important, but the characters might as well be wearing a costume for all the realism there is to be found in the connection they have with the actual animal they are supposed to represent.

As you might imagine, many such terms will be used in a negative fashion, and I feel it is important to comment as follows where that particular topic is concerned: The answer to "Why is your character x?" must always be allowed to be "Because I like it that way". You might replace animal species with any other particular trait you encounter in a person, perhaps gender, perhaps skin colour, perhaps orientation. There should be no expectation that a character must have a particular reason for being any of those, other than because the author felt like they should be. Conversely, that is not to say that there must be no reason. If the author has a specific reason, then certainly that is just as valid.

Why was Robin a fox in Disney's Robin Hood? Why was the poor family of rabbits rabbits? Why was the king a lion? The choices in that story were practically dripping with symbolism. But why is Donald Duck a duck? Well, I'm sure it makes for some good, funny moments of quacking when his anger management issues show up, but his avian nature has little influence on any of the stories you might find him in, and yet, few people question that Donald is, indeed, a duck.

The stories in the collection before you span the entirety of that scale. They are everything from being, in effect, humans wearing a furry costume, which is what zipperback refers to, all the way to animals which have been given some part of human nature to work with, for example sentience as rendered relative to the character's own viewpoint. All of these stories are, in the perhaps not entirely humble opinion of yours truly, all valid, and all equally entitled to being called furry.

As to the jackal who came in from the cold? Well, no jackals were harmed during the production of this anthology, but some foxes, cats, rats and a fair few other more or less animal natured characters arguably were. Not in our world, but in their own, certainly some were. Some quite severely. The jackal succeeded in their mission. A trip into the wild later, and all the data was collected and returned to Auntie. The case is still open, but it is up to you now. Your mission: To investigate all the cases before you and decide for yourself, who is the spy, and to hopefully enjoy the journey through their worlds of intrigue and espionage.

# A TREACHEROUS THING

## C.A. Yates

The barking girls were vicious, frothing at the mouth behind the thick paint and fabric concoctions plastered over their faces, nightmare jowls stretched as they yapped and growled their malice. Demented acolytes of a false god. Murderers of the innocent. All around Lynx Ruffieux lay the bodies of those she was supposed to have been protecting. Betrayal sprayed across the walls and puddled on the floor in crimson accusation. She tried not to look, holding her ground, her face set in grim determination. The frenzied canine wannabes danced around her, their feet kicking up small storms of blood as they waved their knives and now empty guns over their heads, a conga line of corruption, delighting in the knowledge that their work was having its desired effect, no matter the loaded gun pointed at them. It had all happened so fast, she could barely make sense of it. One minute she and her partner had been shuttling their charges into the safe house, the next the shooting had started and the world had turned to chaos. All because of these masked, bewigged jumping jacks. Suspicion niggled at the base of her skull, something she was overlooking, had overlooked, but she shrugged it off. Lynx jutted her chin at the girls, fighting back incipient nausea, every muscle tensed; she was getting out of here and she was taking whatever casualties had anything resembling a pulse with her. She'd had her rabies jab. It was time to finish this.

'Stand down, or I will shoot you in the face, one by one.' The words came out through gritted teeth; their yapping was beginning to test her patience. Howls of laughter filled the air and the pounding echo from the gunshots that had killed so many people so quickly grew exponentially inside Lynx's head. She wanted to close her eyes and sink to the floor with the corpses – she already knew everyone was dead, knew it with every one of her senses – but sheer bloody-mindedness kept her upright, her trigger finger still and ready.

'Hey Mama, what's up with you?' The blue-faced dog-girl had stopped her dancing and was staring at Lynx, head tilted to one side as though something was confusing her. 'Why so sad?'

Three little words, a throwaway sentence. Nothing to lose your head over...

Lynx lost it. Completely. Later, she would tell herself over and over that she should have remembered her training, her years of experience, berate herself for shrugging her self-control off so easily, for folding when the chips were down, really down, with barely a thought... but with the smell of blood and death in her nose, and that noise, the yapping and yipping that would drive a sane person mad, filled her mind with such red hate – *red as blood* – that it coloured every synapse, every nerve ending. Suddenly she hated dogs. Hated them.

'You'll be last then. You can watch your friends bleed out.' Her voice was low and she wasn't sure if the faux-dog girl had heard her. A twitch started to tug at Lynx's right eye. Blue watched her for a moment, assessing her, that grin still plastered across her face, right from ear to ear. Lynx imagined shooting her right in that stupid mouth.

'Big talk, pussy cat, I'd like to see...' The first shot silenced the leader of the pack, the biggest one, the back of her head blowing out across the face of one of her comrades, the bullet downing them both. The two on either side were blinking blood out of their eyes before they even knew what had happened. A split second, hackles raised, Lynx took out the next one. As her target hit the ground, three of the remaining dog-girls turned tail and ran. That left one. Blue. By no means the biggest, but certainly the smartest. Smarts were relative. She was already turning, going low and reaching toward the ground where Lynx's dead partner's gun lay discarded, still loaded. However clever Blue was, Lynx was smarter. Even in her fugue-like state, she had done her maths, her mind on autopilot. She aimed, wanting it done quickly and the shot rang in her ears before she'd even pulled the trigger.

Before.

No smoke curled from the barrel, her finger hadn't squeezed, her shoulder... her shoulder was somehow numb and hot vicious pain at the same time. It hadn't been her gun that fired. The thought was sluggish at best, but the truth of it was fast-becoming all too evident. Blue stepped towards her and Lynx tried to fire her weapon, but what had been almost numb pain suddenly blossomed into excruciating and she dropped it. The sound of the impact echoed around the suddenly quiet room, making her cringe as though she'd sworn in church. It seemed as though her mistakes were still racking up. Trying to make sense of what had happened, her mind plunged through the molasses of shock that came with being shot unexpectedly. From behind. As if anyone could expect that. Realisation hit her as hard as the bullet and, slowly, every move an agony, she turned to look behind her.

One look was enough. She closed her eyes, scarcely able to believe what they had shown her, even as betrayal pervaded the room like ammonia. The man had the decency to look chagrined, at least. She had made it so easy, so damned easy. You trust once in your life and the rat bastard shoots you in the back. She started to laugh, the sound wrenching at the bullet hole in her shoulder, trying to persuade her to stop, but, if you thought about it for too long, it was just too damned funny. Her, the consummate loner, left to fend for herself in her junkie mother's dirty hovel, recruited by the service because no one could control the troubled orphan she'd been... shot in the back by the man she loved.

As Lynx sank to the floor, the pain radiating through her body even as the blood exited it, she tried to say something. The words bubbled to her lips and she hoped they were offensive enough to cause at least some irritation, before letting the darkness claim her, happy for the oblivion it offered.

Break ups were the worst.

\*\*\*

Barely clinging to the ledge, claws wedged into whatever gaps the rock offered, Lynx was buffeted by the merciless mountain winds that seemed to be trying their hardest to dislodge her from their territory. Any minute they might muster a mighty enough blow to dislodge her, but she clung on doggedly. The irony was not lost.

She reflected, and not for the first time, that her life would be immeasurably better with the addition of a sidekick, maybe even a friend. The thought was quickly anaesthetized, and not for the first time, by the memory of how trusting someone had left her high and dry with a bullet in her back and a black mark on her service record. Connections were a liability, and not just in her line of work. Shaking off the intense bitterness that seemed to have been stalking her since then… Lynx swallowed hard, trying to block the details out, like they hadn't taken up residence in every corner of her mind. There was no escape. She felt the claustrophobia of her thoughts closing in on her, narrowing her thought processes into that most primal of reactions: panic. If she panicked now, she'd be dashed to pieces against its stoic face in moments. Her claws weren't the only things that needed to get a grip.

Bare tacks, she reminded herself, tick the boxes, do the job. Mechanically, she checked the sheer rock face above her. Sheer except for her ledge; a ledge that was slowly crumbling. Once the jeopardy would have been exhilarating, she'd been as hungry for it as she'd been for… god, she'd been an idiot, she'd been so hungry for love it had blinded her, made a fool of her.

'Stop it!'

Things were bad enough as they were, and slipping back there every five minutes was not an option. Right now she needed to not fall from the mountain and end up a faint smear across its rocky roots, barely a memory, so she needed to stop wool-gathering and get her backside up onto and then off said ledge before it crumbled to nothing and her chance was gone.

Taking a deep breath and then another, repeating the simple exercise over and over until her breath became everything and not even the mountain winds could claim her attention, Lynx centred herself, focussed on her desired landing spot, and prepared to leap. Her muscles bunched and released, pushing her straight up into the air, her front claws flexing as they made ready to hook into the rock face above her. It was over in moments, chips of rock falling as she scrambled for purchase briefly with her back feet. Resting her face against the unyielding surface she took a deep breath, feeling for the vulnerability in the rock with her mind as she did so. Lynx could get into anything, anywhere in the world, but that didn't mean it was simple or explicable. Sometimes you just had to go with what worked. Dutch Babs, her handler back at HQ, who she'd muted on their audio link after yet another diatribe about inferior British stroopwafeln, said it was her natural cat-instincts, but that wasn't it. Lynx wanted to get into things; she desired it with every fibre of her being. It was what she was made to do, it was coded right into her DNA, into her soul, and she often wondered if she'd been some sort of wraith in her past life, able to slip through solid...

The rock face in front of her suddenly opened up and Lynx fell forward onto the newly revealed floor. Luckily, she'd stowed her human clothes in her backpack to climb up to the hidden lair and her tail was at liberty to balance her before she could sprawl unceremoniously across the cold rock. So much for having been a wraith.

Scrambling up onto her hind legs, she stretched her body into a more human-like frame and pasted herself against the wall of the passage she had uncovered, edging her way along it carefully. The place was musty as hell, but with only a few metres gained it became obvious something was terribly wrong. Lynx could smell something metallic on the otherwise stale air and there was no mistaking what it was. Blood. Fresh blood. No one was supposed to have been in this network of caves for twenty years or more, at least that's what the suits had insisted on in the briefing. So, what a surprise, here she was on a mission that, despite the tricky logistics, was supposed to be a simple retrieval and instead it was very clear her superiors knew jack, *comme d'habitude*. Technically, she was out on a limb, with only Babs in her ear for back up, so it was a good job she'd known all this before she'd set out. Her lessons had been hard learned. She would not forget them.

Something was very wrong up ahead, even if her sense of smell hadn't been as sharp as it was, she would have known it because she had reached the part of the cave with the bloody handprint smeared across the wall. Remote mountain? Check. Creepy caves? Of course. A blood trail? Standard.

Taking a deep breath, although she could feel in her marrow that she already knew the answer, Lynx tried to place the blood. The scent of human in it was unmistakeable, but the underlying stink of canine was too strong to ignore. For some reason she had still wanted to be wrong, even after all this time and effort. Wasn't that a kicker? Of course it was dog blood. Lynx closed her eyes and the smell intensified in her nostrils. Oh god, it really was, wasn't it. She whimpered against the certainty forcing its way in but, even as she tried to dismiss the memories that leapt straight to mind, she knew it was him.

*Him.*

She hadn't thought about him in... Lynx could barely contain the mirthless laugh that bubbled in her throat. She thought about him constantly. Once she had thought about him like that because she had been more in love than she'd thought it possible to be. More in love than she'd ever thought herself capable. Now, however, he was on her mind night and day because he had become her purpose, her reason for being in none of the ways poets lionised. She had stayed alive and in the service despite misgivings from pretty much everyone involved. She had completed her rehab in record time, stunning the doctors and confounding the shrinks, had said all the right words and nodded in all the right places, doing as she was told while all the time working to find him. Against orders. Her country be damned, this was personal and, although she hadn't been sure she'd been right about the tip off she had kept from her superiors, the thrill of the con-firmation of being on the right track was electric. Her hackles rose along her back, tickling her spine with exhilaration. Her shoulder, where his bullet had pierced her flesh and lodged itself so intimately inside her, ached with the force of the memories that suddenly assailed her.

*'God, Lynx, I need you, need to taste you.' His voice, enough to make her come on its own, rolled across her skin like melting chocolate as he kissed his way down her stomach. She burned with impatient desire, urging him to move faster with the desperate press of her body against his. His low chuckle nearly sent her over the edge.*

*'Impatient, little one?' No one had ever called her "little" anything before him; no one had ever used endearments of any kind for her. It gave her a feeling low in her stomach that had nothing to do with the way he was touching her, well not much, his strong hands pawing gently at her thighs, pushing them open, sliding down between them, that long thick tongue of his ready to…*

Lynx shook herself back to the present. It was exactly that kind of obsessive thinking that had got her shot and left for dead in the first place. Nose turned up high in the air, sniffing at the all too obvious signs that her quarry was within her reach, Lynx knew it was a set up. She had also known this from the moment the information had been handed to her. He had left her a trail of crumbs and she had devoured them, gone straight to him when he'd finally decided it was time, as though he was in control of the situation even now. It surprised her how little that mattered to her. All that mattered was that he was within her grasp and this time it would be him who paid the price. After months of planning – after months of agony and confusion – she was ready.

Padding softly along the passage, she came to a large antechamber filled with archaic machinery and dust. Cobwebs decorated the surfaces merrily, spinning and twisting between the rusting edifices of clunky, long dead technology. The only sign that anyone had been here were the distinctive footprints. Four of them, every time. He obviously wanted her to know it was him. He only ever walked on two legs to when it was necessary to blend in… or to shoot her in the back.

Cautiously, Lynx followed the tracks. It was obvious he knew she'd come, and he must have known she would know it. Lynx laughed at the ridiculousness of her train of thought. If she'd known so damned much, she'd have brought a rocket launcher. Despite everything, she'd still listened, just a little, just enough, to the cautions of her doctors and her superiors - white men in suits, saturated in privilege, good backgrounds and costly educations, with a helping hand from Daddy's golfing buddies here and there for good measure. Not a one of them had any more working knowledge of the real world than she had of how to button one of those expensive suits they liked so much. Still not trusting your gut, Ruffieux, she thought to herself, still listening to men.

His scent was getting stronger and Lynx knew she was close. She headed down another passage that ran off the antechamber, leading her deeper under the mountains. Eighteen months of hard work, of scheming, lying, trekking, nightmares, night sweats, panic attacks, and flashbacks; all of it would be worth it once she had him where she wanted him. Once she had payback.

'Lynx.' The sound of her name breaking the near-silence made her jump so hard she almost peed right then and there. Behind her. Again. Lynx whirled around, but the passage was empty. Blinking, she started back towards the antechamber, but there were no prints in the dust other than her own. Not even the ones she'd found in the antechamber. She realised the dirt covering the floor hadn't been disturbed until she'd done the disturbing. The prints she was sure she'd seen hadn't been there. Had the voice been his? Or had it been hers? Had she unconsciously corrected herself, called herself back? She shook her head but suddenly the thoughts that had plagued her for so long, that she was barely able to control at the best of times, flew at her from every corner of her mind, free to bombard her with anxieties and doubts. Her head ached with all the old rhetoric. *Idiot! You've walked into a trap! Again! Not good enough! Another mistake! Always you! Always a loser! Always wrong! Always the common denominator! No one wants you here! He never loved you. No one has. They all know the truth about you, all of them. They all know what you are! Impostor! Stupid! Wrong!*

Lynx cried out against the bombardment, falling to her knees, clutching at her head with shaking hands, trying to keep the thoughts from rattling her teeth, from shaking her to pieces from the marrow out. Her heart was racing; rivulets of sweat trickling down her back, beads of it across her brow, her upper lip, on her palms. She felt the old madness heating up in the depths of her veins, felt it coming ever closer, ready to consume her.

*I love little kitty...*

The familiar song came into her mind suddenly; a whisper at first, but with every line the voice in her head became stronger.

*Her coat is so warm,*
*And if I don't hurt her,*
*She'll do me no harm.*

Lynx mouthed the words, only sounding the last word of every line at first, then growing in strength as the song became everything, drowning out the thoughts, and slowing her heart. The repetition might not have been as soothing as it had been in the safe confines of her doctor's office, but it worked enough to take the edge off the fury that had threatened to engulf her. The fury that had been born in the cold realisation of *his* betrayal.

She stayed on the floor for long moments, her breathing less ragged with every passing minute, but she still felt too shaky to stand. She hadn't had one that bad for a while; even the night terrors had all but stopped; yet here she was almost out of control again. She wanted to howl against the injustice of it. *He* was the one to blame and yet it was she who carried his scars on her body and her mind, weighing her down with what should have been his guilt to bear. Only his. He needed to feel what he had caused her, really feel how much she had borne because of him. She wanted to shove it in his mouth and make him choke on it. The sudden conflagration of hate threatened to overwhelm her again...

*I love little kitty...*

Not like this. Did she want him to see her like this? Let him see how far he had driven her down? A ragged mess, no longer the clearheaded agent she had been before him? Ruled by what he had done to her?

That drove her to her feet. There were days when pride was the only thing that kept her together. She clung to it now like a lifeline, straightening her spine, testing her haunches. Time to pay the piper and the piper didn't accept cheques from beat down cats.

His scent trail was still strong and she made her way back through to the antechamber and down a different passageway. She trusted her nose more than her eyesight, so ignored the fact of no footprints and kept on going. Her fur prickled as she got closer. She knew he was there, knew she would find him at last. Locking down her excitement, Lynx sang her song in her head, murmuring gently to herself, comforting, encouraging. She had this. She would win, one way or another.

The sound of running water caught her attention, getting louder with every step Lynx took. Someone was down there – *he* was down there – taking a shower. A bloody shower! The passage led to another chamber, but this one had clearly been someone's living quarters. A perfectly made bed sat in the middle of the room, incongruous in its neatness beneath a thick layer of dust. No other furniture cluttered the room, and Lynx guessed that wardrobes and cupboards were hidden behind the walls. Evil genius chic. Without thinking too much about it, she pulled back the coverlet carefully so as not to provoke too much of the dust into the air, bundled it up in her arms, and stowed it safely in a corner of the room. She removed the pillows just as carefully and then sat down on the side of the bed, folding her legs beneath her comfortably. She would wait.

After fewer minutes than she would have liked, however, impatience got the better of her. Lynx got to her feet and headed for the bathroom. She slipped through the door, not wanting to alert him to her presence before she was ready. Splashes of blood sat garish on the cold stone of the floor. The puddles grew the closer she got to the opaque cubicle. The air was thick with the coppery smell of blood, so thick she could taste it. The urge to sup at one of the puddles was almost too strong to fight. When had she last eaten?

The water was still running and, even though she could not see through the glass of the cubicle, she knew he was in there. On the floor. What was he doing down there?

It only took her a moment, a flash of recollection. Suddenly she knew.

'No, no, no, you bastard, no!' Lynx grabbed at the door

handle and threw it open, water rushing over her paws, washing through the blood, turning the floor into a swirling pink mess. She didn't think about why anyone would design a shower with a door that opened outwards, all she knew was that she had to get to him before... she cried out with the pain of expectant loss, slipping and sliding on the slippery mess beneath her as she crossed the cubicle. To him, she had to get to him. She knelt down beside the body of the large furry man. His powerful canine hind legs curled beneath him, his more obviously human chin slumped down to his chest. Propped against the wall of the cubicle, his arms stretched out either side of him, he looked like a supplicant to some murderous god. The fur at his wrists was caked with blood, Lynx noticed, and she scoured the floor for the blade that had caused such damage. It was smaller than it should have been. It was then she noticed the word and numbers painted roughly across the tiles behind him. Her name and a set of coordinates. She knew what they were for straightaway and if she'd had any breath left, the realisation would have taken it away with force. After all this time, after all he had done, he was giving her the mother lode. What she had been racing against him to find right from the start. He had got there first, or close enough, maybe he had even seen it for himself, and now... now... Lynx could barely stand the reality of what was in front of her.

She threw her head back and howled.

The sound echoed through the subterranean caves, the only noise to have broken its silence for many years.

***

Secure Unit, The McMillan-Lownds Rehabilitation and Psychiatric Facility, Classified Location, Present

Lynx woke up screaming. She arched off the bed, pulled back down again by the heavy straps around her wrists and ankles. Restraints. For a moment she fought wildly, howling and screeching, kicking and struggling frantically, pulled back onto the bed time and again. A door on the other side of the room opened, leaving a gaping black hole in its wake, and she saw two large men in white uniforms enter, heading straight for her, their faces grim. A smaller lady, clearly a nurse, followed them. Her face was all beatific smile and dimples. In her left hand was the biggest syringe Lynx had ever seen.

'There now, Miss Ruffieux, let's have no more of that.' The nurse gestured to the men to hold her down and Lynx struggled anew. It was futile. They didn't let her get within biting distance and had all the positional advantage. They had her still in seconds, still enough anyway. Lynx wasn't going without a fight.

'Fuck you, lady. You get that thing away from me!' The nurse ignored her and came closer, the syringe looking bigger and more sinister with every step. 'I said get it away!'

'Now, now, Miss Ruffieux, just stay calm and everything will be fine. We're here to help you.' Lynx howled as the tiny woman – maybe the syringe looked so big because she couldn't have stood more than five feet tall in her stockinged feet – plunged the needle deep into her left arm. She dispensed the liquid without missing a beat even as Lynx began struggling again. Before the needle had even been removed, she was feeling drowsy. Her new friends warped and stretched in front of her eyes, one moment their faces leering straight down at her, the next their heads were tiny buds on human stalks waiting to flower. Darkness vibrated around the edges of her vision, stealing across her line of sight in ever-increasing pulses until...

\*\*\*

*His face. Like that of an angel. A hairy angel. So handsome, so hers. But not hers. Never hers. Not really. No one was. She was alone in the dark, always had been, always would be.*

*She remembered fire, the screams of her foster parents. Humans.*

*She remembered blood, his blood, her blood, the blood of twenty people. Dead people. All around her, since birth. She could taste it, like puddles on the floor, lapping them up, delicious, the tang of iron strong on her tongue.*

*His touch on her shoulder. Warm hands, hot hands, burning sharply into her flesh, branding her, piercing her. His face suddenly so angry, full of hate. She wanted to close her eyes against him, to look away, anything, but he filled her mind, his anger now hers, filling her, burning her from the inside out. Would it ever end? Hate and guilt, desire and lust, it bubbled up inside her, threatening to scorch through her skin, to spill out, corroding everything in its path, destroying, her heart pounding, her head throbbing, the blood in her veins boiling. She wanted it to end, she begged, she whined, pleasepleaseplease, over and over, but no one came, no one would. She'd always known she was alone. Hot skin, sweat, she could taste it, she was it. Burning through her synapses, her reactions blurred – did she move forward or back – the flash light of knowledge just beyond her, confusion slicing across her mind, urging her on even as it held her back, frustration like a turned over cauldron, drowning her, she couldn't breathe, she needed to surface. She kicked out, forcing her way up, the breath in her lungs not enough, surely not enough…*

'Butch!' She cried out his name as her eyes opened, the slash of light making her close them again. But she was breathing, she was conscious. She was real. Where had she been?

'Now, now, Miss Ruffieux…'

'Lynx, my name is Lynx.' She growled the words. She remembered the nurse, remembered her syringe.

'Yes, dear. I'm here to help you. It's always difficult at first, acceptance is hard work, but we'll make sure you're comfortable and get the help you need.' Could the woman be any more patronising? Lynx's head pounded, the grogginess of the drugs making her thoughts slower than usual but she knew where she was this time. She knew this place. She'd been here before.

The Facility.

Fighting down the panic her recollection unleashed, Lynx tried to ease her breathing. She swallowed, buying herself a little time, and thought for a moment. Play along. They would be dosing her with all sorts to keep her quiet, to make sure she was docile, that her claws were firmly kept in their sheaths, unthreatening, compliant. They must have found her in those caves, worked out her subterfuge, and seen the rubbed out message on the wall of the shower. They must have known what it was just as surely as she had and, worse, they knew she knew. That was why she was here.

'Are you going to take your medicine without a fuss this time, Lynx? No more of this "I'm a cat," nonsense?' That surprised her. It didn't sound like something she'd say, had been trained explicitly not to do so, and neither did she recall saying it, but if she'd been dosed to the eyeballs she could have said anything. 'Honestly, it's not one of the better ones I've heard, dear. We had someone in here the other day claimed to be Buffy the Vampire Slayer. Got into a right old scuffle with Napoleon Bonaparte over a game of checkers.' Her laugh was a high tinkling cackle and Lynx knew she'd be the first to go when she'd worked a way out of the restraints still tying her to the bed.

Her mind raced. The service had been using furries for decades. Hardly anyone knew they really existed; moreover it was likely that no one would even believe they existed – that would have caused panic in the wider world – but no one within the service pretended they weren't real. The pieces began to fall into place. So, that's how they were going to play it, was it? She was crazy. Not a lynx, not a furry, just a human. Okay. She could play pretend, could play it better than this nurse, that was for sure. She was nothing more than a bit player in the grander theatre of the service's plan anyway. Just doing her job. They all were in reality. The higher ups moving their pawns around like the proverbial chess pieces. Except now this was checkers, like the woman had said, and she was a queen, goddammit, and they would soon know her wrath… okay, that sounded a little crazy, she had to admit it. That kind of talk was best kept in her head.

'Would you like something to eat after you've taken your medication, dear?' Yes, thought Lynx, your liver would be a great start.

'Yes,' she replied out loud, nodding at the question to reinforce just how yes her yes was.

'I'm going to trust you to have one hand free. We have a zero tolerance policy here though. One misstep and it's a feeding tube, do you understand?'

Lynx nodded at the question. Oh yes, she understood. There'd be no feeding tube. Her claws were on fire in their sheathes, her canines elongating nicely. Zero tolerance. There'd definitely be no feeding tube.

# Survivors of the Holocene

## Madison Keller

Tightening her paws around the stock and barrel, Pepperoni clutched her rifle closer. She rocked back and forth on her back paws trying to calm herself while she waited for the frontline troops to drive the enemy towards them. A neat line of animals stretched out on either side of where she stood.

Pepperoni wasn't the only house cat there, but the domesticated cats were far outnumbered by forest animals. Besides house cats, the line contained raccoons, stoats, possums, foxes, skunks, and porcupines.

The quick, larger animals like the deer, moose, and wolves were out in the front lines, while the smaller creatures like the rats, squirrels, and chipmunks had been out earlier in the day to set traps around the woods. That left Pepperoni and others her size that were large enough to handle the over-sized human weapons here as the ambush.

The thought of death didn't bother her; still, she was nervous with pre-battle nerves that would go away once the shooting started. She shifted, pulling one paw from the rifle to run her tongue along the back of it. She swiped her paw up, running it over her ruined eye, ear and back along the top of her head. She usually wore an eyepatch, but she'd found that during battle the straps had a tendency to slip down or catch on branches, slowing her down, so for today she'd left it back in her den. The familiar gesture calmed her.

The cat next to her, a big black Tom, swished his tail nervously. 'We must remain alert,' he hissed at her, 'and ready to fight at any moment. Put your paws back on that rifle this instant. Are you a Survivor or aren't you?'

Pepperoni's tail stiffened, and she placed her paw back on the rifle. 'I'm a Survivor, and proud of it.'

Her answer satisfied the Tom, who went back to scanning

the forest. As if they needed to keep an eye out. Humans in the woods were loud and Pepperoni found she always heard them long before they came into view.

The snapping of branches reached her ear a moment later and she smiled, her tail curling up and satisfaction. A scream echoed out from the woods ahead of them; some human had fallen into one of the squirrel's traps.

As the sounds grew louder, Pepperoni lifted her rifle to her shoulder and sighted down the barrel. Their resistance group had a few smart animals who'd studied the human's technology, and come up with a way to modify the rifles so that they could easily be held and fired by house-cat-sized animals. Pepperoni held one of those very rifles in her paws.

The first of the humans came into view. They wore green and gray patterned clothing that blended into the trees, but their movement gave them away. Her sharp, predator eyes locked on every shift, every twitch. Pepperoni held her breath, and waited for the signal.

Pepperoni watched the human's march closer through the scope of her rifle. They ran, firing their weapons over their shoulders at something behind them, and so they didn't see Pepperoni and her group until they opened fire. Squirrels above them all began chittering, which was the signal. Pepperoni aimed in the fleeing human's direction and pulled the trigger.

The chatter and snap of gunfire roared out over the humans. Pepperoni wasn't sure her shots had hit anyone, but it didn't matter. Her gunfire, combined with that of all the animals in the line, decimated the human ranks.

A few humans survived, ducking behind trees to return fire. While Pepperoni reloaded her rifle, a bullet whizzed overhead and embedded in the bark of the tree behind her. The black-furred Tom next to her took a bullet in his leg. He grimaced and dropped to one knee, but lifted his rifle and fired back. The possum on her other side wasn't so lucky. One of the human's bullets hit him square between the eyes.

A human popped out from behind a tree trunk, firing his gun in their direction. Pepperoni sighted on him and squeezed the trigger. Dots of red appeared on the human's dark green uniform as the human fell back dead, rifle dropping from his hand.

A few hours later, back at the base, the leader of their little branch of the resistance group, Survivors of the Holocene, gathered everyone around to congratulate them on their stunning victory. Besides the possum who had died next to Pepperoni, they had only lost three others: one of the cats from the frontline, a rat who died in a tunnel collapse, and a moose who died herding the humans to the ambush spot. This last death was the worst from a troop standpoint. The big animals provided the bulk of the front-line grunt work and were hard to replace.

They were still counting the human dead, but already the total numbered over one hundred. Compared to that four deaths on their side seemed to Pepperoni like a good trade.

Pepperoni stood at the back of the group with the other cats, ignored by the rest of the forest animals. Since the war had started a few years ago cats had served on both sides of the conflict. As a result, both sides considered them mercurial and untrustworthy at the best of times.

Other domesticated animals had joined the animal resistance group over the last two years since the mysterious virus had uplifted almost all mammals on earth. Most notably cattle, horses, sheep, and pigs; but they were lauded and welcomed with open arms because the humans had treated them as either slaves or food. Many of the forest animals didn't understand why some of the cats, many of whom had been pampered pets of the humans, wanted to join a group dedicated to wiping humans out.

At first Pepperoni had tried to argue with them and educate them as to her reasons for joining, but now she just silently rubbed the fur around her empty eye socket and walked away when anyone questioned her commitment to the cause. As she listened to the squad leader's impassioned speech about today's victory over the humans, Pepperoni's memory drifted back.

***

Pepperoni had been feeling out-of-sorts for weeks, and it wasn't just her expanding belly or the kittens squirming within. Her paws itched and hurt constantly, especially her dewclaw nub that seemed to be swelling and growing with each passing day. Her jaw and throat ached, too, although not as badly.

Along with all of that came the sense that the world itself was making more sense in her mind. She'd always thought of the giant, hairless people she lived with as just strange, giant cats, but now she could see all the ways in which they differed from her. Even more peculiar, the noises that humans constantly made with their mouths started to make sense to her.

Still, Pepperoni went about her daily routine as if nothing was wrong. Today she lay in the window sill giving herself a bath while enjoying the warm sunshine coming through the glass. Done with that, she got up and stretched before jumping down. She landed on the floor with a quiet thump which made her belly jiggle. The kittens within squirmed against her insides. They would be coming soon, she could tell, so she headed deeper into the house.

She passed by one of her human housemates in the hallway. She wasn't sure where the word 'human' had come from to describe this strange creature she lived with, but she knew it was correct. The woman reached down to run a hand along Pepperoni's back, paying special attention to the red and black spots that had inspired her human name. Pepperoni arched her spine and purred, enjoying the attention.

'Who's a pretty kitty, Pepperoni?' the human said as she scratched between Pepperoni's ears. Just a few weeks ago the sounds would've been meaningless nonsense, but now she could parse the noise into words and their meaning. The human moved off about her day so Pepperoni continued her quest to find a safe spot to have her kittens.

Inside one of the bedrooms, she found a closet door had been left cracked open. Pepperoni inserted a paw into the space and with a bit of effort was able to roll the door far enough open to allow her to slip inside. She stretched up balancing on her back two legs so that she could reach the clothes hanging above her, latched onto one of her claws and pulled until it fell on top of her. She climbed out from under it and curled up on top, kneading it with her paws until it was just right. Just in time, too.

There was a bit of pain and blood as each kitten popped forth. Pepperoni dutifully licked each one clean and then rolled on her side so that they could nurse. As the kittens suckled, Pepperoni leaned over and took a closer look at their front paws. She'd noticed while washing them off but the urgency of the task precluded her from doing anything more than taking note of it.

The kittens' fur colors ranged from light gray to calico-spotted like hers. But what most caught her attention was the front paws. The little nub with the dew claw was long enough to touch the pads. In fact, everything about their paw was elongated. Something about the shape of their mouths and muzzles was slightly different too. However, the kittens were healthy, which was all that mattered.

As the days outside grew colder, her kittens grew larger and opened their eyes. Soon they were big enough to leave the closet. The humans noticed and commented on the kittens' paws as well. The veterinarian was the most concerned, but her humans shrugged off the vet's pleas to study the kittens further.

Along with the usual meows and squeaks of newborn kittens, hers kept trying to imitate sounds that the humans made. The humans thought it was cute, but it puzzled Pepperoni. They were sounds she'd never heard a cat make before.

When her kittens were large enough that she felt safe leaving them in the humans' care, Pepperoni made the rounds. Smoke, the big, gray Tom-cat who was the father of most of Pepperoni's kittens, had heard rumors of other cats like her kittens. He directed her to talk to the ring-tails, who lived in the large tree at the edge of the neighborhood. Pepperoni didn't usually go over there, both because the ring-tails sometimes ate cats and because that edge of the neighborhood bordered on the wildlands. But for her kittens' sake she gathered up her courage and made her way over to them.

It was the middle of the day and the ring-tails were gathered high in the branches, asleep. Pepperoni sat at the bottom of the tree and called, 'Good morning, honored ring-tails. This cat would like to talk to you.'

The lowest ring-tail peered down out of the branches

at her. 'About what?' he growled, peering down at her suspiciously.

'My newly born kittens have deformed paws and make strange sounds.' Pepperoni hesitated to mention her own problems. 'Smoke heard rumors about something strange going on with animals, and told me you might know more about it.'

The ring-tail shrugged. 'Everyone has been feeling a little off these days. I've heard whispers from the forest animals in the wildlands, but no one knows what's going on. That's all I know, little kitty.'

'Thank you,' Pepperoni said politely and headed back home. She wasn't brave enough to go into the wildlands to chase rumors. She would just have to raise her kittens as best she could.

Pepperoni ducked through the slot in the door into the kitchen to find the humans in a state of what she could only describe as panic, although she'd never seen them act this way before. The largest male human with short hair and glasses was shouting loudly into the phone, something about demon-possessed kittens. She didn't know what demons or possessed meant, but she did understand kittens. The human's tone frightened her.

Pepperoni scrambled across the slick linoleum into the house, searching for her kittens. She heard the meowing and crying out from a back room, so Pepperoni sprinted down the hall in that direction. The other large human with long hair and floaty clothes that the kittens enjoyed batting at stood outside the closed door wielding an upside-down broom in a white-knuckled grip. Face pale, she stared at the closed door. Pepperoni's kitten's cries came from inside.

The human woman shrieked as Pepperoni rounded the corner, and brought the broom down in a two-handed strike aimed at Pepperoni. To cats, all humans moved slowly, so Pepperoni was easily able to dart out of the way. The straw end of the broom hit the carpet with a loud thwack that made Pepperoni's tail puff out. Pepperoni hissed and swatted at the broom end with her claws.

'Dan!' The human woman screamed. 'You didn't lock the cat door and Pepperoni got back in the house.'

There was the sound of the phone receiver being slammed down and Dan appeared, trapping Pepperoni between the two of them.

'Maybe we can get her in with the others,' he said.

The human woman lifted her broom and stepped back, gesturing to the door. 'If you're brave enough to open that thing and potentially let those Hell-spawned beasts out, be my guest. Were you able to get a hold of anyone?'

Dan shook his head. 'The veterinarian thought I was crazy and said kittens make all sorts of strange noises when they're little. Then I called the priest to ask for an exorcism, but he said the church didn't do those anymore.' The man sighed again. 'Last, I called the news. They at least listened politely and took a report, but I could tell that the woman on the other end didn't believe me, either.'

'So what are we going to do then?' The woman said, pointing at the door and emphatically. 'Those kittens talked, Dan. That isn't normal.'

So far from the other side of the door her kittens began meowing and making strange babbling noises. All of a sudden one word came through clearly. 'Dan. Dan.' One of the kittens chanted. Another kitten took up the cry, and then another. Soon instead of meows and babbling all of them were chanting Dan's name. At that Pepperoni's ears perked up. She wished the ring-tails had been able to tell her more.

The humans both stiffened and backed away from the door. Pepperoni walked forward, scratched at the bottom edge of the door, and then meowed and looked at the humans. That had been the signal for them to open doors for her in the past, but now they both just stared at her.

'Demon – spawned,' the man whispered. The woman edged around Pepperoni and grabbed the man's arm.

'What is wrong with our kittens?' The woman burst into tears.

***

Pepperoni was pulled out of her memories by shouting. She'd allowed her mind to wander while she'd been listening, but the shouts brought her full attention back to the here and now. At first, she couldn't figure out what was wrong. Those near the front of the crowd were shouting and pushing back towards the rear. Then the smell of smoke made it to her.

'Fire!' A squirrel scampered down the branches, shouting as he went.

She reached the group, circling down the bark of the nearest tree until she reached the stump where Twitchell, the mountain lion who ran this branch of the Survivors, gave his speeches. At the moment he was yelling for order, but as the squirrel approached he whirled to address the mammal.

'What is this about fire?' Twitchell yelled.

The hapless squirrel backed away a few steps from Twitchell's snarling visage before speaking. 'The humans have set the forest on fire.'

A hush fell over the gathered crowd. Even Pepperoni held her breath. She knew of the environmental destruction humans had wrought; everyone brought into the Survivors of the Holocene learned of the humans' wanton destruction of the environment. It was why they fought so bitterly over the humans' declaration that the now sentiment animals should submit to human rule and human law. Those of the resistance groups declared that humans should step aside and let the animals run things, since the humans'd had their chance and only managed to ruin the environment. Thus, war had broken out. Even knowing what she did about the atrocities that humankind had committed Pepperoni still couldn't wrap her mind around the fact that the humans had deliberately set the forest ablaze.

Twitchell gasped. 'On purpose?'

The squirrel nodded, nervously rubbing his front paws together. 'They started the fire in a semi-circle, near the southern edge of Mount Hood. They're trying to drive us North and East.'

'Where an ambush surely awaits,' Twitchell snarled, and began pacing. After a few steps he stopped and turned back to the scout. 'How long do we have until the fire reaches us?'

'Not long,' the squirrel chittered. Pepperoni could believe that; the smell of smoke was already growing stronger.

'Everyone,' Twitchell said turning to address the gathered crowd. 'Gather your weapons and as much ammo as you can carry. Larger animals, carry the smaller and slower creatures on your back. We'll need to move fast if we're going to break through the humans' ambush.'

With order restored, the animals all scattered to fulfill their respective tasks. Pepperoni slung two rifles across her back and then strapped a belt, which she'd made herself from human cast-off clothing that she gathered from the dump, around her narrow hips. From that she hung small bags she'd made, into which she stuffed full magazines for her rifles.

The weapons had been stolen from the humans and then modified. For some reason, they discovered pockets of humans living alone in the woods with many storage rooms full of guns and ammo. The first Survivors had made quick work of the humans living there, and then distributed what they found to various branches of the organisation. The newly sentient mammals were still working on producing their own to replenish their dwindling stores. For now, they relied on stealing what they needed from the humans, a task that the Evolved Rats excelled at.

Kitted up, she joined the line of animals making their way out of camp headed northwest. Weighted down as she was, Pepperoni didn't trust herself to be able to climb up into the trees, so instead she walked with the rest on the ground.

By now she could hear the crackling of the fire behind them, and the smoke thickened. A deer bounded by, a line of ring-tailed raccoons armed with submachine guns clinging to its back. Pepperoni would've liked to have ridden, but deer were skittish and temperamental animals at the best of times and didn't like formally domesticated animals like Pepperoni. She hoped that someone was assisting the black Tom who she'd seen shot in the leg. She thought about going back to look for him, but when she glanced over her shoulder the fire was only a few yards behind her; the camp she'd just left had already been engulfed by the flames.

Pepperoni, tired already from the battle earlier that day, exhausted herself further trying to keep ahead of the flames. The fire chewed through the plant life behind them almost as fast as Pepperoni could run. The gear was weighing her down. The first thing she discarded was her spare rifle. She pulled the strap over her head and tossed it to the side. Lighter now, she pulled ahead of the fire.

She ran through the dark with the crowd, the smoke burning her lungs. An animal screamed in pain behind her, a pained yowling that she recognized came from a fellow house cat. But there was nothing she could do but keep running. Other animals fell behind to be engulfed by the hungry fire.

Eventually, Pepperoni threw away magazines from her pouches, but she refused to give up her last rifle. After what seemed like hours of running, Pepperoni heard the crack and pop of gunfire up ahead. Still running on two legs, she unslung her rifle and held it in her front paws.

She broke from the trees into a wide clearing. Large spotlights illuminated the area. Bullets thudded into the ground around her, but she kept running determinedly forward. Squinting at the glare of the bright lights overhead after the dark of the forest, Pepperoni made out the shapes of metal towers with humans standing atop them, firing on the helpless animals below as they came pouring out of the forest. Pepperoni vaulted a dead raccoon and changed course, heading towards one of the metal towers. Bullets peppered the ground around her, but somehow nothing hit her.

When she reached the base of the closest tower, Pepperoni held her gun with one paw and used the other three to climb. In the chaos, no one noticed her ascending the side of the tower. Pepperoni reached the platform at the top and lightly slipped onto it. Her soft cat paws were utterly silent as she snuck up on the two humans on the platform and shot them both in the back. As she pulled the trigger, she imagined the humans she killed had *their* faces.

***

While the two humans huddled in the hallway, Pepperoni tried to get through the door to her kittens. She scratched and meowed louder, but the frightened humans just stared at her. Annoyed, Pepperoni thrashed her tail behind her and stared up at the doorknob. As her mind sharpened lately she noticed that they always grasped that gold knob with her hands and turned it before opening a door. If the humans were not going to open the door to her kittens, Pepperoni would have to do it herself.

Pepperoni stretched her lanky frame up and rested her two front paws on the gold knob. Her dew claw nub had grown long enough to be able to touch the smooth metal along with her paw tips. At first her paws slid right off the slick material. She thought back to what the humans did, how they used their thumb to wrap around one side while they held it with their fingers on the other. Pepperoni twitched her dew claw nub wondering if she could use it in the same fashion. After a couple of false starts she got used to moving the new appendage.

Squeezing down with her dew claw nub and paw pads, she slowly turned the doorknob until the door clicked open. Her kittens pressed on the other side of the door. Pepperoni meowed, telling them to move back and the weight of the kittens moved away. The door swung open, and Pepperoni dropped down and sauntered inside.

Her three kittens swarmed around her, meowing excitedly. The smallest and frailest of her kittens began to say her human name, or at least tried to. It came out 'Pep pa roni.' The other kittens tried to imitate their little brother, but couldn't say the p sound, eventually settling on 'Ronie,' which they repeated several times as the bounced around her.

Pepperoni curled up in the centre of them, lying on her side so they could nurse. The kittens ceased their talking and happily settled in to eat.

The two humans, their faces pale, crept to the open doorway and stared in at them, whispering back and forth quietly to each other. A moment later they were gone. The door to the garage opened and then shut again. Pepperoni ignored this activity, intent on her kittens.

The sound of running water came from outside. Several minutes later the garage door opened and shut again. The male human, Dan, appeared in the doorway carrying a bucket filled with water. The human female came up behind him, her eyes downcast.

'Don't you think that's a little extreme?' She said softly. 'They're just kittens. They aren't hurting anyone.'

'Sure,' Dan whispered back at her, but his voice was louder than it had been before and Pepperoni easily heard him.

'They're small and cute now, until they grow up to full-size demon cats and terrorise everyone. And it's spreading. You saw what Pepperoni did with that door handle. We'll get you a new cat. One that isn't a demonic hell spawn.'

Pepperoni didn't understand what they were talking about. Hell spawn? Demons? These words were meaningless to her. The only part she understood was new cat. She splayed back her ears.

Dan walked into the room and set the bucket down, sloshing water onto the carpet. He reached down and grabbed one of the kittens suckling from her teats. Pepperoni meowed in distress, but the other kittens were too hungry and intent upon their meal to react.

As Dan lifted the kitten, Pepperoni reached out and swiped at his hand with her claws. Her claws caught the skin on the back of his hand, opening up three long gashes. Dan cried out in pain and dropped the mewling kitten. Pepperoni couldn't move with the other two still suckling her, but she meowed at the kitten to come back. Instead, it sat there on the carpet, looked up at the human, and said, 'Dan.' Dan's face turned red and he reached out his other hand is to pluck up the kitten. Before Pepperoni could react, he shoved the kitten down into the bucket.

From the floor, Pepperoni couldn't see what was happening, but she understood her kitten was in trouble. It thrashed around as the human woman began crying. Pepperoni stood, weighted down by the kittens still attached to her. She shook the kittens off her, who cried it out at being removed.

Crouching, she launched herself at Dan, but the human was ready for her. He swung out with his bleeding hand, catching her in the side of the head. The blow launched her to the side and she hit the wall hard.

As she staggered to her feet, Dan lifted his hand from the bucket, still holding her kitten, which was now lifeless and still. He tossed the sopping-wet dead kitten away onto the carpet, and grabbed another one. Pepperoni growled and sprung at him again as he thrust the second kitten into the bucket. She landed on his shoulder with her claws out. She dug her fangs into his flesh through his shirt and raked at him with her claws. Dan snarled and swatted at her, but she hung on tight.

Until the handle of a broom struck the top of her head with the crack. Pepperoni went limp and fell to the floor with a thump. Head spinning, she looked up to find the human woman standing there again wielding her broom. She stared at Pepperoni with tears in her eyes.

Dan tossed away a second dead kitten and reached for a third. Instead of meowing or yowling or growling, perhaps the humans would listen to her if she spoke in their language, like the kittens had. She'd heard this human speak often enough, so she moved her jaw in an unfamiliar way trying to make the sounds that they made.

'No,' she said in human as she staggered to her feet. The words hurt her jaw and tongue, but she did it, forcing out the unfamiliar sounds as best she could. 'Not. Hurts. Kittens.'

She didn't get the reaction she was hoping for. The female human screamed and thrust the end of the broom handle at Pepperoni, catching her in the eye. Dan smiled grimly as Pepperoni screamed. Her eye flared with pain and she couldn't see from that side of her face.

'I told you they were demon possessed,' he snarled, plunging the last kitten into the water.

Pepperoni dragged herself towards him, until the human female whacked her again with a broom handle, hitting her ribs. Her side flaring with pain and the last kitten dead, Pepperoni ran through the cat flap in the door, outside and away.

\*\*\*

Pepperoni dragged herself into the Mount Hood resistance movement's emergency headquarters. The scent of smoke clung to her fur as she staggered the last few steps down the decline. The emergency site was set in a natural depression in the land that was invisible from above. They'd figured out early on that the humans had flying machines, helicopters that they could use to scout the forest from above.

A small and dismal crowd greeted Pepperoni. Twitchell the mountain lion was there, along with most of the faster animals, like the deer and wolves. Other ambush survivors like Pepperoni were slowly trickling in, but even so it was looking grim for this group of Survivors. Pepperoni anxiously watched the newcomers, looking for a black Tom with a limp, but as the flow of new arrivals slowed she was forced to acknowledge that he probably didn't make it. They'd barely spoken more than three words on the battlefield, but the loss still twisted at her.

When it appeared that everyone had arrived, Twitchell got to his feet to address the crowd, holding out his front paws for silence.

'Fellow Survivors of the Holocene,' Twitchell said. 'As you can see, the human's latest attack has greatly reduced our numbers. Half of the forest is gone to the human's flames along with all of our stores except for the emergency supply stashed here. That leaves us less space to hide and less ground to forage for food. If this keeps up, I fear we will not survive until next full moon.'

The crowd began murmuring among itself. Pepperoni remained silent, staring up at the massive mountain lion that towered over most of them. Twitchell let the crowd talk for a moment, before raising his voice once more.

'What we need is a spy. An animal, big or small, willing to go into enemy territory and gather information before the human's next attack. I know you're all tired, so I will not talk further. As you rest, I want you to consider your willingness to take on this role. I only want volunteers, as this mission is a dangerous one. Now --'

Pepperoni jumped up, waving her paw in the air to get Twitchell's attention.

'Yes,' the mountain lion said, as he looked up and down her small form. There wasn't much to see: a small house cat with white fur spotted with large red and black spots. 'Pepperoni, correct?'

'Yes.' Pepperoni straightened her spine and stood as tall as she could. 'I volunteer.'

The mountain lion smiled, his whiskers twitching. 'Excellent. The rest of you, get some rest. Pepperoni, join me up here so I can brief you on the mission.'

Another paw in the audience shot up. 'Does this mean you don't need any more volunteers?'

Twitchell shook his head. 'I need at least one more. This mission is vital to our success, but is also dangerous. Even if one doesn't survive, another might. So rest, and think on it. Anyone who decides to go, come to me in the morning with your decision.'

While the rest of the animals shuffled off to find places to sleep, Pepperoni approached the lion. Twitchell lay down on his stomach and tucked his paws underneath him, bringing one out briefly to pat the ground by his side. Pepperoni curled up next to him.

'You have the gist of the mission. Go to the human camp and find out their plans. I will provide you with a map to the camp's location,' the lion paused and regarded her of the corner of his eye. 'Can you read human script?'

'Yes,' Pepperoni said proudly and confidently. 'Plus, I was a house cat before Evolving. I know humans well and can pass as a domesticated if I must.'

The lion's wide smile widened. 'Excellent,' he purred.

\*\*\*

Her ruined eye throbbing, Pepperoni bolted through the once familiar neighborhood. Grief tore at her heart, threatening to overwhelm her. She ran past Smoke, who called out to her, but she ignored him and kept going. The large Tom heaved himself to his feet and chased after her.

Pepperoni ran past the ring-tail's tree. One of them stopped to watch her go by and then went back to what he was doing.

At the edge of the tree line she stopped. She'd never been into the wildlands. There she sat and stared with her remaining eye into the forest. Smoke caught up with her and sat at her side. Without saying anything he leaned over and begin grooming her face and neck. When his scraping tongue got close to her ruined eye she winced but didn't pull away. He began purring, tentatively at first, and then louder as he went on. Pepperoni closed her eye and leaned against him, basking in his attention.

Twilight turned to dusk, and the sun fell. The ring-tails began descending the tree behind them, prompting Pepperoni to get up and move forward into the trees. Becoming ring-tail food was not on her list of plans for the night. Still purring, Smoke got up and followed after her.

The two of them lived alone in the forest for quite some time. Their bodies continued to warp and change until they could walk on two legs. As they met more and more of the forest animals she discovered the same thing was happening to all of them.

Pepperoni and Smoke taught the human language to those closest to them, as it was a handy way of communicating between species that otherwise didn't speak the same language.

A bit after the snows had melted, a stranger came into their midst. She was a deer from the north, who told them that what was happening to the animals of this forest had happened to animals everywhere. She spoke of fighting between humans and animals, and that she had been sent to find volunteers to stop the humans from dominating over the animals. The humans were trying to kill all the Evolved animals, and a resistance group had sprung up to stop them, Survivors of the Holocene.

Pepperoni was the first to volunteer. A few more of their group decided to join, but most wanted to stay where they were. Smoke was one of those. Pepperoni said her goodbyes to him, and left with the deer to join the Survivors.

When they reached the camp, Twitchell was there to greet them. All of the new members learned about the atrocities the humans had committed against the environment. Pepperoni was aghast to learn how many animals humans had killed over the years, driving some species into extinction.

At that time Twitchell still had a laptop that worked and a solar charger to power it. On it, another house cat who had stayed with her human family longer than Pepperoni had, showed them videos and taught them all to read. Most of the animals had difficulty grasping the concept, but as a former house-cat Pepperoni picked it up quickly.

Pepperoni never asked the other house-cat why she had left, and she never asked Pepperoni. More cats joined their number, but never any dogs. The dogs were too loyal to their human masters and Pepperoni, thinking of her poor drowned kittens, scorned them for it.

*\*\*\**

Feeling naked without a rifle, Pepperoni slunk through the low grass, crouching to avoid being spotted. Twitchell had given her a human uniform to wear, and the cloth was an uncomfortable and unfamiliar sensation against her fur.

The human encampment was just ahead of her. This was the most dangerous part of the mission. If the human saw her approach from the forest, they'd realise she wasn't really a domesticated when she arrived in camp.

On one paw she was terrified of coming face-to-face with a human again after her previous experience with them. Yet on the other she was excited for chance to prove herself a key part of the resistance.

Once she got through the field surrounding the human base, Pepperoni paused, aghast at what she saw before her. For ten feet out from the fence, there was just naked earth. All the trees and plants had been uprooted, and the soil tilled. As she watched, two humans walked by. One of them leading a roaring machine that ripped up the earth in front of him. The other watched over his companion, scanning the area around them for any threats.

Once they were out of sight, Pepperoni shifted so that she could see further down. The grass that she currently crouched in was the last green thing for as far as she could see. Carefully turning around as slowly as she could, trying not to move any of the grass stalks, Pepperoni made her way back to the trees.

From there she spent the next several hours making note of the frequency and timing of the patrols. Ideally she would spend several days scouting the location, but Twitchell needed this information as soon as possible. The longer Pepperoni waited, the more chance the humans would launch an attack that would wipe out the rest of her group.

When she was reasonably certain of her plan, Pepperoni climbed back down the tree she'd ascended and slowly crawled back across the field. During her examination, she'd noticed a small area of the fence where the ground dipped low, leaving a hole below the chain-link. From the distance she couldn't tell if the opening would be enough for her to squeeze through, but it was the only weakness she'd spotted. Armed guards watched from metal towers at each of the corners of the base, similar to the towers that they'd set up and used during their ambush. She couldn't climb the fence and get over the razor wire at top or dig a hole without being an easy target for the snipers on the towers.

As it was she would be in danger for the time it would take her to cross the bare dirt and scrabble through the opening and her white fur would stand out as a beacon against the dark earth.

Pepperoni timed it perfectly. The patrol walked by at exactly the time she predicted. The tower guards turned their heads to watch the patrolling earth tillers, giving her a small window of opportunity.

As he had done before, the guard turned his head to follow their movement. She scrambled up and ran across the space on all fours, aiming right for the opening. The edge of the chain-link scraped her back as she wedged herself through the opening. For a moment the wire caught the fabric of her uniform. It came free with a rip and then she was on the other side, running for the safety of the tents.

She froze in the shadows there, waiting for the guard to sound the alarm or for bullets to thud into the ground around her, but nothing happened. For a minute more, she trembled there, waiting for the beating of her heart to slow back down. Then she straightened up tall on two legs and strolled out into the camp as if she belonged there.

In her experience humans were very social around food, so she followed her nose to the canteen. She figured she could hang around there for a while and see if she could overhear anything useful.

She grabbed a tray and approached the line for food. To her disgust a dog was at the end. She tamped down her natural inclination to hiss and puff up her fur and got into line behind him.

Standing on two legs, the dog was only as tall as her, with short golden fur and big pointy ears. He wore a uniform similar to hers, but his was pressed and fresh. His thin tail wagged as Pepperoni walked up behind him, and he turned to greet her.

'Hi,' he said brightly, his tail wagging harder. 'I'm Scribbles. I haven't smelled you here before.' He stuck out his front paw in a human greeting that Pepperoni recognised from her days as a house cat.

Pepperoni steeled herself and reached out to shake his paw. 'Uh, hello, Scribbles. I'm Pep --'

Her eyes snagged on a human further up the line and she stopped talking. Dan stood there talking to another male human. Her head spun and she staggered back. He had been the last person she'd expected see here, and the sight of him brought it all crashing back to her.

'Pep,' Scribbles said, sounding worried. 'Are you all right? Here,' he threw an arm under her shoulder and dragged her out of the canteen and out into the fresh air of the courtyard. 'The smells in there can overwhelm me, too.'

Pepperoni shook her head, her entire body vibrating with suppressed rage. She wrapped her arms around her chest and squeezed her eyes shut, trying to stop the memory of her kitten's deaths from playing over and over in her mind. She did have enough sense left in her to realise that if she recognized Dan, Dan would surely recognise her. She couldn't let him see her. She gathered her senses together and opened her eyes, focusing on Scribbles.

'I need somewhere private. Do you know somewhere I can go? I'm new here.' She hugged herself tighter.

'Of course,' Scribbles said, taking her arm. He led her to a private spot between two buildings. 'You want to talk about it?' Scribbles asked, leaning back against the wall behind him.

Pepperoni shook her head, already feeling foolish for over-reacting so badly. 'No. I'm fine now. I just got overwhelmed.' Pepperoni started to turn away, but then had a thought. This dog knew camp inside and out, perhaps he could be tricked into giving her what she was looking for. 'Actually, I,' Pepperoni hung her head and let her tail droop, as if ashamed. 'I'm supposed to deliver a message to the person in charge, but I forgot his name.'

Scribbles brightened and puffed out his chest, his tail wagging furiously. 'I can help you with that. His name is Gen. Morin, and I can take you right to his office.'

Pepperoni had to stop herself from purring. 'Perfect.'

While Scribbles guided her through camp, Pepperoni's sighting of Dan gnawed at her. The loss of her kittens still hurt. She and Smoke had talked about going back to get revenge in the early days, but how was a pair of house cats going to fight back against someone ten times their size? That had been before she'd learned about guns, but by then it had been too long and she had no idea how to find him. Now here he was, within her grasp. But then she thought about the mission, and its importance. If someone didn't bring that information back to Twitchell their little resistance group was doomed.

She was so deep in thought that when Scribbles stopped she almost ran into his back.

'Here we are!' Scribbles exclaimed with a wag of his tail. He pointed to a closed door with a little plaque next to it that read 'General Morin.'

'Thank you for your assistance, Scribbles,' Pepperoni said, revising her opinion of dogs up a little in her mind. Although he unknowingly worked for the enemy, the dog had been nothing but friendly to her.

Scribbles wagged his tail and jogged away, back towards the canteen. Pepperoni waited until he was out of sight and then ducked around the side of the building to wait for night fall. She wanted to wait for the general to leave before she tried to break into his office.

Now that she knew where her target was and where to find the documents Twitchell needed, she wandered around sniffing the air for scents of Dan.

After a bit of searching, she scented him near one of the buildings. A television blared from an open window. She stood underneath it and pretended to examine her claws while she listened to their conversation. He sat with a few other humans, watching whatever program was on the television, which involved a lot of whistles and men shouting. Occasionally Dan and the other humans shouted back about plays and referees. For all she knew of humans, their words didn't make a lot of sense sometimes.

She longed to burst in with a rifle in her paws and shoot them all. She hadn't brought one in with her, but she'd seen many of the humans carrying them around. It would be trivial to locate where there were kept and steal one. She had to keep reminding herself about her mission. Twitchell was counting on her to bring back the plans of the next humans attack.

Yet every time Dan spoke her heart broke again.

She stood there until well after dark. Finally, whatever program the humans were watching ended and one by one they filed out of the building, splitting up to head deeper into camp.

Pepperoni trailed after Dan, making sure to keep out of sight as he wove his way across the camp. No one said anything about the cat walking around. In fact, as she traversed the camp after Dan she spotted two more house cats conversing with humans and more dogs eagerly assisting the humans.

Dan entered one of the barracks and Pepperoni circled the building until she found a window open to let in the cool night breeze. She heard Dan say good night to his bunkmates and a few moments later all the lights switched off.

The calm of the camp was broken by the chatter of gunfire. A shout came from the edge of camp. 'Target eliminated.'

The other spy had not made it in.

The commotion died down quickly, when it became clear the gunned-down animal had been alone. Lights turned off all across the camp and soon all she could hear was the chirp of night birds and the sighing of the wind.

This was her opportunity to break into the general's office and steal what she needed.

Yet Pepperoni could not tear herself away from the window.

She imagined jumping up, catching the edge and crawling through the narrow opening. The window was high, but not out of her reach. The opening was small, but bigger than the hole under the chain-link fence she'd used to enter the compound. She imagined finding Dan in the dark, climbing over him in his sleep, raking her sharp claws across his neck. But her claws were small and while she might be able to hurt Dan, the injury would most likely not be fatal. He'd call out, the alarm would sound, she'd be found out, and her mission a failure.

Pepperoni stood there imagining the whole thing. The memory of her kittens danced in her mind one last time. Killing Dan wouldn't help them; they were already dead. The act would be entirely for her. She thought one last time about Twitchell and the other Survivors of the Holocene, counting on her successful return.

Pepperoni said one last goodbye to her kittens, and turned away, walking toward Gen. Morin's office. Towards the future.

# Starlight and Thorn

## K.C. Shaw

The scent of wood smoke reached Starlight's nostrils long before the town came into view. The smell drew her on with the promise of a hot meal, a warm bed. She needed both, but it was tempting to stop where she was and sleep. The road was steep and Starlight had already walked more miles that day than she cared to remember. A sliver of moon rode above the nearly bare trees.

Finally lights twinkled ahead. The trees opened to reveal pastures that smelled of sheep, stubbly wheat and hay fields, and a scattering of houses. Starlight walked a little faster.

She found a tavern, its windows so brightly lit she winced as she entered. She already had coins in her paw.

But she sensed no hostility from the humans drinking in the common room, only mild interest. For the first time in two weeks she felt a flicker of hope.

The innkeeper was a tall man with pale skin and black hair. 'Here to visit Thorn?' he asked with a smile.

'Just passing through. I need a bed and a good meal.'

'You look like you could use a lot of good meals, if you don't mind me saying so. You know we've got bandits in the pass?'

'I know. I'm here to deliver a message to Dunkirk.' Starlight took her pack off with a sigh of relief. 'Who is Thorn?'

'The smith's assistant. He's a cat like you.'

Starlight spoke so quickly her words ran together. 'Is there a colony of us here?'

'No, just Thorn.'

Her hope died. She should have known better anyway: she would have already found sign or scent of a frvaal colony if there was one nearby. 'Give him my regards. I probably won't have time to talk with him in the morning. I must leave early.'

The man nodded. 'Cider, or something else?'

'Cider's fine.'

Starlight accepted the pint and sat at an empty table. It felt good to get off her feet. And when her food came, it was all palatable—no vegetables or sweets she couldn't digest, just a lump of grilled mutton and a bowl of porridge made with chicken fat. No one paid her any attention, so she felt comfortable picking the meat up to eat it, licking her paws clean afterwards.

She yawned. The inn was warm and she had a full belly for the first time in days. She thanked the innkeeper, who showed her upstairs to her room.

It was tiny but private: only one bed, made up with heavy quilts. Starlight sat down and pulled her boots off. She didn't like wearing them, but with the amount of traveling she'd done in the last few weeks, they were necessary. Her paw pads were not that tough.

She was about to undress when someone rapped on the door. It was a polite knock and Starlight assumed the innkeeper needed something. She got up and opened the door.

A frvaal stood in the corridor—a cat, nearly the first she'd seen since she left her clan's territory. He was taller than she was, with tawny fur several shades lighter than her own orange and brown striped coat. A white-tipped ruff accentuated his jaw and thick neck. He had on trousers and a long leather smock of the kind smiths wore.

'I'm sorry to bother you so late. I'm Thorn. Caylor sent me a message that a cat had arrived and I wanted to talk with you for a short while, if I may.' His paws were dark with soot, as though he had rushed over directly from work.

'Come in. I'm Starlight.' She sat back down on the bed and he pulled a chair over from the corner. 'You're a smith?'

'Yes. Indentured originally, but I've worked my way from apprentice to assistant. Caylor said you're a messenger?'

'At the moment. Are there other cats here, a colony or even a clan?' She sat forward. The innkeeper might not know for certain, but Thorn would.

'No, only me,' he said, and killed her hope again. 'It's a comfortable village. I had hoped to attract a colony, but my mate died four years ago.'

'I'm sorry.' Starlight understood his difficulty: immigrant frvaal rarely settled near an unattached male—a superstition based on ancient territorial instincts. If he had no clan to return to, he might end up alone for the rest of his life.

'I might move to Eclin after the new year,' Thorn said. 'I hear there are a number of cats there. Is that where you're taking your message?'

'I'm just going up to the pass. Do you know if Dunkirk is still there?'

'As far as I know. I go up once a month or so to shoe horses and do repair work for his men. He was there last month.'

'I hope he still is.' Starlight sighed. 'I've walked over two hundred miles to deliver this message to him.'

Thorn's eyes widened. They were dark amber, she noticed, with long lashes and a spray of whiskers above. 'It must be important.'

'It is. Very.' She looked down at her feet. At least they were clean, thanks to the boots, although they ached. To change the subject she asked, 'What brought you here? You just liked the look of the town?'

'We were actually headed to Eclin, my mate and I. We'd heard there was a colony starting nearby. But her time came when we were here for the night. Our cub was born here and we decided to stay. I indentured with the smith.' Thorn took a deep breath. 'My mate made extra money by guarding flocks when they grazed near the forest. One day a troll attacked. It killed her and my daughter.'

Starlight sucked in her breath. 'That's awful. The troll— did you…?'

'Killed it,' Thorn said. 'Tracked it down that night, killed it and its young. I have scars on my back from its claws.'

'I'm so sorry,' Starlight whispered.

Thorn flicked his ears. 'It was a long time ago now. I probably ought to move on to Eclin.'

'You should.'

They fell silent, and Starlight wondered how to keep the conversation going. She did not want Thorn to go away with his heart aching from old memories. Besides, he was likely to be the last person she talked to before the two-day hike up to the mountain's pass.

She started to speak at the same time he did. They both stopped and smiled. 'After you,' Thorn said.

'I was just going to ask if you think I should buy a heavier blanket for the trip up.'

'I can loan you my old camping gear so you'll have shelter, if you like. We had frost this morning.'

'I'm not returning this way.'

'A gift, then. I don't need it. I never travel anymore.'

'No. Thank you, but I can't.' Starlight couldn't meet his eyes. She picked up her tail and smoothed its fur, mostly to hide that it was twitching in agitation.

'Starlight.' Thorn's voice was soft. He leaned forward and placed one paw over hers. 'Why don't I go with you, as far as Dunkirk's hold? It's about time I visited up there again, and we can talk more. You're the first cat I've seen in four years.'

His paw was warm and his musky scent reminded her she was coming into season. She nodded.

'Good. Thank you.' Thorn stood and put the chair back where he'd found it. 'I'll meet you downstairs at dawn, if that's all right. We can breakfast together.'

She nodded again and Thorn left, closing the door quietly. Starlight stared at the door for a few moments.

It would be good to have company. Her job might be made easier by his presence, in fact—the bandits knew him and would be more likely to accept her too as a result. Her greatest fear was being turned away before she could deliver the message to Dunkirk.

She undressed and noticed for the first time how thin her fur was where her trouser waistband rubbed. Not that it mattered. It would be cold; she need not undress in front of Thorn, even if he wanted her to.

She wondered if he wanted her to.

*** 

Thorn was waiting in the common room when Starlight entered the next morning. She had overslept and dawn was an hour gone.

'Sorry I kept you waiting,' she muttered as she sat across from him.

'I haven't been here very long myself. I thought I might have to chase up the road after you.'

He smiled, and Starlight returned it with a surge of gratitude. It felt good to have someone who cared about traveling with her. His paws were clean of soot this morning and he wore boots as well as trousers and smock. A backpack rested against his chair.

She ate quickly, a satisfying meal of eggs, ham, and porridge. Then she shouldered her own small pack and they stepped outside.

The morning was sunny but cold. Thorn said, 'Bad weather's moving in. We should be all right tonight, but we'll probably have snow tomorrow.'

'Snow?' Starlight had heard of snow but had never seen it.

'Probably not much. A dusting here, maybe a few inches in the pass. It won't slow us down.'

He matched his stride to hers and she settled into her usual pace. The cold air made scents sharper, sounds clearer. They passed more houses, a few shops, a cobbled square that was probably a market at week's end. A big smith's forge was on the edge of the square, with the usual open front so horses could be brought in for shoeing. One was there now.

Thorn called, 'I'm off to the pass!' and the smith waved back without looking up.

'Your master?' Starlight asked.

'Yes. He's a good man. He took me on even though I had no experience, with smithing or with horses.'

They left the centre of town behind. Houses gave way to farms, then forest. The dirt road sloped uphill again.

'Do you like smithing?' Starlight asked after they had walked in silence for a while.

'It's interesting. I like making things—not just horseshoes and hinges. Decorative things. When I made a gate for the weaver's garden last summer, I decorated it with vines and flowers made of iron. My master thought I was foolish, but it gave me pleasure to make it that way and the weaver was happy too when she saw it.'

'I've never made anything,' Starlight said.

'We don't, mostly,' Thorn said. 'We might be more accepted by humans if we did.'

'We make clothes.'

Thorn glanced at her and she knew he was taking note of what she wore. She wondered if he was considering only her clothing or if he thought of her hidden body also. He must be, after four years alone. She tried to keep her own thoughts from racing ahead to that night.

He said, 'You're wearing human-made clothes, I think.'

'They fit better,' Starlight said with a wry smile. Thorn laughed, showing a glimpse of fangs.

She wanted to make him laugh again. But she could think of nothing to ask him that would not lead back to his dead family.

He said, 'Where are you from?'

'West, from the coast.'

'That far to bring a message?'

'Someone has to carry it.' Starlight looked up, above the trees, and saw the mountaintops grey and white against the sky.

'You've seen the ocean, then?' Thorn said.

'A few times. We lived inland. Have you seen it?'

'Never. My mother told me stories of the crossing from Falarwin, but she made the ocean sound terrifying. What's it like?'

Starlight thought of her childhood visits to the seaside: once to welcome a ship of cats arrived from the war-torn county of Falarwin, two or three times to help harvest unusually large schools of moonfish. 'It's changeable,' she said finally. 'It can be kind or dangerous within the space of two breaths—like the weather. But it's beautiful, and peaceful to listen to. Fun to swim in.'

Thorn laughed again, to Starlight's pleasure. 'You like to swim?'

'Yes. Don't you?'

'Not if I can avoid it. I don't like my fur getting wet.'

'You get used to it. The sea is salty. Tastes funny when you groom afterwards.'

'How big is your clan?'

'A hundred. We split ten years ago so we wouldn't grow too large. My brother went with the travellers, but he visits sometimes.'

Thorn chased that rabbit instead of asking more questions about her clan, as Starlight had hoped. 'How many siblings do you have?'

'Just my older brother. I had a baby sister but she died. My mother still lives, and I have two aunts and five cousins.'

'A good family.' Thorn sounded wistful. 'They'll be glad when you return. Why were you chosen to take the message? The roads are dangerous—not that you can't defend yourself, I'm sure. But you are only one.'

Starlight chose her words carefully. 'Dunkirk might turn me away if he thought I was dangerous. Of all those who volunteered to take the message, I was the least imposing.'

From Thorn's expression, he was torn between disbelief and alarm. 'Truly?'

'Yes. I must be allowed to speak with him.'

Thorn fell silent. Starlight thought he had tired of talking, or had nothing more to ask her. She looked around as they hiked. Squirrels were busy in the trees and birds called occasionally. As the sun rose, the deep shadow of the trail turned dappled and the air warmed. She found it hard to believe it would grow so cold overnight that the very air would freeze into puffs of ice, as she had heard snow described.

Suddenly Thorn said, 'I will go with you on your way back, if you will allow me. As your escort. You must have had a difficult road.'

Starlight said only, 'I told you, I'm going home a different way.'

'Then I'll come with you until I know you're safe.'

'No. Thank you, but no.'

Thorn didn't reply. Starlight knew she had hurt him. He didn't laugh again for the rest of the morning.

\*\*\*

They stopped for lunch in a grassy clearing with a creek, a stone fire ring full of old ashes, and moss-covered hitching posts. 'It's overgrown,' Thorn said, looking at the sapling trees and brush. 'We don't get as many travellers as we used to, not since Dunkirk took the pass.'

'Hasn't anyone tried to drive him away?'

Thorn shrugged. 'Our town is small and peaceful. We don't depend on trade over the pass, and Dunkirk doesn't bother us. He buys and barters with us for what he needs. And he's not there all the time; he leaves a few men to hold the pass while he's away on his travels, sometimes for months.'

'You know what he's done?'

'I've heard rumours.'

Starlight sat down in the grass and took the pouch of dried meat from her pack. 'My clan's patron is Lord Esk, who has given us a tract of hunting land and trading rights with his people. Dunkirk was once a playmate of the Lady Esk when they were young, and claims to know secrets that would ruin her and discredit our lord in the eyes of his peers.'

'Distasteful,' Thorn said, sitting beside her.

'More than distasteful,' Starlight said sharply. 'He is demanding money, goods, women, and arms from our lord for his silence. He will not move on his demands. Our lady lost her unborn child due to distress; our lord is nearly mad with distraction. I am here to negotiate terms. You see why it is so important that I be allowed to speak with Dunkirk.'

'Yes, of course. I'm sorry,' Thorn said, although he had done nothing wrong. Starlight hunched over her meagre meal, her heart heavy with responsibility—and fear that after all her effort, Dunkirk would laugh and turn her away.

Thorn touched her back. When she didn't pull away, he squeezed her shoulder gently and said, 'Dunkirk knows me. I have a little limited influence with him. I will make sure he listens to you.'

'Thank you,' Starlight whispered. She wanted to lean against him. But she didn't move, and after a moment Thorn took his paw away and concentrated on his own lunch.

\*\*\*

Clouds began to gather that afternoon. By the time Thorn suggested they stop for the night at another overgrown clearing, Starlight tasted frost in the air.

He built a fire in a ring of rocks, and soon cheery orange flames chased the chill away. 'I brought us some fresh food to cook,' he said, rummaging in his pack. 'You must be tired of travel rations.'

'Oh yes,' Starlight said with feeling. Thorn flashed her a toothy grin.

He had brought two large beef steaks wrapped in waxed butcher's paper, and a frying pan already smeared with lard. Starlight watched him cook with her mouth watering. He handled the pan deftly, keeping it out of the hottest flame and turning the meat with his claws. When he offered the pan to her to choose her piece, he looked so proud and pleased that a wave of sadness washed through her. She must have been the first person he'd cooked for in years.

She ate quickly although she tried to savour the meal. Thorn still finished before she did. While she licked her paws clean, he took a bundle of leather and metal sticks from his pack and unrolled them on the grass nearby.

He assembled them efficiently into a small lean-to. 'That should be facing out of the wind, and if it gets too cold we can rekindle the fire.' He dug in his pack again and this time produced a sheepskin, which he spread under the lean-to. 'It's more comfortable than it looks,' he said, looking up at her from where he knelt on the grass.

'I have a blanket too,' Starlight said, taking it from her pack.

It was nearly dark already. Thorn sat next to her and poked at the fire, sending sparks dancing into the air. 'If we get an early start tomorrow, we can be at the pass a little after noon.'

Starlight stared into the fire without seeing it. She was close. This time tomorrow—

She would not think of tomorrow. She had fretted away her energy with worry too often during her travels. She knew precisely what she needed to say to Dunkirk, had every word memorised so perfectly she could have said them in her sleep.

Thorn said, 'You don't need to be afraid. Dunkirk's not unreasonable.'

'He won't like what I have to tell him,' Starlight said.

'I won't let him hurt you.'

She turned to him, orange spots jumping in her vision from the fire. 'No. When I speak to Dunkirk, you mustn't interfere. No matter what happens.'

He reached out a paw, then drew it back. 'I won't interfere.'

They talked until the fire died, staying to neutral topics. Thorn spoke of his work, Starlight of her clan. She tried not to appear distracted.

Finally the fire was no more than glowing embers. It still gave off considerable heat, but Starlight's back was cold enough that her tail had fluffed. Thorn said, 'I'm ready to sleep if you are.'

She pulled off her boots but kept her clothes on. Thorn did the same. The grass was chilly when she stood up. 'Will we both fit underneath?' she asked, looking doubtfully at the lean-to.

'Yes, although…if you're not comfortable sleeping so close with me, you can take the shelter and I'll sleep next to the fire.'

'No, I'm fine. We'll share our warmth.' Starlight looked away, embarrassed.

He took the blanket from her and rolled beneath the shelter, pressing his back against the leather. She crawled in after him and lay down, feeling awkward, and realised she would need to press against him or lie mostly outside of the lean-to. She shifted over.

He pulled her closer and spread the blanket over them both. 'Comfortable?' he said. She could feel his voice rumble against her back.

'Yes. Thanks,' she said. 'Are you?'

'Very.'

He put his arms around her. Starlight sighed into the tufty wool of the sheepskin beneath her. It had been far too long since she'd been held while she slept. For the first time since she started her travels, she felt safe. She knew the safety was an illusion but didn't care.

Within minutes she slipped into a comfortable drowse, then a deeper sleep. She roused a few times during the night, once at an animal's howl too far away to mean danger, the other times when Thorn turned over in his sleep. It grew bitterly cold, but as Thorn had predicted, the wind did not find its way into their shelter. They huddled under the blanket, which she or Thorn had pulled over their heads as they slept.

She woke again from dreams of hunger and heat—the kind of dreams that always accompanied the onset of her season. Thorn was licking the pale fur of her throat. His deep purring thundered in her ears, his breath was hot. Each swipe of his tongue rasped pleasurably. His scent drowned her.

He worked his way from her throat to behind her ear. Starlight's purring resonated with his. She felt trapped in her clothes.

Thorn's paw slid beneath her shirt and caressed her belly. She gasped.

His purr died and he raised his head, lifting the blanket enough to let in cold air and pale light. 'Starlight, I'm sorry—I was dreaming. I forgot myself. I'm sorry.'

'I don't mind. It was nice,' Starlight said.

She was about to nuzzle him under the chin, maybe groom his throat too, when something powdery and cold landed on her head. She hissed in surprise. 'What is it?'

'Snow.' Thorn laughed and brushed it off. 'It fell from the edge of the tarp. It looks like we got more than I expected.'

Starlight looked out for the first time. The sun was not yet up but a layer of white covered everything, so that the entire forest seemed to glow in the reflected pre-dawn light.

She reached out and touched the snow. At first it felt firm under her paw, then soft. She licked it from her palm and the snow melted on her tongue.

'It's beautiful,' she said, struggling out from under the blanket. Cold air knifed at her. She stood, and the pads of her feet crunched into the snow.

She bounced over to where she and Thorn had left their boots. They too were covered, and filled, with snow. She shook them out and pulled them on, laughing. Snow still drifted from the blank white sky. It caught on her fluffed-out fur, on her whiskers; her ears flicked at the flakes' light touch.

She examined her own footprints with interest. Her paws had left perfect impressions in the snow, as though she had walked through soft mud. She wondered how long it would take the prints to fill with new snow.

Thorn laughed again and Starlight glanced at him. He had propped himself on an elbow to watch her. 'Never seen snow before?' he said.

'No. I thought it would be more like ice. I didn't know it was beautiful.' Her breath puffed as she spoke.

She was shivering, and despite her excitement at the snow she suddenly wanted to crawl back under the blanket and press herself against Thorn. But he sat up and started folding her blanket.

She brought him his boots. Ten minutes later they were back on the road.

Starlight warmed as they hiked. She tried to focus only on the snow: on the scrunch and squeak of their boots, on how it had transformed the forest into a dreamscape, on the flicker of movement amid the white and grey as birds flew out to investigate. But dread settled into her stomach.

Thorn said, 'See how snow has settled on every twig? It looks like filigree, but white instead of gold. I wish I could make something so delicate.'

'You don't work with gold?'

He gave her a smile that was barely a wry twitch of his whiskers. 'No. Just iron and steel, and the steel isn't as high quality as I'd like. I wish....'

He trailed off, and Starlight prompted him with, 'Wish?'

'I wish I could learn more—about making things. I'd like to work with gold. I'd like to make jewellery as well as ploughshares.'

'Why don't you?'

Thorn spread his paws and let them drop helplessly. 'I'd have to leave to do that. My master is skilled with iron, but he has no desire to learn things just for the interest of it. He makes horseshoes and nails and is satisfied. I try to be satisfied too.'

Starlight hesitated. She didn't want to remind Thorn of his grief, but didn't want to make him think he had a future with her. Finally she said, 'There's nothing keeping you here but habit, as far as I know. You're no longer indentured; you can leave if you want. What's the city you mentioned?'

'Eclin. It lies in the valley beyond the pass, and gets plenty of trade on the river. That's the way you're traveling, isn't it? There's no other road.'

'I'm not going to Eclin, though.' Starlight changed the subject. 'What's that little yellow bird called? I keep seeing them.'

The road grew steeper as the morning wore on, switching its way up the hillside. They stopped occasionally to rest. Thorn didn't press Starlight about her plans, to her relief. They talked little, saving their breath for the climb.

The snow stopped, and the delicate snow filigree melted. The soft plop-plop of snow falling from twigs and branches kept Starlight's ears twitching.

'I like how empty it is here,' she said. 'I walked some empty areas on the road to get here, but nothing like this. It's like we have the whole mountainside to ourselves—just us and the birds.'

'In summer it's busier. We get travellers willing to pay Dunkirk's toll, and there's plenty of game. It's only the cold weather that makes it feel deserted now.'

'It's restful.'

Thorn said, 'I like a bit more bustle, myself. I like to be around people.'

'I like peace, and no one to bother me.'

'Even me?' Thorn said, and when Starlight glanced at him he smiled. She smiled back and shrugged rather than replying.

She caught the scent of wood smoke. The illusion of a world without humans—without bandits, without Dunkirk, without the message she carried—vanished along with her smile.

Thorn raised his head and sniffed. But he only said, 'What do you like to do when you're not acting as messenger? Do you hunt?'

'Sometimes.' The top of a wooden tower came into view above the trees. Starlight's stomach lurched. Almost there.

'What do you do?' Thorn asked again.

She tried to concentrate on him, on her words. Now, with the final step of her journey almost completed, it didn't matter how much she revealed of herself. She said, 'I like to read. My lord taught me and he lets me borrow the books from his library.'

She expected him to laugh the way so many of her clan had. Books were a human thing—stories nailed down to pages, never changing. The frvaal told stories around the fire at night, history and lessons and warnings all rolled up together, never exactly the same twice.

But Thorn said, 'You're a scholar!' He sounded as though he'd discovered something important. 'I wondered why you seem so serious. Do you write books too?'

'No. I can't write, only read.'

'You can learn,' Thorn said, his voice cajoling. 'I can learn to work gold. You can learn to work words.'

'No. There are only a few words left in my future.'

They rounded a last bend as they talked, and the tower came fully into view. It widened at the bottom like a lighthouse, but made of wood instead of stone. Starlight smelled horse manure and saw half a dozen horses in a small paddock, picking at an armload of hay. Their stable was built against a cliff. On the other side of the road was a building that looked like a house.

'This used to be an inn,' Thorn said as they approached. Starlight noticed a man watching them from the top of the tower, thirty feet above their heads. She wondered if he had a bow. 'Dunkirk took it over and houses his men here. I know your message is important, Starlight, but let me talk to the men first. They know me and I can joke with them as usual. It might put them into a better mood.'

Starlight nodded, too frightened to speak. Her paws shook and she had a hard time stopping her tail from lashing in agitation.

A man came out of the inn. 'Hoya, Thorn. Brought a she-cat, have you? No wonder it's been so long since you visited.' He laughed.

'Jealous, Reece? Don't you have a horse?'

Reece laughed again. Starlight followed Thorn up the few steps onto the inn's porch.

Reece ushered them into a common room with a trestle table in the middle. Three men sat at the table with tankards. Another man, skinnier and younger than the rest, was turning a spit over the fire. Starlight's stomach rumbled at the smell of roasting pig.

She looked at Thorn, who greeted the men like old friends. He called them each by name. None were Dunkirk.

'I'll sharpen your blades first, if you like,' Thorn said, and Starlight noticed a grindstone in the corner. 'Hope you haven't been trying to do it yourself, Reece. You know what a damned mess you made last time. Any chance of a bite of that pig later?'

'If we've any left after Roberts takes his share,' Reece said. The young man at the spit grinned.

Thorn sat down at the grindstone and put his booted feet on the treadles. 'This won't take long if yours is the only blade I need to sharpen. No kitchen knives? Well, bring them here.'

Starlight stood by the door, frozen with fear and uncertainty. The men paid her no attention. Two of the men brought Thorn their blades and some knives, which they piled next to him. Thorn took a flask from his pack. When he opened it, Starlight smelled oil.

Thorn started the grindstone moving while he examined the first blade. 'How are the horses? It'll take me a few hours to heat the forge if you've lost any shoes.'

A door opened in the back of the room and a man strode inside. 'Thorn's here? Good.'

'A very good morning to you, Dunkirk,' Thorn said, and Starlight's heart squeezed in fear. 'If you need your blades sharpened, I'll get to them first.'

'I'll wait. I'd rather not be unarmed while a stranger's about.' Dunkirk stared at Starlight.

He was not a large man, to her surprise. In her imagination he had become a giant. He was slender and dark-haired, his pale skin not much weathered—he was still young, no more than thirty. His beard was neatly trimmed and his clothes were of a nicer cut than his men's. But his grey eyes were hard, his mouth cruel.

Thorn laughed. 'She's just a messenger, actually. She came through town and I thought I'd join her for the last part of her trip.'

Starlight took a step toward Dunkirk, but Reece blocked her way. 'Not so fast. Drop your weapons.'

'I haven't any.' Starlight took her pack off and propped it next to the door.

'Strip her,' Dunkirk said.

Thorn said, 'What?' but clamped his jaws closed with obvious effort. He touched the blade to the grindstone and bent over it.

Starlight swallowed hard. 'I don't mind. It's warm in here.'

Her voice trembled.

She turned her back to Thorn and undressed quickly. She thought Reece looked sympathetic.

Dunkirk was still across the room and evidently wanted her to come to him. He folded his arms and rocked back on his heels. 'Skinny, isn't she?' he remarked.

Starlight's tail lashed once but she made herself relax as much as possible. This was no time to alarm Dunkirk or his men, to remind them that even without a knife, even skinny instead of muscular like Thorn, she was still a cat. She had claws, she had fangs. She had a hunter's instinct passed down to her from a million ancestors who had killed to survive.

Dunkirk was no gazelle, Starlight no four-footed lioness. But with every step closer she felt she was stalking her prey.

'That's far enough,' Dunkirk said, holding up a hand. Starlight stopped several feet away. 'Who's your message from, cat?'

'From my Lord Esk regarding your demands.'

Dunkirk straightened and his hand dropped to his sword hilt. 'Is it? Why did he send you?'

'I volunteered. My lord has done me kindnesses in the past. I wished to repay him.'

'What message does he send me?'

Starlight drew a deep breath and spoke carefully. 'My Lord Esk wishes you to know he has considered your demands carefully against the needs of his people and his land. He must decline, but in recompense he offers you an eternity among the gods.'

She did not wait for his reaction. She lunged.

Her teeth closed on his throat and her jaw locked. Dunkirk was as good as dead, although she knew it would take him long, agonizing minutes to suffocate. She had debated with herself for weeks on how best to kill him, and had settled on this one as least likely to go wrong. No outside force could unlock her jaw, not even death.

Dunkirk beat at her back. She felt a knife slide across her ribs, heard shouts and commotion. She closed her eyes and folded her ears back, crossed her arms over her breasts.

It was done. She hoped her death was not too painful. The clan shaman had said she would drop into blackness like deep sleep, and would wake to a new life in a babe's new body—all memories of this life erased to start afresh.

Dunkirk's struggles weakened. He slumped to the floor and Starlight fell with him. She remained where she was even after he had stopped moving.

The room fell silent.

Someone touched her back; Thorn said, 'His pulse is stopped. You can release him.'

Starlight unlocked her jaw with a painful pop and raised her head. Dunkirk didn't move. His face was mottled purple; his neck was mangled where her teeth had pierced his skin. Starlight licked blood from her mouth and glanced up at Thorn.

He had shed his leather smock and was drenched in blood. 'That cut on your side is shallow. Are you hurt anywhere else?'

'I don't think so.' Starlight let him help her up. 'Why aren't I dead?'

Thorn folded his arms around her. She smelled his musk over the stench of human blood. 'Because I knew, Starlight. I guessed you expected to die—although I didn't know you planned to kill Dunkirk. I took care of the others.'

'How?'

'Well, I had most of their blades to start with.' He chuckled. 'I got the watchman too when he came in to find out why we were all shouting.'

Starlight buried her face in his fur. 'I never killed anyone before. I don't even like hunting.'

'You did a good job. I would have torn his throat out, myself.' He stroked her back, his blunt fingers tracing down her spine. He found the spot at her waist where her fur was thin and rubbed it lightly. 'What will you do now? Go home?'

'I can't. They said the rites for me before I left. I'd be a ghost to them if I returned.'

He held her close. 'Then come with me. I can't go back either; once the townsfolk learn I killed six men myself, whatever the reason, they would fear me. Let's go to Eclin, Starlight. Let's go together.'

Starlight breathed his scent deeply, then stepped back from his embrace. She saw the hope die in his expression.

But she said, 'Yes. I have words in my future. You have

gold. Let's go together.'

She took his paw and they stepped outside into the freshly falling snow.

# The Man in the Background

## Miles Reaver

In the late August, the mild afternoon air held a freshwater smell. On the waterfront, the promenade split into a row of umbrellas on the side of the buildings and offered shade to the sidewalk cafes and restaurants. The other side was a free range walkway that overlooked the harbour and the open sea. The days of the three month tourist season were coming to an end and on the far side of the harbour, a long tourist line awaited to board the bigger ships, traveling to and from Dalmatia. The umbrella restaurants were a mass gathering of hoarse laughter, the rattle of cutlery and savoury smell of tilapia.

Angela sat under the cafe's umbrellas and faced the waterfront. She enjoyed a cool drink of Schweppes and chewed on the small ice cube each time she tipped the glass to her muzzle. The rabbit observed the small dock, empty of boats, where a different mass of bodies gathered. A group of reporters armed with notepads, voice recorders and cameras, circled around a trio wearing suits. The tallest of them was a brown weasel that stood in the middle with a wide grin. He was posing for the cameras while the red vixen on his left kept her paws behind her back and looked angry. On the weasel's right, a short and large bobcat wiped his muzzle with a handkerchief.

The journalists, like vultures smelling fresh meat, pressed against the weasel. They asked more questions than the man had time to answer.

'Mayor Pavic, is it true that you're allowing foreign energy contractors to drill in the sea?' one reporter, a skunk, asked and practically shoved the voice recorder into the weasel's muzzle. The weasel darted his head back and brought his paws up to his chest in defence.

'Nothing of such has been decided yet,' he said, shaking his head.

'But you're not denying that there are already eighteen rigs extracting gas?'

The weasel managed a laugh.

'The gas rigs in question extract all gas, safely, and without any pollution or danger to the environment or persons.'

The skunk scowled at the Mayor, but kept the recorder up to the weasel's muzzle.

'Listen,' the weasel tugged at his suit button and grunted. 'No decisions have been made as of yet, but, the new development would bring a better life to Croatian people.' The weasel spread his paws and the reporters up-roared.

Angela shook her head slightly and wrote down the weasel's statement. The bobcat next to the Mayor kept looking at his feet. The vixen's glare only scowled further.

Mayor Pavic cleared his throat. 'If any and all decisions are made, the risk would undoubtedly be minimal.'

The bark and roar of the vultures forced the weasel and his team to take a step back. One more push and they would be swimming with the fishes.

The vixen placed her paw on the weasel's chest and stepped in front of him.

'Enough,' she raised her voice, pushing the reporters back. 'That's all the time we have for today. Thank you for coming.' She shifted her nose upwards and swallowed hard. The reporters protested, but the vixen waved them off. She took hold of the weasel's arm and dragged the Mayor with her, past the crowd. Mayor Pavic held a smile on his face. The bobcat stayed behind and delayed the rest of the journalists. When they turned their voice recorders and notepads to him, he shook his head, waving them off. The journalists gave up after a moment, and then split.

Angela closed her notebook and hid it in her bag. She took hold of her glass and tipped it to her muzzle. The rabbit took short swallows and observed the bobcat over the rim of her glass. The man panted with slumped shoulders. He walked towards the cafe and threw something small into an ashtray. The bobcat stared for a moment, then shook his head and left.

Angela finished her drink before walking over to the ashtray and taking out a crumpled note. Angela opened it in her palm and read 'COCO SHISHA 30 MIN'. The bobcat was careful.

The rabbit crumpled the note in her paw and now it was time to get to work. She grabbed her bag, passed through an alley and got to the main street with a roundabout in the middle. Angela wore a long skirt along with a humble top. The dark-rimmed glasses hid most of her face. She blended perfectly with the tourists.

Angela walked towards the stone stairs, until the shadow of the narrow buildings fell across her muzzle like a drink of cool water. The city was built on a small hill, where at the top, the church tower rose above all the other buildings. Bicycles leaned next to shops and open doorways. Clothes lines ran from one window to another, connecting the buildings together. Rovinj was a colourful city. The red and green wooden shutters were always open, inviting in bits of sunshine that crept over the edge of the shingled rooftops. Local residents lingered in the shade of the open archways, playing cards set on chairs. They smoked, they drank and celebrated the successful tourist season.

The walkways were limited in size as the city itself. The rabbit moved in the sea of people and then just before reaching the very top of the hill, Angela turned east into an alley and went off the beaten path. The unmarked avenue was less populated with tourists and more a home for local only shops and pubs.

The wooden, green sign had a faded colour. In gold, bold lettering, COCO SHISHA was written on top. The door was open and drapes hung above the entrance to keep the smoke inside. Angela removed her sunglasses and entered.

The lounge smelled of sweet smoke and strong coffee. The lights were dimmed for ambiance. A soft carpet led the way inside and across the room. On the sides, the screen dividers gave individual guests a bit of privacy. The guests laid on velvet cushions and sucked on the mouthpieces to inhale the smoke, they drank strong coffee and had whispered conversations.

At the very back, behind the room divider, the bobcat sat

on the bar stool and sucked on the hookah's mouthpiece. His sunken and heavy eyes stared down at the table. The bobcat blew the smoke through his nose and dabbed his fur around his eyes and muzzle with his handkerchief.

Angela stepped to the room divider; turned to make sure no one followed her, and then walked in. The bobcat's head rose and he got caught in a coughing frenzy. His paw held onto the mouthpiece while the other went for his throat. He held it there for a moment until his eyes stopped watering.

'Bogdan,' said Angela with a nod. 'I got your note.' She placed the crumpled note from her bag onto the table for the bobcat to see. The man took the note.

'These approaches, they aren't wise.' They spoke in English, as Bogdan didn't know Croatian.

'Then let's get to the point,' Angela hopped onto the bar stool. 'This oil rig business, how many are built already?'

Bogdan looked at the table and then at the rabbit. His ears twitched, flattened against his head and he sighed. 'Six so far,'

'And they plan to build more?' Angela asked, raising her ears. Bogdan nodded, but said nothing. The rabbit looked at him for a long minute. The bobcat refused eye contact and kept his shoulders sunk to make himself smaller. Angela produced a roll of money onto the table. It got Bogdan to look up. He placed his paws on top of the roll of money and pulled it towards himself.

'Six rigs are built,' said Bogdan, sucking on the mouthpiece. 'Three are operational. One more starts up soon.'

'How soon?'

'A few days? I don't know,' the bobcat shook his head.

Angela sighed. 'Who's paying the bills?'

'Bills?'

'Who's in charge,' Angela simplified it for the bobcat. 'It's not Pavic, he's just a puppet. So who? Serbian, Russian or German? You said you'd know by now.'

Bogdan shook his head again, coughing out the smoke. 'I don't know.' The bobcat growled, pressing a paw to his head.

'It's okay,' said Angela, reaching into her bag again and taking out a bottle of water. 'I need you to stay calm, okay?' she offered him the water. The bobcat fought against the idea, but a moment later took it anyways.

'Thank you. It's the climate,' he coughed, then unscrewed the bottle and took large swallows of water. 'I am not from here. Serbian, Croatian -- it is the all the same to me. I really do not know.'

The rabbit sighed. 'I really will need something, Bogdan,' Angela nodded to him, making sure to look him in the eyes. Bogdan stared, then sighed and slid a black plastic container onto the table.

'Foreign photographer came once and took pictures for newspaper,' the bobcat lowered his voice to a whisper. 'To be released when official paperwork is done.' He slid the container across the table. Angela placed her paws on top of it and slid it into her bag.

'Right,' said the rabbit, twitching her nose. Bogdan tapped the table with his claws.

'The man you want is in one picture. Group photo.'

'Does this man have a name?' Angela asked. The bobcat looked down and to the side. He made a grumbling noise in his throat.

'Victor...' Bogdan trailed off. 'Oleg, Victor Oleg, I think.' The bobcat took a long drag from the hookah, letting the smoke escape from his nose and slide across the table in a wave.

Angela scowled at the bobcat. 'And have you met this man before? Can you describe him? What species?'

Bogdan made a low growl and ran his paws across his head, pushing back his ears.

'A canine,' the bobcat spat out. 'I think, they all look the same. Some kind of dog. I'm sorry.'

The rabbit nodded to Bogdan and offered him a smile. 'That's good,' she said. 'That's good for now.' She looked behind her, through the gap in the room dividers.

'I can't do this for much longer,' said Bogdan, wiping his muzzle. 'They will know it's me.'

'They won't,' Angela reassured him and got up from her chair. 'Make yourself scarce, I got work to do.'

She nodded to the bobcat and Bogdan mirrored her movement. Angela reached into her bag and put on her sunglasses before she stepped outside. She headed up the hill where she mixed with the tourists and disappeared.

***

In Rovinj, Croatia, Angela's home was a small condo, located on the coast of houses and studio apartments. The spiral staircase led down into the flat, where the living room bonded with the kitchen. The dark oak tables and cupboards complimented the white walls and counters. A red rug with Turkish designs tied the room together. Angela's bedroom was behind sliding doors and its window, like the balcony in the living room, overlooked the open sea and the marina to the east.

The nights were cool with a pleasant breeze coming in through the open balcony doors. The surfing waves crashed against the lower walls of the building. The rabbit turned one of her bathrooms into a darkroom. In the bathtub were containers, filled with chemicals and the extracted raw negatives hung from the curtain rods above them. The enlarger, used to blow up the photos, was mounted to the wooden chair Angela brought in and placed between the sink and bathtub. She knelt on the cold floor and adjusted the lens used to project the image from the negatives, to the paper in the tray, and then hit the switch to let the machine do its thing.

While the photos dried, Angela finished her article. She compiled the statement she got from observing Mayor Pavic, but focused more on the information Bogdan gave her. The bobcat's information was good and Angela had enough of it from Bogdan's previous slips to piece together the bigger picture.

The oil rigs were not only already built, but operating illegally. The workers were paid off to be quiet. Part of her had to agree with Mayor Pavic, the oil rigs would boost the economy, but at a high risk of destroying the tourist attraction.

Angela went through the photos once they were dry, selecting a shot taken of one of the oil rigs, and the group photo Bogdan mentioned. On it was Mayor Pavic, standing in the middle, with his large grin pasted on his muzzle. Surrounding him were four others, wearing yellow visibility jackets over their suits and a hand full of oil rig workers in the background. The rabbit traced the photo, finding three canines. Victor Oleg stood on the right side, next to Mayor Pavic. The other two canines were workers.

At least Bogdan got that much right, thought Angela, putting the group photo into a brown folder along with her typed up article. The news would expose people wanting to stay hidden. This was going to cause trouble. At half-past eleven, the runner she called for arrived at her doorstep. Angela rolled the negatives back into a cylinder shape and placed them into the black container, replacing it into the side pocket of her khaki shorts. In this business you never knew who would be bold enough to try something. The boy at the door was a mouse and she handed him the brown folder to take back to the news agency, and get it sorted for the morning paper.

Dawn came too soon. It wasn't the sun shining onto her eyes that woke the rabbit, but the loud banging on her front door. The sound echoed from the entrance hall and kept up a steady pace. Angela pushed herself out of bed with a groan, tied her morning robe around her and stepped into the hall.

Greeting her was a bright smile attached to a small tiger that couldn't have been older than twelve.

The tiger waved a newspaper to Angela. 'Novine!' he cried with a wag to his tail. Angela smiled and pushed the door wide enough to lean onto the door-frame and look up and down the empty street.

'Newspaper' said the rabbit, pronouncing the word slowly and pointing at the bundled up paper. Angela spoke Croatian, and the cub didn't speak English. So she decided to teach him, one word at a time.

The tiger nodded to Angela. 'For you!' he said with a heavy accent that reminded the rabbit of Bogdan. The cub was learning.

Angela perked her ears and clapped her paws together. 'Very good!' she exclaimed. Reaching towards the inner table holding a bowl of fake fruit, Angela picked up two bills. She pressed them together and folded them once with her fingers.

'Very good,' she repeated to the tiger, and then exchanged the money for the newspaper. The cub's eyes widened.

'Thank you, thank you!' the tiger's tail wagged as he chirped with glee. He jumped down the five stairs, separating

Angela's apartment from the street, and waved at the rabbit. She waved back with a smile and headed inside.

The Agency remained punctual with the wording Angela used in her article. The story was on the front page and the title read 'BIG BUCKS, BIG LIES'. It wasn't the title the rabbit chose, but it worked. The picture of the oil rig was on the front cover and easily caught anyone's eye. The full story was on page four, with the group photo now in black and white, and twice as big as the one Angela sent in. The result was a grainy image with hard to distinguish muzzles, but still clear enough to where Mayor Pavic was recognizable.

Angela leaned across the marbled counter and scoffed. Victor Oleg was named 'the man in the background' and made to be a corporate bogeyman who came to a poor country in an attempt to exploit it. The abridged quotes received from the locals were of pure disgust and called for a public lynching.

Angela tossed the newspaper on the kitchen counter, removing herself from the story. Mayor Pavic would respond with a statement soon enough. Bogdan would tell Angela what was going on as long as the money kept coming. The bobcat was a mess, but it was because of that, that she was able to use him. Now she just had to wait.

The sun rose from the east, and come midday, the hot rays would make their way in through Angela's windows. Now was the time to relax.

Rovinj's beaches were a mix of white pebbles and sand. The rabbit marked her spot with a towel on the sandy side, settling between a bear couple and family of foxes. In Croatia, you could sit down and talk with strangers, entering their lives for a day.

Angela swam in the ocean, basked in the sun and enjoyed normality. She returned to her condo later than anticipated. The bear couple invited her for dinner, where they talked and knocked back one drink too many.

The condo was dark, freshly cool and empty. Outside a storm approached. Angela paused in the kitchen to turn on the TV mounted to the wall. It would erase the feelings of isolation. Angela knew a good day when she had it, and her back certainly felt it. There was a pulsing sensation across her spine.

'Not as young as you used to be,' she said to the rex rabbit in the mirror, then took two pills from the plastic container and tossed them into her muzzle. The pills would put her to sleep. It was the swimming that did her in, Angela decided as she got into bed. It was a good day.


The headache woke her up, a pulsing pressure at the back of her head. Angela groaned and turned under her covers. Her throat was begging for water and it followed up with a dry cough. The medicine, while useful, some days took a lot more out of her than any strenuous exercise.

There were voices coming from the living room, shouting and roaring. She'd forgotten to switch off the TV. Now the bark of the soccer game sounded like it was happening *in* her living room instead of on the TV. She rolled to the edge of the bed, then dragged herself out. The window in her bedroom, that overlooked the sea, was dark. She stepped close enough to peer out and was able to see the lamplights shine on the far side of the marina. She knew the pills would let her sleep, but not knock her out for nearly a full day. Angela sighed and walked to the living room and turned off the TV. Then, using her paw to support her weight, she climbed the stairs up to the front door and opened it. The newspaper waited for her on the doorstep but the tiger that brought it each day was nowhere to be seen.

Of course he wouldn't be waiting, thought Angela and scowled with a shake of her head. She picked up the paper and climbed back down into her den, tossing the paper on the counter. The clock on the wall showed a quarter to seven and the storm they promised would come, was just an hour away, perhaps not even that. She would have to find something to do to occupy her time -- to not feel so bad about sleeping the day away.

The rabbit sat on the barstool by her counter. She opened the newspaper, saw the headline and dropped it like it was hot. The title was a hit, written in big bold letters, 'VICTOR OLEG, SUICIDE'.

***

There was a captivating and morbid curiosity to the front page photo. They covered the head with some sort of rag, but the body's limp tail and paws were recognisably canine. He wore a suit and hung from the edge of the oil rig, with a rope tied around his neck. Talk about a public lynching, this was not what Angela imagined when she read the quotes in yesterday's newspaper.

The rabbit held the paper in her paws, reading through to the end, and then starting all over again. The article talked about the backlash and the oil rigs, rather than about Oleg. And yet, his body was found this morning by the workers on site. It had all happened too fast. Angela named the wolf, and in less than twenty-four hours, he winds up dead.

Angela lowered the paper, her eyes dancing across her counter. This didn't feel right. She needed Victor Oleg and now she had a body. It was generous to call the situation complicated. Then the phone screamed and brought her out of her daze. It was the wall mounted phone, the kind with the mile long wire to be able to reach through the entire condo. Angela observed the phone for a moment, letting it go through a few rings, and then picked up the receiver.

There was a click, followed by hoarse breathing and a frustrated grunt. The rabbit's ears cupped and she said nothing.

'Alo?' the voice snarled. 'Alo?'

'Bogdan?' Angela's ears pushed to the side. She recognised his breathing. The bobcat was in a panic before he even started talking.

'Where have you been?' Bogdan groaned. 'I have called all day!'

'You're panicked,' she said. 'What's wrong?' Angela brought her paw up to her muzzle. She immediately regretted asking; of course she knew what it was about.

'Wrong? What,' Bogdan took a breath. 'A man is dead. Dead and hanging from a rope!' The rabbit nodded to herself.

'Yes, I just saw the paper,' Angela sighed. 'I need you to calm down,'

Bogdan went into a coughing frenzy. 'Calm down?' the bobcat raised his voice. 'It is my fault the man is dead – my fault.'

'No, Bogdan,' Angela clenched her teeth together. 'If it's anyone's fault, its mine. I put his name in the paper.'

'No,' said Bogdan. 'The man in the picture is not Victor Oleg!' his words were followed by a click.

Angela's ears perked. She moved the phone receiver from her ear and looked at it. Her muzzle gaped open for a moment as the rabbit gathered her thoughts.

'What do you mean?' there was another click, followed by silence. 'Bogdan?'

'I'm sorry,' said the bobcat, quieter. 'They all look the same to me, but I know that was not Victor.' A third click echoed on the line.

'Bogdan, what is that clicking?' Angela asked. 'What are you doing?'

'Nothing,' the bobcat cried. 'I thought that was you.'

It could have been anything, only it wasn't. A man ends up dead, followed by clicking on the phone. This was Croatia after all and not long since the wars ended.

'Bogdan, get off the phone!' Angela yelled, leaning her paw against the wall.

'What? Off phone?'

'Hang up, someone is listening in. I'm coming over,' she slammed the receiver back onto the forks and ran into the bedroom. She put on her khaki shorts and a top, then manoeuvred across the living room and hopped up two stairs at a time to get out the front door.

The first sprinkles of rain hit the pavement moments after Angela made it towards the main street. At the end of it, she turned and dashed through a yard that was always open. It brought her onto the main, one way road that led up the hill to St. Euphamia. She went the opposite way, towards the centre of town. The buildings and alleyways twisted like a labyrinth, obscuring her path and slowing the rabbit down. There was no time to stop and think about it, Angela knew where to go and now the trick was getting there fast.

The rough asphalt under her feet changed to a polished stone surface as she passed the museum and turned right to go past the bank. She slipped on the smooth ground and landed on her hip. Angela shut her eyes and groaned. She cursed, then got to her feet and limped until the end of the street. Once Angela passed the bank, she went into a jog, and then turned left onto the empty road. She ran right in the middle until the halfway point, turning at the fork in the road, she headed down the right alley.

Thunder struck somewhere in the distance and heavy rain accompanied the storm. From a distance, Angela saw the open area where the alley widened and split sideways, down a new path. The tall buildings loomed over her and squeezed into claustrophobia. The hanging lamps lit the dark patches of the alley. Angela approached the illuminated corner.

The rabbit turned into the open space, exhaled the last of the air left in her lungs and brought her paws up to her head. She could see Bogdan's room on the very top floor. The wooden shutters were wide open and light escaped into the night. The mosquito net, attached to the top of the window was torn and hung on by a single edge as it flapped in the wind.

The bobcat lay on the stone pavement with his head twisted to the side. The splash of blood, which formed a puddle, was flowing down onto the alley in streams with the rain. Bogdan was dead, Angela could tell by the empty look in the bobcat's eyes.

Angela squeaked, as no other sound would come from her muzzle. Her maw shook before she clenched it shut and clamped her paws around it. There was no stench other than the fresh smell of rain and steamed seafood coming from a nearby restaurant.

The rabbit's ears twitched, a pair of feet splashed in the rain just behind her. She turned and faced the unknown muzzle. The rabbit took a step back and took hold of the assailant's paw. She let the momentum throw the man off balance, before delivering a kick to the back of his knees and sent him flying to the ground with a groan. Angela slammed her weight onto the man and twisted one of his arms behind his back.

'Wait, wait!' the man howled. He was a coyote, American, near as Angela recognised.

'Who the hell are you?' The rabbit demanded. 'Why did you attack me?'

'I didn't, I-' the coyote shifted his head and found it on eye level with the bobcat's corpse. 'Oh, god, no!' the coyote screamed. 'Bogdan, no!' the man struggled against Angela's weight, but locking his arm further up, she kept him from breaking free.

'I asked who you are,' the rabbit grit her teeth together. 'Did you kill him? Did you?'

'No, god, no.' the coyote shook his head. Slowly, he calmed his movements and leaned his head against the stone ground. 'Listen, listen,' he began, panting. 'We have to get out of here, if anyone sees us with him, we're doomed.'

The coyote's eye stared at Angela. There was something in his eyes that made her want to believe him. If he killed Bogdan, he wouldn't stick around. It wasn't unreasonable to think that the coyote might still be up to something. For now, his ears were splayed back and his struggling stopped.

Then there came a sound Angela didn't want to hear. A scream, loud enough to echo among the buildings. From down the alley, the guests huddled outside the restaurant. A woman, a tall cheetah, kept her paws on her muzzle.

'We have to go,' the coyote groaned underneath Angela. She released her grip on the coyote and took a step back.

'Run,' she said, looking into the crowd's direction. The coyote scampered up from the ground faster than Angela thought he could. He took the rabbit's shoulder and tugged into his direction.

'Follow me,' the coyote broke out into a sprint and a split second later, Angela followed.

They ran quickly down the alleyway and turned a corner from the fork in the road. They went back up the street, making a U turn around the murder scene. The streets were mostly abandoned in the rain and that gave them some breathing room. At the end of the street, the coyote turned left and traced the side of the buildings facing the pebbled beach. Angela followed close, gasping for air and wiping away the rain dripping down into her eyes. A few feet ahead, the coyote turned left again and down another alley. He waited for Angela to catch up, before turning into an archway.

The coyote panted when Angela reached him. He kept his paws on his hips and then stretched his back. He wore beige shorts, similar to Angela's. On top he wore a white, unbuttoned shit that exposed his chest and stomach.

The two exchanged glances, keeping a reasonable distance between each other.

The coyote sniffed. 'You really kicked the hornet's nest, didn't you?' he said between breaths of air.

'Me?' Angela scowled. 'What do you know about me? Who are you?'

'Tom Perry,' the coyote offered a paw. When the rabbit didn't move, the coyote shrugged. 'I know you wrote the article about the oil rigs. About Victor Oleg.' Angela straightened her back, rising to match Tom's height.

The coyote tilted his head. 'You didn't think you were the only one running Bogdan, did you?'

'You're a journalist.' Angela stated and scoffed.

'New York Times,' Tom confirmed and offered a smile. 'You're Angela Mlakar, Croatian reporter.' Tom knew enough about Angela to make her suspicious of him.

Tom's smile died. 'You exposed a spy.'

\*\*\*

Angela stared at Tom, rain dripping from her fur.

She brushed at the fur with her paw. 'That's ridiculous,' the rabbit argued. 'It doesn't make sense.'

'It makes perfect sense,' Tom mirrored Angela's movements and dragged a paw across his head, then flicked his ears. 'Who provides energy for most of Europe?'

'The Russians,' Angela responded. She assumed what Tom was going for.

'The war wasn't that long ago. Who do you think helped this place rise again?' Tom pointed out. 'Why would Russia let the Croats run their own oil rig if there wasn't anything in it for them?'

'I think I see what you're getting at,' Angela crossed her arms, observing Tom.

'Right. This deal would generate millions. It's an eighty-twenty split. Rovinj is a place of national pride; they don't want to scare away tourists.'

Angela nodded. 'So they never officially green-light the

project, but make money anyways.' The rabbit finished Tom's sentence. The coyote nodded, stepping to the edge of the archway and looking up and down the alley. In the distance, there was a faint sound of approaching sirens.

'So who killed the spy?' Angela asked. 'And who killed Bogdan? He said the man in the picture wasn't Victor Oleg.'

'He's right. Who the man is, I don't know, a stiff from the hospital maybe. Though, if I know the FIS, an agent who is exposed is dead either way.' Tom explained, crossing his arms and looking out into the street.

'And Bogdan?' Angela's ears flattened.

'I don't know,' Tom flapped his arms, then turned to Angela. 'The FIS probably. They knew Bogdan talked and they needed to tie up loose ends.' Angela tilted her head. Her nose twitched. Something didn't feel right. She mirrored Tom's movements and leaned on the opposite wall of the archway.

'How do you know that?' She asked, looking at him sideways. Tom turned his head to the rabbit, maw closed shut.

'Let's not do this.' Said Tom, shaking his head. Angela opened her muzzle, but the coyote waved his paw at her. 'Bogdan was on the take. You paid him for information. I bought him booze. We're reporters, it's what we do.' Angela closed her muzzle and bit the inside of her cheek. 'Though there is another problem. You heard it too, didn't you? The click?'

'Wiretapping,' Angela nodded. 'It's why I rushed over.'

'Same. I must have gotten the call after you.' Tom said. 'If they listened in, then they must know where we live. We should expect trouble.'

'Right,' Angela moved away from the view of the street, keeping her arms locked around her. Tom reached into his pocket and took out a cigarette packet. From the wrap around the packet, he pulled out some folded bills. The coyote licked his thumb, counted them, and offered half to Angela.

'It's not safe to go home,' he said. 'We should stay in a hotel for tonight.'

Angela observed the coyote and the money he was offering. The rabbit's pockets were empty and the coyote had a point, if anyone was listening in, then they would know where she lived.

The rabbit made a step and took the offered money from Tom, who nodded in return.

'Let's split up. The people at that restaurant saw a couple, so we shouldn't be seen together.' Tom replaced the cigarette pack into his pocket.

Angela squeezed the money 'And then?' she asked.

'We meet at the Gallery. You're from around here, you know where it is.' The rabbit nodded. 'Take the money, get a room and we'll meet there at say, around eleven? Follow the news and see what the word is.'

Tom turned and tugged at his shirt collar to push it up against the wind.

'Tom,' said Angela, making the coyote turn around. 'Do you have a card? You said you were a reporter.'

'Ah, sure,' the coyote stepped back under the archway, then reach to pull his wallet from his back pocket. He opened it, searched one of the sleeves and handed the rabbit a dark blue card with white writing.

'Thanks,' Angela smiled and accepted the card. He offered her a grin with a nod.

'Good luck,' he said, and jogged into the rain and down the way they came.

The rabbit waited in the archway for a moment longer and let Tom get a head start. The rabbit sniffed the card for a scent. Not a coyote. Oleg was dead and now so was Bogdan. Angela thought about extracting, shedding this place off her fur and leaving it all for someone else to pick up. Though there was an anchor that kept her from bolting. Tom hit a lot of things on the nail; he knew all of the answers.

The money Tom left her was enough for a hotel. She chose a room away from the elevators but close to the stairs. She let her clothes dry while she stood by the window and watched the glow of the police lights attract to one area.

Morning came fast and there was too much on Angela's mind. Checkout was at ten, but the rabbit changed the plan. She left the hotel at eight and took her time walking across the marina. Angela had to make sure she wasn't followed.

The bars and restaurants were opening their doors, setting up tables and chairs, sweeping away the gathered water in front of their doors.

Angela walked through the city and all the way back to her condo. The street to her flat was, as always, empty, but the knocking could be heard from down the farthest alley. She approached her door, where the small tiger greeted her with a newspaper and a smile.

'Newspaper!' he shouted this time, remembering the word. She praised him and handed him the rest of Tom's money.

'Is everything working now?' the tiger asked in Croatian.

'Working?' Angela tilted her head. 'What do you mean?'

'The repairman was fixing last night.' said the tiger. 'But you weren't at home.'

'Fixing? What was he fixing?' The small tiger shook his head, his ears going down. 'What did he look like?'

'Like a repairman,' the tiger's smile broadened. 'A wolf, I think, slim muzzle and all!' Angela's eyes narrowed on the tiger. She glanced at her condo apartment, closed and undisturbed. She faced the tiger again and squatted down to his height.

'And have you seen him around anywhere else? Any other houses?'

The tiger looked up, shifting his eyes and then to the ground. His ears came up.

'By the old factory,' he said. 'It has been abandoned since the war, but he says he was fixing things. We saw him when we played hide and seek there.'

Angela smiled and patted the tiger between the ears, letting him go.

Once alone, the rabbit opened the door to her condo and entered. The same fresh smell greeted her. She descended down the stairs and walked into a clean and undisturbed flat. She stood there for a moment, taking it all in. It was due to how clean and tidy it all was that made Angela suspicious. Not a single clump of fur was on the floor, not even her own. First things first, she checked the nearest bathroom where her equipment was. The red light bulb was smashed, so she had to turn on the light above the mirror. The photo enlarger was in pieces, screws and bits of plastic laid around the bathroom floor. She shoved them away with her foot before stepping in. The chemicals, the copies Angela set to dry were gone, even the collection of negatives. The rest of the condo appeared untouched, though the rabbit could imagine someone went to a lot of trouble to make it look that way. Whoever it was, focused on destroying the darkroom.

Angela sat on the edge of her bed and kept rewinding the scenario over and over, until she remembered. She tapped the left side pocket of her khaki's, and there it was, the plastic container Bogdan gave her, the original negative. She forgot she had hidden it before the runner from the news office came for the article. Thinking about it, it wasn't hard to make a few guesses about what was going on, the only thing left was to prove it.

Angela had another hour to waste before she agreed to meet with Tom. She could have eaten or showered, but instead she got up from the bed and headed back into town. The newspaper put Bogdan's murder on the third page and labelled it an accident. Funny that.

The Christine hotel was new, expensive and an eyesore when it came to architectural design. It stood on the hill and overlooked the island of St. Catherine by the port. Coincidentally, it was also where most reporters, with well-off backers, stayed. Angela walked into the cool lobby, with the morning sun's heat warming her back. She produced the card Tom gave her last night and showed it at the reception desk.

The antelope at the desk typed it into her computer, cringed and shook her head at Angela.

'There's no one here by that name, I'm afraid.' She handed the card back to the rabbit.

'You're sure? Coyote, working for New York Times?' Angela asked, but the antelope shook her head again. The rabbit knew better than to pry the desk for information. She didn't look the part and at the moment it was more trouble than worth being kicked out by security.

Angela turned and took a few steps down the wide corridor before she spotted him. The coyote walked from the elevators and into the lobby, then as if by chance, turned his head to the right, spotted Angela and froze. The coyote's ears pushed back and his tail squeezed between his legs. Angela knew that look; it was a man with his paw caught in the cookie jar. A second later, Tom's ears perked up and a smile appeared on his muzzle.

'Hey,' he said and approached the rabbit. 'You surprised me.'

'You surprised me,' said Angela in return. 'They say you're not registered here.' The two walked side by side, out the door and onto the road that headed to town.

'I never stay in hotels under my name,' the coyote explained. 'Makes finding someone too easy and based on the kind of work we do – you know?' Tom trailed off.

'Sure,' Angela nodded. They walked in silence until they got to town.

'So,' Tom then broke the silence. 'Any new developments? Everything okay? You okay?'

Angela kept her paws at her sides. The thought of the cartridge in her pockets brought a weight to her shorts. 'Sure,' she answered. 'They're treating Bogdan's murder as an accident.'

'Figures,' said Tom. Angela spared him a glance. His ears and tail were neutral, his eyes kept forward. 'I mean it's something the FIS would do, is what I meant.'

Angela stopped in place. A second later, so did Tom and turned to the rabbit.

'Tom, someone was in my apartment last night.' She said. The coyote flicked his ears.

'In your hotel room?'

'No,' the rabbit shook her head. 'In my condo. I went back this morning and some of my stuff was smashed up.' Tom glanced at Angela, his ears flicking up and down.

'Do you think it was them?' Angela asked, wrapping her arms around herself.

The coyote nodded, looking away. 'I think so, yes.'

'But why? I don't understand.'

Tom rubbed his muzzle with his paw, his eyes gazing around the area slowly filling up with tourists. Then, the coyote snapped his fingers. 'The photo,' he said, turning towards the rabbit. 'Bogdan said that Victor Oleg was in the photo, right?'

Angela nodded.

'In that case, they might want to destroy the originals, keeping anyone from making a high resolution picture.' He turned to face Angela. 'Where are the negatives?'

The rabbit shook her head. 'Most were hanging out to dry,' she said. 'They took those.'

'Most?' Tom's ears perked. 'You hid some?'

Angela nodded again, rubbing the back of her head. 'The stove. It's old and still has a compartment at the very bottom.'

Tom was taken aback. He grinned and shook his head.

'Smart thinking,'

'I don't want to go back there alone,' said Angela. 'Actually I don't feel like I want to go there at all. Would you be able to do it?'

Tom turned, fully facing the rabbit. 'Me?' he asked. 'Well, sure.' He extended his paw and Angela searched her pockets to hand Tom the key.

'Let's meet at the Gallery, like you suggested.' She nodded to the coyote.

Tom nodded with her, smiled and walked towards Angela's apartment.

***

Angela hurried up the hill towards the old factory. Things were easier once she knew what she was looking for. The rabbit followed the telegraph wires around the building. At the back, branches and leaves covered a door that was built into the hillside. She tried the door and found it locked. The rabbit didn't have time to think about it much. The large and unevenly shaped rock did the trick. Angela bashed the rock against the lock, pushing the door wide open with a screech.

The rabbit recognised the equipment. An old switchboard that made wiretapping child's play was pushed up against the wall. Next to the switchboard were pictures pinned to the wall. Of Angela, and Bogdan with the middle one missing. The label SVR was taped underneath the missing picture. Bogdan's just said PAWN. Under the Angela's photo, the labels read REPORTER OR SOA and an assortment of question-marks. The problem with privacy was that people were too honest when they thought no one was looking.

On the table, next to the typewriter was the needle in the haystack. An enlarged image of the group photo Angela sent into the paper. The image was blurry, difficult to enlarge without the original negatives, but someone made a lot of effort to clean it up. In the back row, facing sideways, the coyote wore the work clothes of the oil rig engineers. That's how Tom blended in, that's how Angela exposed him. The man in the background, a spy pulling the strings.

There is no worse feeling than knowing you're being played. The key part is always to know your enemy, once you're aware of how they operate, things get simpler from there.

Not all spies operated alone. They had agents and handlers, people who were in contact with the agency when the spy was undercover. The map left on the table had marks of meeting locations, drop-off points and codes used for emergencies. Angela recognised it all.

A point at the marina had a label reading RADIO on it. It was an old school trick, harmless but effective. A tape recorder wired to a broadcast station would play an emergency signal to anyone listening in. To the right person, it would signal that things have changed, to anyone else; it would look like the radio DJ played the wrong song.

Angela hit the radio switch and played the tape. It would broadcast across all radio stations in Rovinj until someone shut it down. A few seconds was all it took to signal the person listening in that a meeting had to happen. The rabbit grabbed the enlarged group picture and left while the tape was still playing.

The marina was full at daytime, and the contact wasn't hard to spot. He was a chipmunk and wore a bright yellow Hawaiian shirt with blue shorts. He surveyed the area, his eyes moving left and right. He held an envelope with both his paws. The thing about runners was that they don't always know who to expect.

Angela approached the chipmunk with a nod. 'Contact,' said the rabbit. The man looked her over, as if unsure if he was talking to the right person.

'Sorry,' he said. 'Who are you?' Angela snatched the envelope the chipmunk carried in his paws and shoved the picture his way. He was startled for a moment, but looked at the image once Angela pointed to it.

'I found your spy,' said Angela. 'He's got a burn notice on him and he's already producing bodies.' The chipmunk's ears rose to alert. His eyes narrowed and he looked at the picture again.

'Wha, who?' he began, but then shook his head. 'Not my business. What do you need?'

Angela shook the envelope at the chipmunk. 'Gallery, ten minutes. Bring a short leash and come quick.' She nodded to him with a smile, tossed him the black cartridge, then turned and headed down the walkway. She turned once to look back, but the runner was gone.

Angela had the boat tickets to Dalmatia and all the time in the world. The Gallery was a short walk from the marina. It was modern looking, with the outer side walls filled with graffiti. With the free entrance, people moved in and out as much as they pleased and that gave Angela the perfect opening. She walked into the air conditioned room and placed herself in front of an obscure painting. Thirty minutes later, the rabbit spotted Tom tracing the edge of the building. He entered, looked around and then closed the distance between him and Angela.

'The negatives weren't there,' said Tom, holding his paws on his hips. 'Something isn't right either, I feel it.'

'I guess the FIS really took everything and its gone forever.'

'No, impossible,' Tom shook his head, his eyes darting across the room. 'It doesn't make sense,' He looked at Angela again. The rabbit's muzzle spread into a smile.

'What-' the coyote began to say, but then their ears picked up the distant sounds of approaching sirens. Tom's muzzle fell open. It was a shock to know when the sirens were meant for you. He looked around, then back to Angela.

'What is this?' he asked.

'This is it,' said Angela. 'End of the line for Victor Oleg.' The coyote observed Angela for a long moment, his ears flicking back and forth, and his tail turning into a lash. A smile grew on his muzzle, twitching.

'You played me.' The coyote chuckled.

'I played the game, Victor,'

Spies operating under non-official covers had no diplomatic protection. Burnt spies had nothing at all.

The coyote chuckled and dragged his paw across his muzzle. He threw a glance around the room. The sirens were enough to attract the people's attention and dragged them outside to see. The exit was blocked; there was no place to run.

'What are you? MI6? Croatian SOA? It's CIA, isn't it?'

'None,' the rabbit shook her head. 'I'm freelance. It's why I get to do stuff like this.'

Victor scoffed. 'Play journalist?'

'Hunt burned spies.'

In front of the Gallery, the vehicles stopped with a screech. The authorities were making their way past the crowd, attempting to enter.

'The Russians are SVR not FIS.' said Angela. 'A card that doesn't hold your scent and way too many coincidences. It's what gave you away, in case you wanted to know.' Victor stood before the rabbit, but didn't say a word.

'Tom was investigating you, it's why he had to die, didn't he? Once that picture was out, you knew you were burnt. You thought you could make a switch, a coyote that looks like a wolf.'

Victor listened and said nothing. His tail lashed behind him.

'They'll hang me for this, you know.' The coyote managed. A moment later, a tactical team of uniformed officers made their way into the Gallery. The chipmunk and ferret wore bulletproof vests and held a pistol each.

'Better than the Gulag, no?'

The coyote smiled, shaking his head. 'A burnt spy is a dead spy.'

The officers surrounded Victor, yelled orders at him, making their intent obvious. Victor raised his paws and slowly got to his knees. There was no reading of his rights. His people would take care of the rest.

'Good game,' Victor nodded as they handcuffed him, and then pulled him back onto his feet. The chipmunk holstered his gun as he stepped closer to Angela.

'I had no idea you were CIA' he said.

'I'm not.' Angela replied. 'I'm freelance. Tell Langley they can reach me in Dalmatia.' Angela waved the envelope at the chipmunk and the man nodded in response.

The tactical team accompanied Victor towards the exit. With locals and tourists standing shoulder to shoulder, they chatted, took pictures and then, they screamed. An echoing shot of a rifle came from somewhere outside. The tactical team held onto Victor's limp body for a moment longer, trying to register what just happened. Then they let him fall to the ground and searched for the shooter who was already gone amid the chaos.

A burnt spy is a dead spy.

# Dirty Rats

## Jan Siegel

*When men discuss the things which are to be, the rats laugh in the raft-ers.* **Chinese proverb**

Like all good rats, I hate humans. Not deep-down gut hate, the way you hate your bitterest enemy, just gen'ralised hate, cos they're such a bad thing.

Think of the *space* they take up. The Big Red – he's the big-gest of the urbin vermin – he'll hunt over a huge territory, but his den'll be small, just enough room to sleep out the day. Us rats, we've got the Tunnels, we're the kings of the Undercity, but hell, there's lots of us in every cranny, eating and snoring and fighting and shagging. Being Rat, that's about being part of the gang, part of the pack, part of the Mischief, friends and enemies and endless sprawling families all huddled up together. But humans, they build these nests, tall nests going up to the sky and wide nests rambling over huge areas like anthills gone mad, and in some of them there's a few humans, and in some there's maybe just one – just one human in a den as big as a warren! – and in some there's none at all. They build the nest and leave it, coming back once in a season, to check it's still there. It's like those great mountains of rubbish they leave, except at least you can eat the rubbish. What's anyrat meant to do with a load of empty space? You can't eat it and it don't keep you warm – it's a lot warmer snuggled in a small hole with your mates. Space, who needs it?

That's the thing about humans, Muzza says. Muzzletoff, he's my friend, though he's not lean and strong and tough like me. There's plenty rats would kill him for a runt, they says to me: 'Ripper –' that's me, Rippercheek '– why'd you bother with him? He's the kind who's dead meat the moment he's born'; but they don't get it. Muzzletoff is smart, not sewer-smart but brain-smart, more'n anyrat I know. He figures out stuff most of us don't even think about. He knows how humans *work*. That space thing, he says it's all about *not sharing*. All creatures share, he says, whether it's cockroaches or mice or us rats or even the Big Red – he's meant to be a loner but he'll scavenge with his mates when the bins are full and the shes curl up with their cubs like all the urbin vermin. Human shes don't even sleep with their pups. That's not natural, right? Muzza says, being human is *about* being unnatural. In Human, if you're king of the heap you gotta have a great big empty den to prove it, and then you don't even live there.

Talk about dumb.

'Course, leaving those big empty dens around means sooner or later – probably sooner – somebody'll move in. That's just common sense. This is the city, and in the city we all share, whether humans like it or not. We share with them and they share with us. We live in the Tunnels but hell, we're all upwardly mobile if there's stuff to eat and stuff to chew on and those soft cushiony humps humans have in their dens what are great for nesting. You gotta be careful cos sometimes they leave traps, what'll catch you and hold you till you die, and sometimes they leave poisoned food, but you can tell if there's traps and poison, cos other rats or mice'll be there already, dead and rotting. You don't want to eat them, neither, cos if they're poisoned the poison'll get into you and kill you too. Dead humans are all right, there's loads of meat on 'em; a dead human's a real treat. But mostly humans take their dead away to eat private, though Muzzletoff says they don't eat them like we do, they bury them in the ground for later, or burn them, the way they burn all their food, and sometimes they don't eat them at all. How wasteful is that!

In nests where there's humans actually *living*, they have cats. You gotta steer clear of cats. Even the ones what *look* fat and lazy, like they've eaten so much they won't even bother to lift a paw, they'll go for you in a heartbeat. You don't want to mess with cats. But the vacant dens, the ones with acres of floor and coils of wire to gnaw on and huge mounds of the cushiony stuff to burrow in – they don't have cats there. You only get cats where there's humans: it's what Muzzletoff calls *syn-edgy*. (That means living on the edge of each other.)

Cats are like, half-pet half-urbin vermin, and they can't make up their minds which: they take food from humans and they hunt anything that moves, and they live in human dens and go out on the streets at night and yowl at the moon like the Big Red. Muzza says cats have got it made, but they're not cool like rats. We own the Tunnels – we own the whole damn city. There's loads more of us than cats, loads more than humans, which *proves* it.

Talking of cats, well, after Skroat got his guts ripped out by that white cat he'd been keeping, he took a long time healing up. Most rats would've died, but not Skroat, you can't rely on him for anything. He hung on and he healed and he came loping back to Hole 101 meaner and wickeder than ever. Skroat's a big piebald rat, even bigger'n me, half hairless and with more scars than space in between. He thinks he's the boss of the Undercity: he's got a load of henchrats what do everything he says, a whole gang of them, and his does are the glossiest, slinkiest mousies you ever saw, except the slinkiest of all was Shagrat, and she left him for me. Which is one reason why I'm not too popular with Skroat right now. There's more reasons, since it was me what released the white cat (well, my mates Longeye and Weezil, but I told them to), and killed his top henchrat Lockjaw, rat to rat, what makes me a mugging *legend* in the Tunnels. But that's another story. Point was, when he healed up Skroat got his gang looking for me and my mates, so we thought it was a good idea to move out for a while. I mean, there's loads of them, and there's only the four of us, and I can't kill everyrat, can I?

So Muzzletoff says he knows where there's one of these big empty human dens, with just one rat living there, though he's a gerb what escaped and went native. (Gerbs are foreign rats from places a *long* way away. Humans bring them here for pets, so we think they're pretty low, but Muzza will make friends with anyrat; I've talked and *talked* to him about that but he still does it.) This gerb, he's got a posh human name, on account of having been a *pet*; his name's Cholmondley-Botham, like *Bot-arm*, but they call him Chumlybum. He stands kind of hunched, the way gerbs do, balanced on his hind legs and looking down his nose at you cos his nose is that shape. First time I met him, I noticed he kept touching his whiskers, like he was afraid they might fall out, and he spoke very soft, more whimper than squeak, but Muzza said that was just cos he was nervous.

'Ain't got no call to be nervous,' I said, 'so long as he don't play games with us.'

'He ain't scared of you,' Muzzletoff said. 'It's just jenna-rick nervousness. He's a nervous type.'

I don't know who Jenna and Rick are, but I didn't ask. Sometimes Muzzletoff says stuff that's so random it's better not to, cos the answer'll take forever and tie your head up in knots.

This gerb Chumlybum, he shows us round the biggest den you ever saw. He told us he used to live there in a cage, and one of the humans, a pup, would feed him and fuss over him and even let him out sometimes, so he runs away and hides, and the humans think he's gone, and then they went too, and they don't hardly come back no more. That shows how important they are. Anyway, this den was *huge*. There was chambers as big as a whole city, filled with those giant cushiony mounds to nest in, and poles to climb with platforms on top, and cloth to nibble and wood to gnaw, and great stretches of ground covered in thick furry stuff like animal skin, only it wasn't cos it didn't taste right. There was even one with a kind of lake in it, bright blue and funny-smelling. Weezil said the blue was poison, and if you jumped in it you'd die, so of course I dived in, and splashed about a bit, and I didn't die at all, I just came out with a weird stink on me, but it wore off later. Anyway, this den was so high, there was too much light coming in, from holes and wall-spaces, and the shadows were huge and pale with nowhere to hide. The spookiest thing, suddenly we sees these other rats coming towards us, and I show my teeth and so does one of them, and we go towards them, all snarly and angry, cos they don't look friendly at all.

'They're not really there,' says Chumlybum. ''San illusion. Try fighting 'em, you'll see.'

We got right up close so we could see the glint in their eyes, and then we hit this hard cold surface, like ice or something, between us and the enemy rats, and we couldn't get through. And the weirdest part, there was a rat looked like

Muzza, and one like Weezil, and Longeye, and Chumlybum, and a big mean-looking rat in front facing me, moving when I moved, but we couldn't get through the hardness, we couldn't even bite through, it was so smooth.

'It's a *reflekshun*,' Muzzletoff said, 'like you see in a puddle somedays, when there aren't any waves to break it up.' He said the enemy rats were us, staring back out of the hardness – it was a kind of trick, a magic thing which humans have. After a bit I could see he was right – the mean one was me, natch – but it was so creepy, we got away from that part of the den as quick as we could. I really don't get humans. Why would they want to be bumping into themselves all the time? They have this *not sharing* thing, and then they want to share with a spook-self? That's freaky shit.

After that, we found the place with all the paper. Don't get me wrong, paper's all right to nibble, when you haven't got anything better, but this was like a whole world of paper. Racks and stacks of it in great thick layers, climbing up the walls, the sheets squashed together into solid blocks – it would have taken a year to gnaw through the half of it. Normal paper is scrunched up in a bin or gutter, and sometimes it's got grease and food on it, which is pretty good, and sometimes it's got funny markings, but we've never much bothered about that. But Muzzletoff's intrested, cos he's intrested in all sorts. This paper had marks, lots of little black marks close up. Muzza said that's human talk, turned into paper: *talking paper*. It sounded mad, but I could believe it, cos you've only got to be inside a human den like that place to see how mad humans are. Muzza said if we knew the secret we could understand the talk from the paper, but, I mean, *why?* Still, that's Muzzletoff. He's my mate, so it don't matter if he's a bit barmy. It's allowed.

Anyway, Chumlybum says the humans what made this den aren't never coming back, not for *ages*, so we gnawed through some old animal hide and burrowed down into the fuzzy stuff underneath to sleep. I felt pretty safe cos this ain't the kind of place Skroat's gang would invade; they don't hardly leave the Tunnels at all. I'm lying there dreaming of Shagrat who's got pups at the moment, probly mine, and there's the den stretching away through all those empty chambers, so the quiet actually seems to echo, and the air moving gently like a great big sigh, and those soft shadows making the sounds shadows make, what only rats can hear. A sort of rustling, shifting, whispery sound, like two ghosts rubbing shoulders on a dark night. Suddenly, there's a noise, bursting into my dream – the sort of noise that might be ordinary in the Upper City but sounds huge in that quiet place. Paws. Big, heavy paws, a hundred times bigger than ours, and thumpier. *Humans.*

We all wake up quick.

'You said they never come!' Longeye hisses to Chumlybum. 'You said they're so grand and important, they never come here. You useless piece of mouseshit!'

'They don't come... they ain't come in ages...'

'Shhh!' I shut them up fast. We needed to get out of sight. Wasn't difficult in that place; plenty of cover. We got under one of the mounds and I squinnied out to see what's happening. Chumlybum squeaked a bit, he was so scared, on account of being a nervous type like Muzzletoff says, but Longeye clamped a paw over his snout to keep him quiet. There was one of those moveable walls in the way – humans make those, to close off the gaps between different parts of the den, but the ones in this den hadn't been closed tight so we'd been able to get through. It's more of their *not sharing* thing, so they can keep themselves apart. We heard this one sliding open wider, making a scrapy noise across the floor. Then the big thumpy paws coming into the room.

'Something's wrong,' Muzza whispers.

'What d'you mean? We're stuck in here with a pair of humans – of course something's wrong!' I said. But I was listening good, cos if Muzza says *something's wrong* he's usually got a brainy reason for it.

'They haven't put on the firebulbs,' he says. 'Humans don't see normal the way we do. That's why they have the firebulbs. There's a couple in here; I noticed. But these've brought their own, small ones.'

He was right. There were two of them, carrying firebulbs what they pointed round the den, running the beams up and down the walls. Muzzletoff and I crawled out to see what they were up to. It was a bit risky, cos the firebulbs might have pointed at us by accident, but they weren't aiming at the ground and anyway, humans couldn't see a whole ratpack if it was under their noses.

They can't smell for shit either.

They were talking too, really loud – though everything humans do is loud, cos they're so big and ugly and clumsy, not quick and smart and cool like the urbin vermin. We couldn't understand them, natch, but you could pick up an idea from the *tone*, which was sort of urgent, even *desprit*. When you come into your den you curl up or roll over or do a bit of grooming, but this pair were prowling round and sounding more nervous than Chumlybum (and he's a nervous type).

Muzza said: 'This isn't their den.'

'It's empty,' I said. 'Maybe they're moving in.'

'Humans don't do that. It's the *not sharing* thing.' He went on: 'They're acting like we would, if – if we found Hole 101 empty and sneaked in to have a look around.'

He was right. I saw that straight off. It's hard to tell with creatures that big, but they were being *cautious*, pulling the cloth together over the outward holes in case anyone beyond saw their firebulbs. Then they started moving things, not the mounds where we were hiding, thank the Great Mother Rat, but things on the walls, flat things covered in fancy markings, all shapes and colours, and even one of the huge racks filled with blocks of paper, swinging it across the ground. There was something behind it, squarish and made of metal. They got really excited when they saw it; I could feel their excitement through my whiskers, all tingly on the air. It was frightening, being so close to them, when they're that big, and getting so worked up, like they might stampede or do something dreadful. Longeye and Weezil kept Chumlybum quiet under the mound, but Muzzletoff and I, we crept nearer, shaking a bit, catching the excitement. I crept cos I'm brave, but Muzza, he's just so curious about stuff, he calls it *scientific*, so there's times he oughta be afraid and he's not.

The humans were fiddling about with the metal thing, then that swung back too, and there was a hole beyond it, and they were groping inside and pulling stuff out, and their tone changed, and the vibe coming off them, like they were excited in a different way, excited and pleased. As if we'd sneaked into Hole 101, and found a secret stash of ripe dogshit, and we were stealing it for ourselves. I said so to Muzzletoff, and he said yeah, but it's got to be very ripe dogshit, to be hidden away behind that metal square so no one else could get it. That would be something very special in the dogshit way, right?

I told you Muzza's smart. That's brain-smart, that is. But I was pretty smart too, figuring the humans out. There's not many rats can figure out humans like that.

So we watched, while the pair got all the special dogshit out of the hole in the wall. We couldn't see too good but one of the humps was pushed up against the stacks, and we shinned onto the wooden ledges to get close, moving very quiet, though humans make so much noise, they wouldn't have heard the Big Red if he'd barked in their ear. What they were getting out, it looked like more paper, different paper, tied up in bundles, with the markings all thin and curly. We'd seen paper like that before, 'course, lying in the street sometimes, but it don't get left around. Humans *really* prize that paper: they'll scrabble around for it in a pile of good rubbish even though there's no food on it, like it's the best dogshit ever. But this pair just put the bundles aside and went on groping in the hole.

At last they get out this flat brown package, and they open one end, and there's more paper inside, not curly-patterned paper but the other kind, with regular black markings, and now they're so elated, you can feel the air crackling. This is what they were looking for. You can tell how pleased they are cos their smell changes. The fear smell is *sharp*, kind of acid; it stings inside your nose. These humans had been channelling fear since they came in, fear and excitement all mixed up.

Human smells are really complicated: Muzza says it's cos they wash a lot, they wash off their natural stink – how weird is *that?* – then they put other smells on their bodies. Like the extra skins they wear, called *clothes*, what smell like flowers and soap and stuff, with the human smell underneath. Apparently, the more important they are, the more they wash, and the less natural they smell. Somerats go crazy around them just from the muddle of all the different smells.

Anyway, these humans, they were stinking pretty strong, what with the fear and everything, but now it changed, they was almost relaxing, smelling softer, smelling *satisfied*. Their voices go softer too. Next thing, they're sticking all the bundles except the brown one back in the hole – though one human, he tucks a curly-patterned paper bundle in a pouch in his outer skin when the other isn't looking.

The other, he don't see, but somehow it seems like he knows, he knows there ain't enough bundles to put back in the hole, and suddenly they're arguing, shouting at each other. Pretty stupid when you're trying to be sneaky, but of course there aren't any more humans near, and humans are no good at *sneaky* anyhow. Not like urbin vermin. We grow up doing sneaky.

Muzzletoff and me, we're creeping back along the ledge, away from them, when suddenly there's Chumlybum scrambling up towards us. He's all trembly cos of being a *nervous type*, but he's still climbing, what's pretty impressive: bigger'n braver rats than him would've stayed safe under the mounds.

'We gotta stop them,' he says.

'*What?*' That was when I was really surprised. Gobsmacked. Really for real. 'They're *humans*. How'd we stop them? And – *why?*'

Then all this stuff comes out about the pup what looked after him, and the family, and how they fed him nice food, and stroked him, and all that peaches, and how, while they were away, he had to look after the den for them, like it was his den now. I said that was nonsense, his brain was all messed up from living with humans, this was pet-thinking, but he kept on and on about it, and behind us the two intruders were still arguing, louder and louder, like they were heading for a fight, though humans never fight proper cos they don't bite. The whole huge place was fizzing with all that anger – it was bouncing off the walls – my whiskers were twitching with it – and maybe it got inside our heads and made us crazy, like human stuff can. Chumlybum says I'm *scared* – scared, ME! – and then he dropped down to the floor and scurried towards the humans, what're grabbing each other by their skins and shaking each other, the way they do, only not real fighting, like I said, not biting or clawing. Humans must be big cowards cos they never fight for real.

I wasn't scared, natch – well, only a little, since it was human giants, and anyrat with half a brain would be scared of *them* – so I slithered down after the gerb, and caught up with him on top of a platform, where they'd put the brown bundle. He was tugging at it, but he ain't strong and he couldn't move it much, so I got a grip with my fangs and pulled it hard. It slid along the platform and fell to the floor – I was sure the humans would hear, but they were busy with the shouting and the shaking, and anyhow, humans never hear nothing. We got it under one of the mounds, and Muzza and Weezil and Longeye joined us, and I said: 'What do we do now?'

Mostly, I'm the one what decides what we do, but this was Chumlybum's den, in a way, and he was the one all worked up about it, so I thought he oughta have a plan.

'We eat it,' he says. 'Then they can't get it.'

We're rats. We eat *anything*. (Except peaches, cos they're disgusting.) All the same, it was a big wedge of paper, and we'd have to eat it quick, before the humans found us.

We start chewing, and chomping, and tearing at it, and there's a big crash as one of the humans falls down, or maybe the other pushed him, but he gets up again – I take a quick squinney – and they're trying to hit out with their paws, but they keep missing, or not hitting hard enough, and knocking into the mounds so they slide about, and it's all getting pretty dangerous. We dragged the brown bundle across the room, crunching at it all the time, mashing up all the markings and things so, like Muzza said afterwards, the paper wouldn't talk any more, wouldn't tell any secrets.

It seemed like ages while we were ripping and champing – I'm good at that: they don't call me Rippercheek for nothing – and the humans were banging about, then abruptly they stopped, and they must've noticed the bundle was missing, and then it's panic time.

You don't want to be near a panicked human. They rush about and shove and bump and yell like it's the end of the world. These two were jerking those big mounds round the place like pups playing with balls of grit. They were peering under things and poking the firebulb-beams into corners and saying stuff in tones all sharp and worried. And angry, cos humans are often angry. This pair were angry about everything, angry-scared, what was different from the way they'd been scared before. It smelled different.

'They're scared cos they've got their own Skroat,' Muzzletoff whispers. 'They're meant to bring *him* the special dogshit, and if they don't, he's going to be in a screaming rage.'

It seemed funny to think of there being a human like Skroat, with his gang-rats and his lair in Hole 101, but I did think Muzza might be right, cos he so often is.

Then they started finding the chewed-up paper, and that made them *really* mad. They were upsetting things and yelling louder'n ever, and Chumlybum, he goes from being bonkers-brave to being totally petrified, so he won't even move, and one of the firebulbs picks out his tail, and the humans give a great screech, worse than the Big Red in a rage. Weezil – he's the fastest of us, the fastest rat in the Tunnels – he runs around in and out of the mounds and even between the human legs, and they're hitting at him with the biggest paper wodges, and throwing them at him, but he's too quick, they can't get him. Longeye and me, we grab Chum and start pulling him away, and then he's moving again, and somehow we all get out through the open wall, into the next chamber, with the humans coming after us. We keep running – we can hear their huge paws pounding along behind us – but pretty soon they stop, cos humans never run for long, and Chum sort of wakes up and leads us to another part of the den where we're safe.

There's nothing like that moment, when you all curl up together, and scratch each other, not rough but gentle, and nuzzle snouts and touch whiskers, and tell each other how brave you've been. That's *sharing*, that is. Humans don't do that.

I've had a plenty adventures, what with Skroat and his gang, and killing Lockjaw – once I fell into the water with the Crays, and they come after me with pincers snapping, pinching my tail, but I got free and my tail healed up, and in the Big Heat the water shrank and I got one of them, when he was left high and dry – but nothing, *nothing* was as scary as that time with Chumlybum and the humans.

It was funny, we never really knew what it was all about. Much later, Chum's humans came back, with their pup, and found some of the chewed up paper, and the silly gerb went back to them, back to being a *pet*, which shows you how stupid gerbs are, and they seemed pleased with him. We knew, cos we visited him. He was in a cage, and I said I'd gnaw the bars and let him out, but he wasn't having any, he liked it. Sick.

But I'll always remember how brave he was, totally bonkers-brave, going after the human invaders. No rat would've done that, not Skroat, not *me*.

It just shows you.

# The Sentinel

## Will MacMillan Jones

Listen.

*They* are coming. I can feel the pressure on the Portal from where I stand on this side. It is something that you learn through experience. At this stage it is not possible for me to tell how many of *Them* are trying to pass through at this time. Who are they, and why did they choose our world as their target? That is not known to any Sentinel. Yet we all know, at our deepest level of understanding, this: that *They* come from beyond our reality, from somewhere outside. This place is the object of their desire, and they seek to tear their way into it, and to eject us from the planet, system, universe itself that is our home. *They* hate us, and wish us harm and it is not necessary to know more than that.

I sound the alarm, as is my duty.

Then I concentrate of the focus of the Portal, the first point to fall open if the attack is pressed home. It isn't always. Sometimes, just sounding the alarm is enough to deter *Them* and the Portal isn't assailed. A feint, to test my readiness to action, maybe? Anyway, today the pressure is still there. Building.

I sound the alarm again, with a little more urgency.

This time, I begin to think, will be the time that a full attack takes place. I've only experienced that once since I took over the Duty from Ted, my predecessor. The task fell upon my shoulders when he became too elderly to be a reliable Sentinel any longer. He tried to carry on, of course, and finally he fell in a desperate fight one night. Luckily, I had been with him by then and was able to stand over his body and repel *Them* before they broke through. I grieved for my lost comrade and mentor, but of course I now had the Duty and the responsibility. I had been born to the Duty, Ted having been my father. I knew from the start that this was to be my role and purpose in this life, to guard this Portal and prevent the enemy from ripping a breach in the time-space continuum, and invading our reality.

I sound the alarm, giving warning to both sides: here to raise the alarm and on the other side of the thinning Portal to Them that a Sentinel is here, standing guard and prepared for battle. I can't hear any nearby answering call though, as I sometimes do. That is alarming. I am in the prime of my strength, confident that I can fight and repel any attack: but the knowledge that some backup is available would be comforting. It is the nature of the Duty that we each stand watch and fight alone, until we need to train our successor – but I suppose that every lonely warrior can sometimes feel the need for companionship. I do miss Ted.

Is this, I wondered at first, the only such Portal? Were we - Ted and I, that is - alone in the Duty? As I grew older in my training, before Ted went down fighting on that dreadful night, I found out that there are in fact many such Portals and each one has a Sentinel. In fact, as no Sentinel can be on duty constantly, we do have a specialised rota for time off, a break, and sometimes on these I meet others of my ilk who also stand guard. It's good to know that I am not alone on those nights when the pressure mounts against the Portal and the enemy feels strong. It would only need one of us to fall unaided and alone, and the consequences would be terrible. I hope that I will soon get a trainee of my own, someone to teach, and to take over the Duty when my time comes to follow Ted.

Sounding the alarm helps. It deters *Them*, and it helps my morale and confidence. When the alarm alone repels an attack, I feel good. The alarm. I sound it now.

Yes, I've had to fight. Once a strong attack came through, and I had a dreadful time. In fact, I thought I had lost the battle - that was when Ted came from his retirement to help me, and although he lost his life that night the Portal was held. *They* have not tried to break through here in such numbers again, for Their losses were very heavy. *Their* dead were dragged back through the Portal in the retreat, so at least there was nothing for me to clean up after the assault and I could attend to Ted and vent my grief at his death. I suppose it is a good way to go, and hope that when my time comes I will be as brave.

The pressure from beyond the Portal builds to a crescendo of force. It pounds against the Portal, and pounds inside my head. I stand before the Portal, sounding the alarm and making it clear that I shall do my duty, shall defend the Portal to my last breath. It's two in the morning. *They* like to attack at this time of night. I suppose that it is because *They* hope that the Sentinel will be sleeping. I have been better trained than that. I will not be caught sleeping, and fail in the Duty.

I sound the alarm a last time and prepare for battle: but then for some unknowable reason *They* fall back into wherever it is that *They* come from. The Portal has held, and I have won another night in the long, unending battle.

My reward for the small victory comes. The words are in another tongue, and I do not understand them – yet I know that they are full of love, praise, and appreciation for my efforts. For my bravery. For my steadfast resolve. The words, whatever they are, encourage me to continue. Perhaps one day their full meaning will be revealed to me. I hear them now:

'Stephen, the bloody dog's barking his head off at that empty wall again. It's two in the morning!'

'I'll go and sling a slipper at him, then. Rats. Missed him, but he's shut up now.'

# Pay the Piper

## A McLachlan

THE KITTEN'S WHISKER

Dazed by sunshine, vibrating with the early morning hum of honeybees, Cloaca scuffles the cottage path with her belly now. The pups are getting heavy; they have reached a size where she can count them when she rests her hand against the strained velvet pelt below her ribs.

She stops beneath the bird table to collect a handful of black sunflower seeds. The old lady has noticed her condition and puts seed on the ground for her now. Next to the seed is a bundle of silver hair, pulled from the brush. Lately there has been sheep's fleece and a twist of sweet smelling hay, and even an old mitten, carefully washed. Cloaca chews with her eyes half closed. Between the lids, her eyes dart left and right.

None but the sharpest of trained eyes would have noticed her pause by the pot of motherwort where she keeps a slice of broken mirror.

At the entrance to her tunnel she stops, a spine of fur bristling up her back. Her rodent synapses spark. So: the kitten's whisker she had placed in the entrance has been moved. She rears, catching scent in her nostrils. Male. Juniper. Soul of an empty sandwich wrapper.

She goes inside.

'Looking for this?'

He is laying on his back, sucking on a piece of bacon rind she had put by. He flourishes the whisker. 'Bit old fashioned of you,' he drawls.

'You know me, Morgagni. I'm old school.'

He sits up. 'Nice set up you've got here. Cushy.' He points the whisker at her belly. 'When are you due?'

'Whatever you want, you're wasting my time. I'm retired.'

'Retired? That's not what I heard. But I don't blame you for going soft. Motherhood and all that. You're bound to want an easy life after what happened. To try and forget.'

His eyes slide away.

Cloaca does not want to forget. She summons Paneth in her thoughts to ask him – what happened? Paneth's drowned eyes contain a warning when he comes.

She turns her back and begins to weave the clump of silver hair into her nest.

Morgagni pours a layer of oil on to his voice. 'Q Fever would like to make amends. She always was the sentimental type. She wonders if perhaps you had had more support, maybe you could have stopped the Piper at Hespe.'

'Are you saying she wants me back in? Q Fever?'

'For now. Depending. Have you heard what happened at Hameln last night?'

'Go on.'

'Thirty thousand. Piped into the Weser. Not a single one left alive.'

Cloaca stiffens. 'He's escalating.'

'Plenty of time to think about it. The offer has been made. I'm sure it's pretty cosy for you here, playing mother.'

Cloaca's tail goes hot.

'I'd want Cowper and Villi.'

'No can do. Cowper took ship. And Villi is – well, you know Villi. Holed up at an inn somewhere. Besides,' Morgagni becomes brisk. 'The Cellar is stocked with bright young things nowadays. You'll have plenty of top drawer assistance.'

Cloaca tucks in the end of the hair and regards Morgagni. 'What's the brief?'

'Usual stuff – pamphlets and such. Spread a little misinformation about the Piper, put off a few customers.'

'That's it? Then why do you need me?'

'We don't, frankly. It's a little favour. Clear that dark cloud that hangs over your name. I'm sure that's important to you.'

'Your definition of important was always different to mine, Morgagni.'

He grabs her hand, spreads her claws. 'You've let your nails grow.'

She snatches it back, too quickly. She looks at her hand. He's right. The nails have grown; they are all the same length now, and uniformly sharp at the ends.

She scratches the end of her nose and draws the scent of Morgagni through her nostrils. She senses a note of something beneath the juniper but cannot place it. There is a juniper bush at the entrance to the cottage, she remembers. Perhaps he brushed against it on his way in. But the pungency is too strong... he must have rubbed himself with crushed leaves. He had left it late, to disguise himself. She considers this a discourtesy.

'All right. I'll do it.'

As Morgagni lets himself out he gestures to her belly. 'Mine?'

'How would I know? I never look round.'

## THE CELLAR

The Cellar, on the face of it, seems unchanged, except Old Sigmoid who guarded the entrance has become two sleek rats who keep their names to themselves. They sniff her from nose to tail, even flip her on her back so they can sniff her belly. Her pups huddle inside her.

She allows scent to drift through her nostrils during the inspection; the sleek rats smell of wormwood.

She goes straight to Q Fever who makes her wait.

The faces that pass through the tunnel are unrecognisable. She searches for an old one, a friendly one, but they carry on past her without a glance. She lets their scent in: wormwood.

Sprigs of wormwood are everywhere, she sees: at each entrance and exit, and at intervals along the walls. She watches these new rats, these fresh rats whose glossy coats have never been near a sewer, rub their bodies against the wormwood and self-anoint.

Every rat reeks of it.

Wormwood is bitter, camphorous, sharp and cooling on the nostrils, but far from invigorating the rats the Cellar has a languorous air, and no more so than in Q Fever's lair which Cloaca notes when she is finally allowed in.

'Nibs! Oh, Nibs, you've let yourself go.'

Q Fever is reclining on a soft fleece bed. She has become vast. Solicitous rats in constant motion make a fuss over her, plumping her pillows, proffering mounds of steamed corn, tucking a blanket around her feet. Cloaca had brought an offering of innards from a new cushion, and they are propping it under Q Fever's head.

Cloaca pulls her hand back from Q Fever's prying claws. 'I brought you these as well.'

'Rapunculus seeds – delicious! Where did you get them? The old hag?'

Cloaca watches as Q Fever nibbles. Her mind wanders, as it so often does these days, back to Hespe. How had she missed it? Maybe she really had let herself go. But it hadn't just been Hespe: watertight ops had been going wrong for a while. And key rats had been reassigned at critical moments.

'Your assistant will be Lumen,' Q Fever is saying. 'You can have your old office back.'

'I'll need my papers, inks, stamps.'

'And a little knife to carve your nibs, Cloaca! I must see them when they're finished.'

'And the Bremen customs seal.'

Q Fever's mouth stops. Then: 'Of course. Everything you need will be provided.'

Cloaca senses the dismissal, but: 'Don't you want a more permanent solution to the Piper?'

'Permanent? Of course. But not right now. He would only be replaced. For now we only want a little trouble, send a little warning shot across his bows. That's all.'

Cloaca wonders: when did Morgagni and Q Fever begin to speak so alike?

'We could send in a team. Shit in the pantries. Let them think he only did half the job.'

Q Fever sets her pink eye on Cloaca. 'I prefer a more elegant solution.'


The office is bare. Next door a scrabble of young rats laugh and plan a weekend away at one of their houses. One of them tilts back on Paneth's chair, chewing a weasel rib.

'Lumen – where is everything?'

'You can get what you need from the store cupboard. Ma'am.'

'And a candle stub and a knife.'

Cloaca taps her nails as the clerk disappears down a hole. Then she turns the ledger around and checks the entries. One item catches her eye: yesterday, Morgagni signed out a parcel of cotton wool.

Her whiskers warn her the clerk is approaching, and she turns the ledger back around.

***

Cloaca is paring her nails into nibs – she can remember by heart the differing widths and slants of the quills used by the burghers and mayors of eighteen different towns, the idiosyncrasies of their writing. For instance: the merchant Grenz uses a particular blackness of ink, and since he broke his wrist last winter after slipping on ice and landing heavily on the flat of his hand he wears his nibs down on the right. His letters are scratchy. Grand Burgher Rennacker is profligate with his quills; his clerk passes a freshly sharpened one for each letter. His ink contains crushed lapis lazuli, and he writes with a serene hand. Citizen Jantzen, however, has a wife who stands at his shoulder reading his correspondences as he writes them. He writes with a flinch in his quill.

'Any news on my inks, Lumen? My papers?'

He has been watching her carve. He shakes his head. 'The clerk says they are at the far end of the hole, where the bricks fell when we expanded. He's going as fast as he can to clear a way through.'

'And the Bremen seal? Did that get flattened under a ton of bricks, too? It's useless.'

He shrugs.

***

Cloaca waits outside Q Fever's lair, watching the comings

and goings of the Cellar. Everyone appears to be busy, in the middle of something, going or coming back, but no actual work is done. Hands and fur are clean and glossy, teeth are unbroken, eyes are bright, tails – despite their baldness – are bushy.

'Oh, your nibs – your nibs are back. Aren't they wonderful? You have quite the skill.'

'I need to go to Hameln while I wait for my inks to be recovered.'

Q Fever lets her hands go, and Cloaca tucks them into her rolls of fur where she counts seven moving inside her.

'Of course. I'll send Lumen with you – travelling must be so uncomfortable for you now, you poor thing.'

## DEAD IN THE WATER

Lumen stands on the Weser bridge, a soft summer breeze riffling his whiskers. His eyes are watering. He speaks from behind his hand.

'This is where the worst of it happened, ma'am. Not entirely sure what you can glean from it – there were no survivors.'

Cloaca looks down the wide river. She remembers trying to swim across it once, as a dare. She had been tumbled and spat out on to rocks a mile later. Now it is still, clogged with gently bobbing corpses. I could walk across it now, she thinks.

'I'd like to go down to the shore.'

'Do you mind if I stay up here, ma'am? I can still keep an eye on you from here.'

I bet you can, she thinks, as she picks her way down the greasy mud.

She walks to the edge of the river where the bodies make a brown froth. Each rat has a look of ecstasy on its face. The rats that still possess eyes have a faraway look in them.

Damn that magic flute.

She continues downstream until she comes to a bend in the river, where a clump of dead rats has snagged on a fallen bough.

She falters and turns, glancing up at Lumen who gives her a pasty wave with his pale spare paw. He watches her as she staggers up the bank and makes her way back to the bridge gasping and holding her belly. He helps her up on to the road and she stumbles against him.

'It's a bit much, isn't it, ma'am.'

Cloaca leans against Lumen. She sets her eyes to soft-focus. 'I've seen enough. The smell is making me hungry.'

## THE GOOSE AND APPLE

The cock is still on his perch at the Goose and Apple, but Hamm is already up and having a fight with his horse.

This morning, of all mornings, the beast has become head shy and refuses to take its bridle. It repeatedly throws its head up as Hamm, in no mood for he has been pissing hot needles since the three o'clock bell, dances around beneath it trying to keep his hand on its nose.

Goslar, the stable boy, watches this entertainment from a crack in the hay barn door until it gets old, and then he goes to help.

The horse gets bridled and hitched to the wagon, and the carter goes on his way looking worse for wear than usual.

The horse tosses its head and rolls its eye all the way to Hameln, and it doesn't settle until it steps on the bridge, where Cloaca lets herself down from the hammock she has knotted in its mane.

She clambers down the mud bank and walks downstream. Two hundred and forty seven steps from the bridge, just beyond the clump of rats on the log, she finds what she is looking for – a set of footprints leading out of the river.

The footprints drag themselves up the slope and into a hole under a birch tree.

Cloaca rears up and takes in the scent. Young. Frightened. Female.

Her whiskers lead her down the hole, and she is ready when the rat flies at her. She steps to one side and it slams

111

into the wall. It lays there, panting, its fur sodden with fronds of trailing algae.

'You're safe with me,' says Cloaca. 'You're with pup, aren't you? Same as me.' She indicates her belly, the mounds of her pups. 'I bet you're hungry.'

The rat, still pressed against the wall, nods.

'I'll fetch you some food. You'll feel better.'

As she runs down the river bank Cloaca wonders what the rat is so frightened of. It has been presented with a golden opportunity. It should be having fun in the grain stores while the burghers sleep complacent.

She drags a burst rat back to the hole.

The pregnant rat nibbles at it, shaking, barely able to swallow.

'What's your name? Mine's Cloaca.'

'Crypt.'

'You look like you're due any moment, Crypt. I can see your pups moving. Why don't you go back to Hameln?'

Crypt shakes her head. Her teeth are chattering. A lump of green meat falls from her mouth.

'What is it, Crypt? You can tell me.'

'That night – that night. You heard?'

'I did. What happened?'

'The pipe, I – I couldn't resist, I just couldn't. I don't know why. I thought I was strong.'

'You are strong, Crypt. You survived.'

'Only because I was so slow. These are my first,' she cradles her hands around her squirming belly. 'I can't get used to being so big. I got there last, but I still went in. I got swept down on to a pile of rats clinging to a log and managed to scramble over them and away when the music stopped. That's when I saw them.'

Cloaca's whiskers twitch. 'Them?' A thrill of bristles runs up her spine. 'Who?'

'The Piper and... you won't believe me.'

'Go on.'

'He was with a rat. I mean – it stood with him on the bridge. You must think I'm crazy, but it's true. The rat didn't go into the water, it watched. It watched as we drowned. I looked back and saw it.'

'Can you tell me what it looked like, Crypt?' Cloaca gentles her voice. 'The rat?'

'It was huge. And it had one pink eye.'


Crypt has eaten and is curled up, her eyes half closed, as Cloaca's tongue rasps algae off her fur. Velvet blooms on her pelt as it dries.

'The last one to do that to me was my mother,' murmurs Crypt.

Cloaca finishes with a few quick rough licks to Crypt's neck and sits up to regard her.

'Much better. Now, Crypt, I want you to listen to me. You aren't safe.'

'I know. Please help me.'

'I will, but I need you to wait here. I'm going to get help. Now, don't trust anyone who comes here, don't go anywhere with them unless they give you one of these –' From her ear she takes out a piece of paper folded to the size of a barley grain and opens it out. Inside is a dot of blue ink, or rather Oxford blue, since that is its exact shade. One of eighteen from her old collection.

'Memorise it. If they bring one of these you can trust them. You have my word.' She replaces it in her ear.

Crypt says, wide-eyed, 'Thank you. You've been so kind to me.'

Cloaca hurries away across the mud to the bridge, her mind as sharp as broken glass.


VILLI


Villi's network has been broken. Villi cannot, or will not, be found.

Cloaca has been to the rye store but was met with a hail of stones from flint-eyed boys and their catapults. All the holes have been cemented up at the bakery, and the baker's wife chased her off with a besom. At the old river the Ferryman sees her and whispers to a pedlar as he poles across the water.

The old network is a masquerade of veiled eyes, eyes that glance down and away, a network that refuses to say 'no' in case even that forms a commitment.

She is on the verge of doing something reckless: setting up a safe hole from scratch. Any other rat she would have put on a cart in a barrel of cherries and sent it far away to be dealt with later, but Crypt is due any moment.

Cloaca is about to make discreet enquiries in a timber yard when she scents Villi behind her. She turns and finds a rat, sitting on its haunches, its face a mess of scars and both its eyes missing.

It is holding up its hands and from one of them comes the scent of Villi, tinged with fruit sugars.

'Can you take me straight to her?' Cloaca asks. 'I don't have much time.'

The blind rat says nothing, but leads with its whiskers, and they take a journey of back alleys and hedgerows, they run through the fresh dung of slop buckets and carters' horses to disguise the smell of their feet. They stop, briefly, to anoint themselves on a patch of sweet basil, and soon they arrive at the back yard of the Castle of Comfort where the blind rat slips away.

Villi is passed out and reeking of fermented apples.

'You,' she says, when Cloaca has finished dunking her head in cold water. She swings a fist at Cloaca's throat which Cloaca catches and turns. Villi staggers against an empty barrel.

'I need your help, Villi. It's urgent.'

'So urgent I'll go half prepped? Not this time. Not after Paneth.'

'No-one is more upset than me about –'

'Catscat.'

'Listen to me. Something has happened at the Cellar –'

'So you're still working there. How nice for you.'

'No. They've brought me back. Everyone's been cleared out –'

'Except you. Evidently.'

'Q Fever runs the whole show.'

Villi puzzles. 'Q Fever? How?'

'That's what I'd like to know. And Morgagni's with her.'

Villi's expression opens slowly. She reaches out and snatches Cloaca's hand; Cloaca lets her. Villi sniffs each nib, each pad, she sniffs her ears, her face, her whiskers. She puts her hand in Cloaca's mouth, touches her tongue, feels around her teeth. Hostility drains from her eyes.

'What do you need me to do?' she asks.

'Have you heard what happened at Hameln?'

Villi slumps. 'I did. And I can't stop thinking what it must have been like at the end for Paneth.'

'I'm pretty sure he died happy, but that's not the point. Why did he have to die at all? I'm a great believer in balance, you know that, but what's happening now is excessive. Tell me –'

She, Cloaca, scents misery, puts her hand on her old comrade's back. 'Tell me – this Piper appeared out of nowhere. Nowhere. He arrives at Hespe, in broad daylight, on our patch, and it's the first time the Cellar has heard of him? I don't buy it.'

'There was something. A whisper. Paneth came to me...'

'And?'

'Do you remember that time Morgagni went missing?'

'There was talk he'd been dismissed. I never set any store by it.'

Villi turns to her with ghosts in her eyes. 'Could I have stopped it? Could I?' She collects herself. 'Listen – I'm a bit parched. Need to wet my whistle.'

'Tell me first,' she says gently.

Villi looks down, away. Sags against a barrel. 'You know Paneth never trusted Morgagni. Paneth thought in between things, he was always drawn to what we weren't allowed to know. His whiskers led him to a musical instrument shop on the outskirts of Brunswick. He sniffed around. And what turned up? The scent of Morgagni.'

'So Morgagni knew about the flute?'

'It's worse than that. Paneth believed he designed it. He found the scent of Morgagni on the blueprints.'

'So.' Cloaca thinks – why does this not surprise me? 'So. Morgagni is wiping out large numbers of rats. Why?'

'To disguise the fact that they are targeting specific rats, perhaps? There's more. Paneth told me an interesting thing but he couldn't be sure. Some soft knowledge. He was going back to check, and then –'

'And then. What was it?'

'He thought the music didn't work only on rats.'

'Ah.' Cloaca tries to digest this information, order it. 'Morgagni and Q Fever are working together. They've brought me back to the Cellar to discredit the Piper.'

'Oh – they must have decided to finish him off. Maybe they planned to use the pipe on something else – maybe he went rogue.'

'No. That's just it. They've only brought me in because they think I'm off my game. They don't want to stop the Piper, they want to be seen to be doing something, that's all. It's just like it was before – my inks and papers have gone missing. And the Bremen seal has been broken in two.'

'The Bremen seal?' Villi's eyes mist over. 'Whoo – that was a close shave! Remember? Thought we'd never get Cowper out of that scrape.'

They smile together for a moment, thinking of Cowper. She had been the bravest of the lot of them. Always first to go in.

'Does Cowper know about this? Where is she?'

'Morgagni told me she'd taken ship.'

'I don't believe it.'

'Neither do I. Anyone with any intelligence, any skill, has gone. No-one's hungry anymore.'

They sit for a moment and watch the Weser creep past the inn's garden. The river has swollen and breached its banks; it laps at the feet of summer tables and chairs.

'Paneth...his face haunts me. So... he knew too much. Is that why he was sent to Hespe? Is that how the Cellar works, these days?'

'There's more, Villi. The Cellar thinks every rat in Hameln died, but I found a survivor. And she has a tale to tell. Are you still in touch with your old network? The one the Cellar never knew about?'

CRYPT

As they turn off the bridge Cloaca notices another set of footprints running alongside them in the mud. She sprints with Villi up to the hole. Rearing together, scenting, Cloaca and Villi exchange a look. They go inside.

Crypt is curled up into herself, dead. There is a single bite mark to her neck. Beside her is a piece of paper, crinkly where it has been folded down to the size of a barley grain. It has dot of blue ink in the middle. Oxford blue, to be exact. Camphor perfumes the air.

Her paws cradle her belly; it moves as her thirteen pups squirm.

## What the Papers Say

The inks and papers are waiting for Cloaca when she gets back.

Lumen looks up. 'Feeling better?'

Soon her nails are stained with eighteen different shades of blue and black ink, and a sheaf of correspondence between the burghers and mayors of eighteen towns describing their various dissatisfactions with the Piper's work are ready to be sent out.

'You've excelled yourself, Nibs. We will bear you in mind if another job comes up so keep those little nibs sharp! And in the meantime, have fun finishing your lovely little nest!'

They are taking apart her office – everything tossed into a box: candle stubs, inks blue and black, parchments, papers, desk and chair; even the knife she used to carve her nibs. 'Can I keep that?' she asks, and they look at each other until one shrugs, why not.

The rats in the office next door are laughing, likely at the same joke, making the same plans for next weekend as the last. Without even looking she can feel Paneth's chair tilting backwards.

As if she had never been there the Cellar goes on about its business.

There is only so much I can do, she thinks. But I do it well, she adds.

Lumen is nowhere to be seen.

She walks home clutching her belly, stopping half way to crouch beside a wych elm whose trunk has been cleaved by a lightning strike.

A ramekin of scrambled egg waits by the entrance to her tunnel, and after eating it she rolls on to her back and falls flat asleep.


## THE MAYOR'S FEET


Villi waits until the pasty looking rat who has been trailing Cloaca has scuttled past her scat pile, its hand to its mouth, its eyes watering. She reaches into the cleaved wych elm and out of it she takes a piece of folded paper, heavy with a wax seal. The seal has a faint line through its middle, imperceptible to a casual glance.

She is out of practice and slow, and so she only has a moment to time her run up the tails of a brightly coloured coat as it is borne into Hameln Town Hall by its wearer. This is just the sort of thing Cowper would have been up for, she thinks with a pang.

The Piper is ushered into the Mayor's office and he presents his invoice for one thousand guilders.

The Mayor nods to the Banker who begins to count the guilders from an oak chest into a large leather bag.

'We're very pleased,' says the Mayor sidling up to the Piper, 'with the job you did for us. Now –' he drops his voice. Behind them, the chink, chink, of coins into bag. 'Tell me. What sort of commission could I expect if I recommend your work to other towns?'

Villi chooses this moment of closeness between the two men to drop the sealed paper at the Mayor's feet.

'Allow me,' says the Mayor, bending down to pick it up. He glances at it, and his face gathers with bafflement as though a string has been pulled tight around it.

'What's this?' he asks, holding the paper up to the candle

on his desk.

The Banker leans over his shoulder and squints. 'Well well. It's a bill of lading from the port of Bremen. For a cargo of thirty thousand rats, shipped live from Felixstowe.'

The Mayor and the Banker turn their eyes on the Piper.

'Let me see that!' His harlequin arm reaches out and snatches the bill. His eyes run up and down it twice. 'This is a forgery! A lie! What are you playing at?'

The Banker drops a coin he had been holding back into the chest. He narrows his eyes. 'The Bremen seal does not lie, Piper.'

'But – this – I don't!'

'Get out. If you think we're going to pay you now, you need to think again.'

'This is poor, very poor,' says the Piper. 'I've never seen this paper before in my life. You've cooked this up to avoid paying me.'

He puts his face into the Mayor's. 'You will regret this.'

The Mayor turns to the Banker as the door slams. 'What can he do? Our own rats are already dead, he can't bring them back. What a piece of luck!'


PLAY THE PIPER


It is dusk on the Saints day, John and Paul. Sunset has turned the stone bridge over the Weser to mottled gold. The river is a brown sludge.

From the Hameln side walks the Piper, dressed in green. He walks with wings of flame as behind him the torchlit townsfolk fan out across the hills, calling for their children.

From the opposite side of the bridge walks Cloaca.

They meet in the middle.

Cloaca studies his face. He is sour looking, stubbled. He does not wear his revenge well, she thinks. But he does not know that, yet.

'Here is the proof I promised you,' she says, holding out the two pieces of the Bremen customs seal.

He tosses them like dice in his palm. If only you knew, she

thinks, what it took to get that seal. If only you knew what courage can do.

The Piper fits the pieces together and stoops against the bridge parapet to compare them to the wax imprint on the bill of lading.

Cloaca watches his mouth, carefully.

It moves. 'Bastard rats. Bastard rats.'

His eyes slide towards her from beneath his matted yellow fringe. His lips move again.

She interrupts: 'And here is the address of the Cellar. But you don't have much time, they move every day. They'll be gone by the morning.'

He snatches it from her hand, runs his eyes across it and looks down. 'You're all as bad as each other. You're all filthy. You're all scum.'

Cloaca flinches when he pulls the pipe from his coat and puts it to his lips, laughing. She turns and rushes away, but she is slow, dragged by her belly. She puts a hand over her pups as she scurries.

The music plays down the fur of her spine. She feels the pups turn towards it inside her, feels them push against her spleen. She can feel the shape of twenty eight battering feet desperate to dance behind the flute.

Cloaca knows men, so she has taken precautions. She has cotton wool stuffed deep into her ears and is deaf. If she runs fast enough she will be home in time to beat the rooks to the first ribbons of bacon rind put out by her tunnel, and to birth her pups in peace.

And Villi? She is already back at the Castle of Comfort, raising a toast to Paneth. She wishes she could tell him the tale of how she pissed on the pipe's mouthpiece while the Piper argued with Hameln's mayor. She makes Paneth a promise: that not long after he pays his visit to the Cellar, the Piper's skin will turn yellow, his limbs will swell, and his lungs will beat like blooded wings inside his chest.

She watches the river flow past the inn's garden, low and swift as though a blockage has been cleared further downstream. A late bee browses on water mint pollen. Villi tastes fermented apple on her tongue, and takes another mouthful.

# The Long Game

## Neil Williamson

*March 7th 1974, 1.30am*

*When the moon comes out,* Fred thinks, *it's all over.* Craning his neck upwards to reassure himself, he makes out the satellite as a diffuse radiance behind the slow-shifting clouds. Not unlike a corpse light out among the river reeds back in his childhood home, really.

*Now, there's a cheery thought.* As Fred ponders that notion for a moment, the corners of his mouth crinkle. Then he forces himself to concentrate. *Mustn't get ahead of myself.*

The question is, how long have they got? It's too dark out here behind the village main street to determine the extent of the cloud cover. Just as it's too dark to gauge the length of this field with any real accuracy, the distance to the safety of the trees. And too dark too for Vizsla, prowling behind the coach house hedge, to make them out.

For now.

As Fred watches the clouds hurry across the moon, he turns his leathery cheek incrementally, trying to detect the direction of the breeze that moves them. He feels nothing, but the clouds rush on whether he's ready or not.

He's getting too old for this… Scratch that, he was too old when he retired the first time.

\* \* \*

*March 6th, 9.05am*

'Come and sit down, Jackie.' Framed in the doorway between the kitchen and front room, Fred tried to keep the weariness out his voice. *Christ, what do they teach these lads of the craft these days? Daytime surveillance. Shadows behind the curtains, old son. Those blasted, ever-twitching ears of yours.* 'I've made breakfast.'

According to the lease, the little flat above Dreyton's village post office technically still belonged to the premises down-stairs but there was no post master now, just a trenchant local called Mavis Davies—a name so unlikely it could only be real—who ran the place as a general store. The shop still had the red signage above the door and the post box embedded in the wall, still sold stamps and postal orders, and accepted parcels too. They even still offered the forms for applying for passports and driving licences and the like, but you had to send them away now. Times had moved on. These days many of the smaller villages like this one were no longer afforded the luxury of a post master.

So, this empty first floor flat, facing the old converted coach house inhabited these four and a half months by a certain Mr Collins, had been a stroke of luck. A holiday letting sign had gone up and the villagers had got used to seeing new faces coming and going. Couples, families, and now an old man on a pastoral retreat. And a younger one, his amanuensis or his carer, the villagers might think. Or perhaps they might imagine a different relationship. It didn't much matter. One story was as good as another.

Young O'Hara took a last squint through the long-lensed SLR, scribbled the time in the log and came through to the kitchen. 'I'm telling you, he's bolted.' That delightful soft-quick Liberties brogue. 'He's made us the minute we got here and now he's fecked right off, hasn't he? We should have pinched him right at the start. What's this?' He picked the breakfast bowl up and wrinkled his nose at the contents.

'Dandelion salad,' Fred replied. 'Mother's recipe. The secret is *beaucoup de* parsley.' Picking up his fork, he felt a dull throb and bit down a grimace. He'd never had nimble fingers, but over recent years they'd become knuckled by arthritis too. He speared a forkful and began to chew, taking his time, savouring the childhood memory as much as the flavour.

Apparently convinced, Jackie shovelled some leaves into his own mouth, bolting them down like they might be snatched away at any second before going back for another forkful, and another. 'It's good,' he said, the bowl already half empty.

Fred finished chewing his first mouthful and swallowed.

'Mother would be gratified to know it. And, no. Our friend Vizsla is still there. At least his car is. It's a nice car that, the new Princess. He's not one to panic. He wouldn't leave that behind.'

O'Hara's smoothly-bearded jaw froze in mid-mastication and those languid brown ears pricked up. 'He might have, if he's made us. You said he was clever. We should have pinched him.' The ears subsided slowly and the young Irishman continued to eat his breakfast. 'It is a nice motor, mind. The Princess. No Capri, of course, but nice. Have you seen my bandana, by the way?' He patted his forehead as if Fred could have missed the red and yellow kerchief the lad had been wearing yesterday.

*Gone missing has it? No great loss if you're trying not to be memorable, son,* Fred thought. But what he said, with a lugubrious shake of the head, was: 'I'll keep an eye out for it.'

O'Hara pushed his empty bowl away, the fork rattling around inside it. 'Thanks. I'll be getting back to it then.'

Fred raised his eyes to watch the lad scamper back through. The slender, hirsute muscles extending from the rolled-up sleeves of the denim shirt. Those long legs shrink-wrapped in the jeans they all wore now. Flared at the hem, tight around the arse, they didn't leave much to the imagination, and Fred so liked to use his imagination. If only he were a few years younger.

*Age was never a barrier to you, Freddie. What's stopping you now? We already know he enjoys your cooking.*

*Ah, Tommy.* Fred smiled at the thought, but it was hard won.

*It's even legal in Britain now.*

*Oh, behave. That's not what this is about. This is serious business.*

*Of course it is. Why would the Zoo bring you back out of retirement, if it wasn't serious business? Still, being cooped up on a stakeout in the middle of nowhere…you can enjoy the perks, eh?*

*The perks? You're incorrigible, you bastard. I'm too old for perks. I'll settle for advantages.*

Fred swallowed his food, then took another considered mouthful of dandelions. His smile turned from wistful to sad.

Regrettably, if this was to work, he'd need all the advantages he could get.

* * *

'So, you see, we're just not sure,' said Keeper from behind that ridiculous, monumental desk. Not the same Keeper, of course. The old one must have retired not long after Fred and, judging from the preened gloss of her neat fashionable do, there must have been at least one more in between Fred's Keeper and this one. It didn't matter. Fred could tell from the fussy neatness and the way she looked down her beak at him that she was very much of the same type. Call me, Clarice, she'd said, in her clipped, public school tones.

It was the same desk, though. That ancient monster of ornately carved oak, so solid that if any Keeper *had* wanted it removed it would probably have meant demolishing a wall. Right now, there were files on it. Forms filled with Fred's own cumbersome handwriting, with black and white photographs he'd taken paper clipped to them and stamped Secret. The date was smudged but Fred didn't need to read it to know what he was looking at. He remembered perfectly well.

Thirty five to thirty seven. Bärstadt, East Mitteland. Sandor bleeding Vizsla.

'And you think I can help?' he replied. He meant it meekly, but even to his own ears it sounded somewhat truculent. 'Of course, if I can help, I'm only too happy to, Keeper.'

'That's awfully good of you,' Keeper said. 'You see, it's quite a surprise to see this ancient old codger,' she checked the file, '*Vizsla*, turning up on our patch. Retired, our sources over there say. Something of a falling out with their new guard. What's he doing, hmm? Is he genuinely out of the game—as he should be at his age, bless him—or is he sitting there waiting for us to pick him up? Maybe he thinks he can sell us something we don't already know, hmm? But if that is his game…well, he's been out for so long, why now?'

'And you want me to tell you it's safe to approach?' Fred said, keeping his voice level. 'That Vizsla isn't here for some *other* reason.'

Keeper smiled. 'Quite so.'

'I never *knew* him, you know,' Fred said. 'Not face to face.'

Keeper tapped the file. 'But you were our watcher over there. No one on our side knew him better.'

'I'll need to see him.'

'Of course. It's all arranged.'


*March 7th, 1.37am*

'Fred!' The urgent whisper comes from the right and perhaps twenty feet ahead. 'Fred! I'm going. I have to.'

*Shut up you stupid fool. You'll get us both killed.*

Instead of replying and giving their presence away even more surely than O'Hara may already have, Fred blows out through his nostrils twice.

The signal means: *Wait.*

Then he listens for Vizsla. He can hear nothing but that doesn't mean the old dog hasn't located them already. Sandor's eyes were never the best and his sense of smell was reported to have been impaired by the accident but judging from the speed at which he exited the back door almost the instant O'Hara had set foot in the coach house grounds, those ears of his are as sharp as ever. Fred imagines him now, alert and scanning these waving meadow grasses, lingering over each hunched shadow, every seeming rock. Listening for them to betray themselves.

*Did he recognise me?* Fred thinks. *I was mostly hidden behind the lad, it's been almost forty years and we never officially met, but still... Did he?* He tells himself it's just the old watcher's paranoia flooding back. That sense of getting to know the target so well that you find it hard to believe it's not reciprocal.

The boy is right, though. The situation is untenable.

Fred inches painfully out of his crouch and creeps forward. One foot, two. A yard. That's enough in one go. He pulls his neck in beneath the collar of his hunched gabardine overcoat. Becomes the rock again.

Two more snuffles. *Wait.*

'Fred. I can't. I have to...'

The gunshot he's been anticipating is not after all a

shotgun blast ripping open the night. It's a perfunctory, mechanical snap. A distance to Fred's left a clump of tall lilac foxgloves lose their heads. Not too close, but closer than he'd like. Another reminder that, though Vizsla may be missing some faculties, he's still very dangerous. Fred hunkers and hopes that young Jackie's nerve holds.

Fred waits for another shot. It doesn't come, but the first one tells him several things. Either naughty Sandor has held on to his old Service equipment or Keeper's suspicion about him still being active was right on the money. And interesting, too, that he judged it a bigger risk to use the shotgun he'd used to bag a brace of pigeon the day before, which might attract attention this late at night but could conceivably be explained away, than to use a rifle and suppressor of East Mittelland manufacture that, while quieter, could not be explained under any circumstances.

*Well, Sandor. It seems we really have you spooked, me and the lad.*

The third, and currently most important, thing Fred has learned is that Vizsla doesn't yet know exactly where they are. Thank Christ.

Fred gives O'Hara the wait signal again and this time the response is two slow taps of a size twelve training shoe on the ground.

*Good lad,* Fred thinks. He cranes once more to watch the clouds passing across the moon, and makes himself ready.


*March 6th, 3.41pm*

'You've got quite the reputation.' From back in the dimness of the room, O'Hara rustled his newspaper. 'Back at the Zoo.'

There was a seagull on the window ledge across the street. Big old sod, its hooked orange bill scratching at something on the plinth. Fred couldn't see what, not even through the scope. He frowned and adjusted the focus, trying to penetrate the white reflection. A moment before, Vizsla had been raking out the fireplace, but where was he now?

Then the old defector's hangdog face was right there at the window. He wore only a vest. There were smuts in the grizzled, once-russet bristle on his hands and forearms, and his muscles strained as he threw up the sash so that he could shoo the bird off with a bark of credible estuary English. Hardly even a trace of an accent from the man known to his neighbours here as Collins. If only they knew that this harmless-seeming elderly gentleman had been involved in chemical and biological research for the enemy before the war. Aluminium Phosphide gas. New strains of myxomatosis and VHD. Nasty stuff.

The urge to flinch never leaves you, Fred mused, resisting exactly that impulse at the old dog's sudden reappearance, so clear and so close that you'd swear he must see you, and instead reaching slowly for the camera on the tripod. *Click click click,* as Vizsla leaned over the sill to watch a mustard-coloured Maxi navigate its way around a fish van and a giggling knot of uniformed school children absorbed in a comic, tails waving excitedly. Then, as Vizsla straightened, he looked directly across the street to the window where only the fagsmoke-yellowed net curtain screened Fred and O'Hara and their various tripods and lenses. The eyes were rheumy, the scar tissue across the cheek and nose, white like lace. There was no suspicion in Vizsla's face, however, just a sort of pensive introspection.

'He hasn't made us,' Fred said once Vizsla had closed the window and retreated inside. As he leaned over to jot the event in the log he wondered at his own certainty, pleasantly surprised that the skill hadn't atrophied in his years away. 'And of course I had a reputation. I was at the Zoo a long time and I was very good at my job.'

'Small mercies. I still say we should have pinched him though.' The chair creaked again as O'Hara rearranged himself. Unable to sit still, that lad. 'Tenacious as a terrier you were, so they say at the Zoo.'

Fred looked slowly around at that comment. Beyond the bony hunch of his shoulder, the television was on. Some programme for children, one of the ones with stiffly animated models. Soldiers in red tunics with white crossbelts, wearing shakos on their little squirrel heads and lined up for inspection by a moustachioed CO. The sound was off, of course, but the picture silvered O'Hara in the threadbare green chair.

He had the paper folded on his lap, a pen poised, forgotten out of distraction or disinterest over the quick crossword Fred had suggested to stave off the boredom, and his long legs extended uncomfortably, but his face was as big-eyed and disingenuous as ever. 'Tenacious? Not really,' Fred replied. 'Just very patient.'

*Oh, your infamous patience. Such a virtue.*

*I don't remember you complaining, Tommy.*

*Not once I'd got your attention. Positively a boon in the right circumstances, in fact. But I practically had to write you a letter of invitation. And between your side and my side, that wouldn't have been…*

*The done thing? That would rather precisely have been the point.*

This generation didn't know the meaning of the word *patience*. Especially not O'Hara's sort. Here they were, barely into the second day of a surveillance detail that, for someone of Vizsla's experience, Fred would have expected to take weeks before it revealed anything of value, and the lad was probing already. And so inelegantly too. No one trusted anyone any more.

'Who have you been talking to?' Fred said, affecting casual curiosity as he returned his attention to the window. He forced a chuckle into his voice. 'Who's been tattling?' If he put his mind to it he could probably guess. There weren't many who remembered him left in the sprawling national intelligence complex bordering Regent's Park. He'd outlasted most of his contemporaries by the time he retired and that was over a decade ago. Of course, it took time for reputations to fade, but to all and sundry his should have been one of long and doughty service. Good at what he did but undistinguished. The kind of chap who kept his head down and just got on with things. Hardly the sort you'd bring up over a pint of mild at The Watering Hole. No one ever said: 'Now, Fred the Tort. There was a spy.'

*Then they didn't know you, did they?*

*Bless you, Dear Tommy. No, I don't suppose they did.*

'Bob Whitrat briefed me fully on all the actors.' Dispensing with any pretence, O'Hara sounded as if he regretted having to continue the conversation now that he'd brought the subject up. As if it was routine these days to be asked to inform on one's colleagues. As if Fred's decades of good service meant nothing.

Fred didn't look up from the telescope. Across the street Vizsla passed the window again. He had a shirt on now and was buttoning it at the collar.

*Whitrat, though? And under Keeper's nose, I'll bet. Sneaky old weasel. Never trust a burrow-dweller, Clarice. Wonderful at ferreting out secrets, but you never know when they'll turn out to have been a mole all the time. Sooner or later, everyone is true to their nature.*

Fred couldn't help rolling an eye in O'Hara's direction.

*Not him, Fred. This lad's no burrower, you know that. You're thinking rabbits. Big difference. And you're letting your prejudice show.*

*Oh, Tommy. Won't you allow me even a small amount of indignation in my own thoughts?*

*You're just worried he's on to you.*

'So what did Section Chief Whitrat tell you,' Fred said, 'about Sandor Vizsla?'

'Nothing that wasn't already in the file,' O'Hara replied. 'Only that you were brought in because you had history with him.'

Fred snorted. 'I was a watcher,' he snapped. 'Vizsla was a mark. We never met. We don't have a *history*.'

*Well, Tommy, right as always. The lad ought to leave it there. If he's looking to get a reaction, he's got it now.*

O'Hara waited long enough that Fred thought that might actually be the end of it, but of course that characteristic impatience won out. 'Not even after what happened to your boyfriend?'

Fred sighed. That wasn't the word he would have used. Not ever. Not even in private to Tommy. Back then they didn't have the luxury of *thinking* that word. But it punctured his shell all the same. Straight to his soft heart. 'Even though I was just a watcher,' he heard himself trotting out the standard story with impressively weary patience, like a school master to a slow pupil, 'I had to maintain a cover over there. My friendship with Tomasz Fousek was part of that cover. We drank coffee and played chess in the afternoons in the café across the square from the Factory. That's all.' Saying the words brought the memory to mind. The leisurely tour of the sun around the square, the dappled shade under the almond trees, the music of starlings and chinking porcelain, the sweet-dark coffee in the little cups. The sweet-dark of Tommy's eyes, laughing and open, as if there should be no secrets in the world, ever.

Across the way, Vizsla had his coat on now. 'Look lively, Jackie, boy,' Fred said, unexpectedly hoarse. 'Our man Collins is on the move.'

*March 7th, 1.51am*

*You kept your secrets very well, you know. You were a mystery to us right until the end.*

*Did I, Tommy? I always rather thought I was an open book to you.*

*Not at all. We watched you, we suspected, but... well, no matter how well trained they are, sooner or later most spooks succumb to impatience and take risks to snap that photograph or file that vital report. To get the job done. You just carried on with your little emigré academician life. Taught your classes at the École in the Western Quarter. Did your crossword puzzles in your foreign newspapers. Played chess with attractive young men in bars.*

*You know there was only one attractive young man. But if you thought me of so little importance, why did you spend so much time in my company?*

*Why do you think, you old fool?*

*I need to believe that, I really do.*

Fred unfolds, totters forward another yard, then hunkers down again. Becomes the rock, motionless and still, although he feels far from safe. He's close to O'Hara now, though. That thicket of cornflowers just ahead. A different kind of stillness to Fred's own. A hair-triggered tension.

And then, above, there's a chink in the clouds and the moonlight shines through, illuminating the field like a searchlight for—one two three—seconds. Fred freezes. He can see the cornflowers trembling with tension. *Stay, Jackie. Stay.* Somewhere behind him, he can hear Vizlsa now. A soft throat-growl from this side of the hedge. *Stay, Jackie.*

Four five—and the field is dark again. The cornflowers settle, but Fred can't relax because now he knows for sure that Vizsla hasn't given up. He's hunting them the old fashioned way.

*March 6th, 3.49pm*

Fred watched the Princess pull away from the front of the house, circle around in the car park of The Bull public house up the street and then pass beneath his window again, heading out of town in the direction of the city. A few moments later the lad's red and black Norton roadster followed, Jackie hunched over the handlebars now jacketed in black leather, eyes peering through goggles, long ears pinned back as the bike picked up speed and left the village.

*Off to town, Sandor? Why stick your head above the parapet now? Going to make contact with your handler? Is Keeper right after all? Or is this just an innocent shopping trip?* Fred recalled that look of introspection when he'd seen Vizsla at the window. He knew that look. The old dog had been calculating. Planning. And if Vizsla was anything, he was loyal. Dogs were like that. True to their nature.

Fred had been counting on it.

This absence gave Fred perhaps a couple of hours. It wasn't long, not if he was going to do this properly, but it would have to be enough.

Slowly but deliberately, he moved around the flat, picking up the things he would need from the secret places in which he'd hidden them. Then, his old knees complaining with every stumpy footfall, he descended the stairs and donned his gabardine and trilby. Gloves too, mustn't forget those. Outside, he found spring sunshine and raised his leathery face to enjoy it. Walking along the pavement, he passed through the life of the village. He nodded to the proprietor of the ironmongers who was struggling to get a display of hoes and rakes to stand up straight. He tipped his trilby at a young mother, rocking a pram. He stopped to smell the flowers outside the florist, a sweet glory of daffs and tulips and purple hyacinths, but the aroma made him hungry so he moved on. Slowly, steadily, evincing a benign air as he went. People parted around him and smiled at the old fellow, humpbacked and ponderous, but out enjoying the day. If he doddered with a little more exaggeration than was accurate, that was all well and good.

There was a café across from the Bull. *Daisy's Milk Bar*, the sign bedecked by cartoonish flowers read, but it sold teas and coffees too. Fred sat outside and sipped his coffee. He hadn't made a fuss about the milk and it didn't spoil things too much. It was how they drank it here, after all, though he'd never got the taste for it. He closed his eyes and enjoyed the flavour, the sunshine, the song of starlings.

*Peace*, he thought. *That's all I've ever wanted. To live in peace, the way I choose.*

When he'd drunk his coffee, he left a modest tip—although if ever there was a time to make a grand gesture, it was now—crossed the road and began his slow return down the other side of the street. At the newsagent he bought a broadsheet newspaper and made a point of griping mildly to the proprietor about the red top the lad had purchased that morning. When he was opposite the post office, he feigned absorption in the weather report—cloudy with clear spells—waiting patiently not only until the traffic had cleared but the street was empty of pedestrians too. Then, decades of experience compensating for his cumbersome digits, he deftly let himself in through Vizsla's front door using the duplicate key he had filched from the property rental office while picking up the post office flat's keys the previous day.

It wasn't what you'd call a homely home. It was well kept, tidy in fact to a military degree, but there were no personal touches. Not from Vizsla anyway. From the little pottery vignettes of sailing boats on the wall behind the door to the dried flower arrangement Fred discovered on the table as he went through to the kitchen, to the stodgy airport novels—Harold Robins, Jilly Hooper, and the like—crammed into the living room book case, the place was as it had been rented to him. Not that Vizsla was much of a one for books these days, it appeared. The single armchair had been pushed close to the television, a copy of the TV Times jammed into the cushion, a black felt pen circle around *The Liver Birds*.

Despite its banality, it was still the den of a predator. Fred struggled to master the urge to jump at every little thing that caught the corner of his eye. He had a job to do.

As Fred toured the rooms he carried O'Hara's bandana, wiping it on doorknob, stair banister, kitchen chair back. In the living room he carefully extracted two of the lad's long brown hairs. One, he laid on the carpet, one on the chair arm. That should be more than enough. He barely felt any remorse for the lad. Especially now he knew he was one of Whitrat's boys.

Fred took one more look around, returned to the front door and opened it a crack. When the street was empty again, he slipped out, locked up, crossed the road and let himself back into the post office flat.

Fred made tea, crushing the nettles with the teaspoon to master the shakes. He sipped it in the green chair. It was done. There was no going back now.

*Bärstadt, East Mittelland, August 17th, 1937*

Fred's heart was hammering when he got back to the apartment on Grunewald Strasse, shutting the street door against the taint of smoke and the sound of distant sirens. As he climbed slowly to the second floor, he noted that the landing bulb was out. He'd have to have words with the superintendent again and he so hated to make a fuss.

'Where have you been?' Tommy lurched at him out of the shadows, eyes wild, his shaggy mop of hair even more deranged than usual.

'Christ, don't do that.' As the eddy of relief washed through him, Fred attempted a creased smile but it felt paper thin. 'Man of my age. Are you trying to kill me?'

'This is important.' Tommy gripped his arm, the pressure points of his claws, painful. 'Where *were* you?' That wild look, the searching intensity.

'Out,' said Fred defensively, staring back into his lover's eyes as if he could stare away the hateful suspicion. 'I went to the gardens and then came back via the Kohlmarkt.' Now he wished he had something to show for it. A paper sack brimming with those wonderful cabbages. 'And then, when

I heard the bang I came straight back here. Tommy, what's happening?'

Tommy shook his head but his grip lessened. 'You have to leave. Right now,' he said, guiding Fred back down the stairs.

'Leave?' Fred shrugged him off. 'I don't want to leave. I haven't done anything.'

Tommy's dark eyes were full of fear. 'There's no time. They're coming.'

'But I didn't *do* anything.'

'I know.' Those two words were a balm. Even if they were a lie. He couldn't know. Not for sure. 'But that doesn't matter. They're still coming for you.'

It was a short walk to the bahnhof, but a fraught one. Every corner they turned was preceded by a prayer, but the only time they saw the polizei was the uniformed officers manning the roadblock across the street that led to the Factory square. The plume of acrid smoke was starting to drift south across the city.

'Vizsla?' Fred murmured as they hurried past.

Tommy nodded. 'He was in there. That's all I know.' It was the first and last time they acknowledged the man's name to each other.

'He'll be dead then.' They were at the station now.

'Yes,' Tommy said. 'Believe that. Now get on the train. Any train.'

The next departure from the great palace of iron and glass was heading to the Balkans, but it was as good as any. Tommy was right. It was all over and, while Fred hadn't known the action was coming, he'd supplied the information that made it possible.

'Come with me,' he said from the step as the whistle shrilled, but Tommy was already hurrying away. Fred watched him weave through the crowd to the exit. Saw the black car pull up and the men emerge, shouting. Tommy's hands raised to the heavens. But he never once looked back.

And Fred knew he had made a terrible mistake.

*March 6th, 8.12pm*
  *You'll be older now too, I expect.*

*It has been forty years, Fred. Assuming I survived the gulag.*

Fred blinked in the darkening living room. It was gone dusk and the sodium orange lights had stuttered and sparked in the street outside, casting unfamiliar shadows around the room. Everything in this country was unfamiliar. Had been for forty years. Fred thought that, maybe even deep down, he'd felt it since his mother had brought him here as a child all those decades ago.

*Don't say that,* he thought. *I should have stayed. I should have gone there with you. We'd have been all right. Together. We still can be.*

But Tommy didn't answer.

Across the street, Vizsla's bedroom light came on. From the chair, Fred could see movement in the room but he didn't move.

Ten minutes later, he heard the front door opening and O'Hara's feet on the stair. The Irishman was griping as he climbed. 'Waste of bloody time,' he was saying. 'Bastard didn't go to the city at all, did he? Just drove around the countryside for hours. Stopped for a pint. Drove. Stopped for another pint. Drove. Didn't speak to no one the whole time. The whole thing was a wild goose chase.' This last was spoken as he entered the living room. 'What's up? He's been back for fifteen minutes easy. Why aren't you watching?'

*Because now he's made us,* Fred thought. What he said was: 'We have new orders.'


*March 7th, 2.11am*

*When the moon comes out,* Fred thinks, *it's all over. And it has been such a long road getting to this point.* All he's ever wanted in all the years since Bärstadt was the peace to live his own life, with the man he chose to live it with. In the years that followed, he'd made investigations. Vizsla was still alive. Sooner or later he would resurface. Although Fred had expected it to be over there rather than at home, he had been ready for the call and wherever it would take him.

A little peace. Did it really matter whose peace it was?

The call had been a long time coming, but at last it had come.

Could the old bastard have turned? It was laughable. The one thing he could have told them right at the start was that Vizsla was a dog, and dogs remain loyal their whole lives. True to their nature.

*Just as old torts are known for their patience and determination?*

*Quite so, Tommy, old son.*

*And hares?*

*Quite the opposite I'm afraid.* The shifting clouds above have started to tease out. And everyone knows that hares lose their senses in the moonlight.

When the clouds break, the radiance that lights up the field is cold and without mercy. Under his gabardine and trilby, Fred is the rock, so he hears rather than sees Jackie's nerve break in a fluster of undergrowth. He's fast, the lad, but the safety of the woods is well out of reach.

Fred hears the shots. The cry. The sound of a body falling.

The he hears the savagery of an embittered and furious old dog.

So, he waits. And he waits.

At last, slowly, he unfolds himself and stands with his hands raised.

'Please,' he says. 'Take me back with you.'

# 'Agent Friendzone'

## Kyell Gold

The Sett, a large basement tavern with loud music and a bar in the centre room and table service in two quieter rooms, never got completely full on Thursday nights, but even a modest crowd overwhelmed the antiquated ventilation system, whose constant whine of protest scored the background of every conversation. Kirk liked the miasma of scents, the feeling of being lost in a crowd, but one of his three friends usually complained whenever he brought them here. Tonight, though, they hadn't. Lonny's nose twitched constantly, but the jaguar, sitting across the table next to Porta, was playing a musical demo he'd made for her and was intent on her reaction. Martin was usually quickest to complain about anything from scents to noise to the temperature of his fries, but tonight the cacomistle's sensitive nose was for the moment buried in a fragrant strawberry daiquiri.

Kirk sipped his own drink, waiting for Martin to answer the question he'd asked, but when he turned to repeat it, he only got as far as, 'So what did you think—' before he stopped. Martin's gaze was not on Lonny, as Kirk had thought, but past him, at the dance floor and the bodies moving to the music there. A fox in a shimmering pink satin shirt paused at a bar table, his thick white-tipped tail waving just beyond the door frame, and Martin's ears perked forward slightly.

Oh no, Kirk thought, and searched for some way to distract the cacomistle, but he couldn't think of anything before Martin nudged him.

'What about that guy, the fox?'

'Let it go,' Kirk snapped, and then felt bad about snapping, so he turned to Lonny and Porta. The otter had taken the headset off her ears. 'What'd you think, Porta?' the badger asked, louder than strictly necessary. 'I thought it was great, Lonny. I love the bass line and you're bringing in some amazing stuff. You gonna play it at the club?'

'I just thought he looked like your type,' Martin muttered, lapping up his daiquiri with a reddened tongue as his ears flattened.

'Gonna run it by them, see what they say. Thanks, dude.' Lonny reached out a yellow-furred paw toward Martin and tapped the table. 'And you. Better watch out or the badger here will bite your ear off. The guy's only been single for a month.'

Martin eyed the jaguar balefully. 'Two weeks.'

'Whatever, he's still in the mourning period.' Lonny turned to Porta. 'How long's that supposed to be?'

The small otter shook her head. 'Don't ask me. My mourning period is as long as it takes me to put on a tight outfit and get my ass to a club. You gay boys got your own rules, I got no idea how it works. You, I get.' She patted the jaguar's shoulder.

'Thanks, I like being reduced to "that guy who doesn't have relationships."'

'The thing is,' Martin said to Kirk. 'You can't just come here and not at least look at other guys.'

'Looking, sure. I don't need them pointed out to me.'

Porta leaned back, tipping her chair and using her thick tail for balance. 'If you guys want to go cruise, you can. Lonny and I will still be here when you get shot down.'

'Ha ha.' Kirk flicked his ears back to the side and stared back into the dance room. The fox was gone, disappeared back into the cluster of moving bodies. He felt no compulsion to go join them. Van had dragged him to dance a few times, even when Kirk had said that he preferred to sit home and watch a movie, which was true in the specific case of evenings spent with Van, if not generally in his life.

'No judgment.' Porta grinned. 'I ditched you guys a bunch of times when Kalvin dumped me. Some stuff you gotta work out of your system.'

The scrutiny did nothing to decrease the warmth in Kirk's ears. He turned his black-and-white muzzle fully to stare down the cacomistle, who ducked his head. 'I know usually when I get out of a relationship, I'm mopey, but honestly it's such a relief to be done with Van that I feel light. I mean, that guy was—'

'Stifling.'

'Velcro.'

The badger lay his ears back, then relaxed and laughed. 'You guys are tired of hearing about it, I know.'

'It's cool,' Lonny said. 'We've all been there.'

'But it has been almost a month,' Porta added. 'It's, like, part of the past.'

Martin lifted his head long enough to say, 'Two weeks.'

'See,' Kirk said, spreading his large paws, 'that would make sense if I were hung up, or something, but—'

He turned back to Martin, intending to go on, but over Martin's shoulder he caught sight of a pair of large ears pointed in his direction from a few tables away. Of course, there could have been any number of fennec foxes in The Sett, but how many of them would have a cluster of pride rings in one ear, or own a lime green patterned Taro Zelmani shirt? Kirk leaned back to get a better look, and sure enough, it was Van, pretending to study his menu with his ears positioned to listen to everything Kirk was saying.

'But clearly you're fine and maybe we should talk about the Galahads' new album.' Porta shook her head. 'Mia turned me on to them last week. Lonny, you'd like it. There's one track I think you could sample.'

His ex was spying on them, and Kirk couldn't say anything about it because Van would hear everything he said, and if he said what he wanted to, something like, 'Hey, my creepy ex is spying on us,' Van would know that he'd seen him and then he might come over and confront him and then there'd be a scene, or at least an argument, and telling Martin to 'let it go' twice had filled up Kirk's minimal tolerance for arguments and scenes.

'You did actually break up with him, right?' Lonny leaned forward. 'I didn't want to ask, but before we move on to alt-punk...'

'New punk.' Porta rolled her eyes. 'Alt-punk sucks.'

'Yes.' Kirk kept his voice low, aware of the large fennec ears just a few tables away.

'Like, you said the words—'

'So.' The badger turned to Porta. 'The Galahads, huh?'

Lonny gave him a look, but Kirk ignored it. He navigated the rest of the conversation without further reference to the ex-boyfriend sitting nearby, keeping his voice low so that Van wouldn't overhear anything even as personal as what album he was currently listening to. If the fennec found that out, chances were one of the song titles would end up as an email subject or text message or something.

It wasn't a bad evening out, all in all, but Kirk couldn't enjoy it properly. Even though he looked away from Van and spoke quietly, the fennec's presence weighed on him and he couldn't tell any of his friends about it. For one thing, Van would overhear. For another, he suspected that one of them was responsible.

*** 

'You think one of our friends is telling Van where you're all getting together?' The polar bear filled up the small Skype window, blocking out most of the bamboo scrolls hanging on the wall behind her. 'Don't you go to The Sett all the time?'

'Not all the time. And two days before that it was at the freaking mall, for crying out loud.' Kirk stared out into the darkness beyond his bedroom window. Could Van be out there watching him now? Was he that much of a stalker?

'Wait. You guys went to the mall? The Chester Mall? Was this a high school nostalgia trip?'

Kirk scowled. 'C&R were having a sale and Lonny wanted to get me some new shirts.'

'Is that one of them?'

He pulled at the collar of his blue paisley Zelmani and glanced again at the window. 'Mia, be serious.'

'I am. If it is, then you should let him get you more shirts.'

'The point is, Van has shown up three times in the two weeks since we broke up and I'm not talking about the places we're going on Twitter or anything, so how is he finding out?'

'You check everyone else's accounts?'

'Yeah. Lonny posted a shirt picture but not where it was from, and anyway that was like five minutes before I saw Van. He couldn't have gotten to the mall that quickly.'

Mia shook her head, smiling. 'All right, look, I gotta go get breakfast here in a minute. What are you going to do about it? You can't just stop hanging out with everyone. Who don't you trust?'

'That's the thing.' Kirk rested his head against his paw, his blunt claws pressing into his temple. 'Couple weeks ago I would've said I trusted them all. But I can't figure out any other way that Van knows where we are.'

Mia shook her head. 'Maybe it's coincidence. Maybe he's going out to a bunch of places all the time and he happened to run into you a few times.'

'No.' Kirk straightened. 'No. Once is happenstance, twice is coincidence. Three times is enemy action.'

The polar bear snorted, a concussive sound that popped the microphone. 'You read too many spy books. You're reading into it.'

'Then how's he doing it? It's got to be one of them'

Mia leaned in close enough that he could see her black nose glistening. 'Maybe you should tell them that the group is getting together somewhere in the next day or two, but tell everyone a different place. Wherever Van shows up, that's the person you want.'

The badger stared at the screen. 'That's right out of John Le Carre. How come I didn't think of that?'

'Because it's night and you're tired and you're angry, and plus I'm studying historical court politics and if you think your ex-boyfriend spying on you is bad, let me tell you, the emperors of the Edo period would have laughed at you.'

'I won't tell them, then.' Kirk stared at the screen, already forming a plan in his head. 'That's brilliant. I'll figure it out that way.'

Mia shook her head. 'Also I was being sarcastic. Oh my God, Kirk, people don't do this kind of spy stuff in real life to their friends. Nut up and ask them if any of them is talking to Van and why.'

'They'd never admit it.' His ears folded back.

'Then talk to Van. Tell him to stop coming around. Kirk, I know you hate to hurt people's feelings, but don't you think it's hurting him more—'

'Go get breakfast,' he said. 'Thanks for the advice.'

He was already clicking on the red 'Hang Up' button as

Mia said, 'It wasn't—'

***

Lonny was his top suspect because the mall had been the most unusual place for Van to turn up and it had been the jaguar's idea. They already had a weekly Wednesday night dinner, and this week it was set for Red Hook Pizza, but Kirk could adapt to that; he'd just reverse his plan. So he called Lonny an hour or so before the pizza and said he might not be able to make it. Lonny wasn't likely to call either of the others or text them just to say that Kirk was buried in work, but if he were the spy, he'd for sure tell Van not to bother showing up this time.

And half an hour into their meal, Kirk looked up and noticed the fennec sitting at the bar in the back of the room. He must have come in the back door, and he was trying to make himself inconspicuous, but big-eared species were really bad at that unless they folded their ears down, which a fennec trying to listen to a conversation halfway across the room wouldn't ever do.

Mia's advice came back to him—why not just go over and confront Van?—but as Kirk pictured doing that in his mind, he kept seeing Van's eyes bright with hurt like they were every time Kirk hadn't wanted to do something the fennec did. He knew the flattening of the fennec's ears, the sagging of his whiskers, the guilt that wormed its way into Kirk's heart because he was letting someone else down. Even if he knew intellectually that it wasn't that big a deal, that Van was over-reacting to his comment, he couldn't chase away the feeling that somehow it was still his fault for not being accommodating, or for expressing himself poorly, or something.

So he hunched over, turned his body away from his stalker, and made sure to keep the conversation to subjects he didn't mind being overheard. The longer he sat, the more he felt Van's scrutiny like a heat lamp, until he grabbed the check when it came and tossed his card onto it, not wanting to sit through a round of 'how are we going to split this up?'

Nobody said anything except 'Thanks'; each of them sometimes picked up the tab for any number of reasons. And

142

Kirk, already in his head moving on to the next plan, said casually as they walked out the door and out of Van's hearing, 'I want to try this new bar over in the West Side. Friday night?'

Porta said, 'Sure. Good cocktails?'

'Good beer selection.'

'What's it called?' Lonny asked.

'Ah… you know, I forget. Let me check.' He took out his phone and pretended to look things up for a minute. 'Can't find it. I'll text you guys the address.'

'Cool. Hey, there's my Lyft.' Porta waved to them and hurried to the curb, where a black sedan had just pulled up.

'See you guys then.' Lonny headed down the street to the bike rack where he'd left his bike.

'So,' Martin asked, pulling his tail into his paws like he did when he was thinking about something, 'this a gay bar?'

'Just a bar.'

'Oh.'

If Martin started trying to hook him up with someone again… . Kirk fantasised about walking out on one of their gatherings, knowing he wouldn't ever do something that dramatic. 'I'm really looking forward to seeing it with just the three of you, though.'

'Sure,' Martin said, and cleared his throat. 'Yeah, that sounds fun.'

Spies always trusted their instinct, and Kirk's was telling him that Martin was the one who was telling Van where to find them, but he could not for the life of him imagine why. Martin had bent a sympathetic ear when Kirk complained that Van needed someone who could discuss boundaries with him, and that Kirk needed someone who didn't have to have that discussion started for him. So why would the cacomistle be responsible for what Kirk could only assume was a clumsy attempt to get him and Van back together? Like, if he noticed Van he'd eventually go over there and talk to him? Was that what they were waiting for, the two of them? That was the only explanation he could find that was remotely plausible, and maybe, just maybe, Van had convinced Martin that Kirk had broken up with him prematurely and Martin had been sympathetic enough to help the fennec with a second chance.

That seemed like something the big-hearted cacomistle might plausibly do.

On thursday, Kirk sent Martin the address of a newly-opened bar and then sent Lonny and Porta the address of a nearby bar they'd never been to, setting the same time for getting together. If they talked to each other, he hoped they wouldn't get too specific.

Hope, he found over the rest of Thursday and Friday, was a poor companion. Every time his phone buzzed, he expected to see a message from one of them saying, 'Hey, you told us different places, which one are we meeting at?' But the days passed without any of his friends questioning his complicated plans, and he met Martin on Friday night with the feeling of—well, not a master spy exactly. The master spies in the books weren't generally the ones making the plans; they were solving puzzles put down by villains. Trying to trap a spy didn't make him a villain, though, did it? He was the counterspy; that felt better, and made him feel a bit less guilty about lying to some of his friends.

The first half hour of drinks with Martin passed quickly. The cacomistle kept looking around and saying things like it wasn't usual for Lonny and Porta to both be so late, and when Kirk deflected that conversation, they talked about the latest Bond movie, comparing it to the other recent few. Martin could talk acting for hours, and Kirk had worked in theatre design in college, so they usually enjoyed discussing those aspects of movies they'd seen, and while neither acting nor set design were what you went to Bond movies for, they still killed half an hour on that topic.

But when the conversation flagged, Martin went back to picking out cute guys at the bar for Kirk. 'How about that badger, the one in the nice jacket?'

'The jacket's just this side of pretentious,' Kirk said. 'But how do you even know he's gay?'

'I don't.' The cacomistle sipped his cocktail. 'But it's fun to pretend, right?'

'I don't want to meet a guy in a bar.'

'Then why do you keep looking around? You think Lonny and Porta might be sitting somewhere else? Oh hey...'

Kirk's phone buzzed at the same time. They both looked at

the message from Lonny: Where are you guys?

Before Kirk could stop him, Martin was texting back. *We're here, where are you?*

While Martin was sorting out the fact that they were at two different bars, Kirk scanned the room one more time. If Van wasn't here, then maybe he was over at the other bar where Lonny and Porta were, and Porta was the—

At that moment, the fennec walked through the door. Kirk's eyes met his, and Van stopped.

They stared at each other, neither one moving. Slowly, Van scanned the restaurant, like he was looking for another friend who wasn't there, and then he turned and walked right back out the door.

'Ah, you must've sent them the wrong address,' Martin said. 'They're over at this place on Rosen. It's just a few blocks, so they're coming over here. What?'

Kirk had shifted his stare to Martin, his claws tap-tapping on the table. 'So you're the one who's been telling him.'

The cacomistle turned quickly toward the door and his ears went back, though he tried to put on a brave, innocent smile as he faced Kirk again. 'Telling, ah, who? What?'

'Van just walked in.' Kirk nodded to the door. 'How'd he know we were here?'

'I don't know. What—you think I told him where we'd be? Why would I do that?'

'I don't know.' Kirk's muzzle felt warm. He rubbed his other paw over his whiskers. 'I thought maybe you were trying to get us back together, but as soon as he saw that I saw him, he left. He showed up at the movie, and the mall, and… and The Sett and Red Hook. And now he's here and you're the only one who had this address.'

Martin's brave smile struggled a moment longer and then creased into anger. 'I'm the only one—did you tell Lonny and Porta another bar? Was this a *trap*?'

The pride Kirk had felt in the success of his scheme remained with him about as long as Van had stayed in the bar. 'Maybe, but—but it worked. So tell me. Is Van following me and then waiting half an hour to walk in? Or are you telling him where to spy on me?'

'It's your fault,' the cacomistle snapped. 'If you'd just tell him it's over.'

'I told him.' Kirk shifted in his chair. 'I mean, I said I was gonna be real busy—anyway, why does that make a difference? I know he's clingy. You don't have to help him.'

'Because he still thinks he has a chance with you!'

People around them turned their heads and ears. 'Quiet down,' Kirk said, leaning forward.

'He still thinks you might get back together with him!' Martin ignored Kirk's words. 'Because you don't have the balls to go tell him it's over. So I told him to come watch us and be discreet, and I thought maybe he'd hear you talk about someone else, about going on other dates. But you can't even commit to that. So he thinks you're still hung up on him.'

Kirk waved the cacomistle silent. 'What do you care? Let him figure it out.' Even as he said the words, they sat uneasily with him.

A fox at a nearby table made a sound like a 'tsk' that might have been directed at him, but as soon as Kirk half-turned, Martin replied. 'Oh my God. "Figure it out." Are you—are you serious? Do you understand how people work?'

'Look—' Kirk turned from one side to the other. As Martin had moderated his tone, people had lost interest in their conversation. Or at least they'd figured out how to disguise their interest. 'Can we discuss my relationship issues later? What does this have to do with anything?'

'You don't have a clue.' Martin shook his head. 'It's dumb, never mind. I'm sorry, I won't tell him where we're going anymore.'

He stared down at his glass as though he wanted to dive into the pink liquid and disappear. And Kirk, who did manage to think things through once in a while, got a glimmer of the answer. 'Wait, you want to date him?'

'No,' Martin muttered, his ears back and his tail curled tightly under his chair and still staring down at his drink.

'Cripes, Martin, why didn't you say something? If—look, I'll talk to him. I mean, if you're interested. He's not a bad guy, just…'

'I know.' The cacomistle kept his eyes on his drink. 'We hung out with him enough. You don't have to say anything.'

'No.' Kirk took a breath. 'You're right. I need to tell him

plain and simple, if he can't pick up on what "I'm busy" means…' He took a breath. 'I'll text him tomorrow.'

Martin looked up. 'You're going to break up with him over text message?'

'I haven't been seeing him for three weeks! You think he hasn't picked up on that?'

The cacomistle shook his head. 'I don't think he has. Or maybe he has but just doesn't want to admit it.'

'So I have to go through this whole thing again?'

'Again?' Martin laughed. 'The whole point is you haven't gone through it at all, dude. Do it in person. Or at least call him.'

'All right, all right.' Kirk sighed.

'If you'd just done that in the first place,' Martin said, 'you wouldn't have to do all this lying and sneaking around. Wait.' He squinted. 'Did you think you were James Bond?'

'No.' Kirk's ears flattened.

'Oh no.' Martin giggled.

'Hey.' Kirk grabbed his glass with a scowl. 'It worked, didn't it? Anyway, you're also doing spy stuff, sneaking intel to Van.'

Lonny walked into the bar and scanned it. Kirk waved him over, and the jaguar waved behind him, presumably to Porta.

'Don't call it intel.' Martin turned to see who Kirk was waving at, and so both of them froze as Porta walked through the door, talking to a visibly reluctant Van.

'Why are they bringing him in here?' Kirk asked. 'They're not going to have him sit with us—are they?'

They were. Lonny took an unused chair from an adjacent table and swung it around for Van while he and Porta took the seats next to Kirk and Martin. The fennec stared at Kirk, and spoke before the badger could. 'Lonny said it'd be okay if I joined you.'

'Uh, yeah,' Kirk said.

Martin, Lonny, and Porta all waited, and he knew what they were waiting for him to say. 'The beers here are pretty good,' he said, staring at his menu.

The jaguar and otter looked at each other. Porta cleared her throat. 'So hey, Kirk, didn't you wonder where we were? It's a nice place but we were waiting for half an hour.'

'He set me up,' Martin said.

Kirk reached out to stop him, but Martin shook his paw off. 'I've been telling Van where we're hanging out, so he could maybe see Kirk dance with someone else or at least talk about breaking up, maybe, but so far Kirk hasn't obliged.'

'Ahh,' Lonny said. 'That's why you were trying to get him to dance with other guys.'

Van cleared his throat. 'I know this is all a misunderstanding. Kirk's been pretty busy, and I know you guys are important to him so he makes time for you. But he hasn't— he hasn't told me we're over. He hasn't told me to my face.'

This was very much like one of Kirk's nightmares, caught in all of his past mistakes in front of the people he liked most in the world. He tried to think of some way to change the subject, but nothing came to mind.

Porta leaned forward. 'Did you really send us someplace else instead of just asking Martin if he was talking to Van?'

'Oh, hey!' Lonny slapped the table. 'That's why you said you might not show up the other night! Hey, that was a test. I passed!'

'Of course you passed,' Porta told him. 'You weren't doing anything.'

'I'm sorry!' The words burst out of him. 'It was—kind of fun, setting it all up. I just didn't want to accuse someone if it turned out not to be that. Imagine how stupid I'd have felt.'

'As opposed to now?' Martin folded his arms and leaned back.

'But look—it worked!' Kirk insisted. 'Martin's been trying to get me to break up with Van because—'

The cacomistle's eyes went wide. 'Kirk.'

'If I have to tell him, you do too.'

'Tell me what?' Van looked from badger to cacomistle. 'Guys, seriously, can we just have a straightforward conversation?'

'Technically,' Porta said, 'if you'd just called and asked Kirk flat out what the deal was instead of stalking him all over the city, you could've avoided all of this too.'

'You guys want us to go?' Lonny pushed his chair back. 'Seems like this might get personal.'

'"Get"?' Kirk said.

'Shut up, Lon.' Porta put a paw on his arm. 'Kirk used us to set his trap. He owes us.'

He shook his head and stood, pulling the otter to her feet. 'You guys wave us back when you're set.'

'Ow. Just because you're bigger than me, you can't just ow okay fine fine.' She followed Lonny over to the bar where they pointedly kept their ears perked up at the television.

The remaining three sat in silence for a moment. Kirk hoped one of the others would start, but it was clearly up to him. He was going to have to deal with Van's disappointment, but the sooner he did, the sooner it'd be over. He took a breath. 'Okay, fine. Van, I'm sorry, you're a nice guy, but I can't keep dating you. There's just too much pressure and I can't handle it.'

'Pressure? When did I ever put pressure on you?'

There it was, the hurt in his eyes, the flattened ears, and the feeling that it was all Kirk's fault, that he'd screwed up somehow. He started to talk, but Martin cut him off. 'Van—don't question how Kirk feels. It took him way too long to do this, but he did it, so be gracious about it.'

The fennec looked down and rubbed his eyes. 'I didn't really believe it,' he said softly. 'I mean—sorry, Kirk, if I made you feel… I didn't mean to.'

'It sounds dumb to say it's not you, it's me, but it sort of is.' Kirk steeled himself and reached out. 'I'm sorry too.'

'And I'm sorry for stalking you. That's not cool. I just really needed to know and you weren't telling me anything.' Van rested his paw in Kirk's. The contact, warm and pleasant, didn't upset Kirk as much as he'd thought it might.

'Speaking of that.' Kirk turned to the cacomistle.

It was a little fun watching Martin stumble over his words, and fun watching Van take too long to get what he meant. Then Van asked if it would be okay with Kirk, and Kirk said it would be fine, and that seemed to upset Van again too, so the fennec stood and said good-bye to all of them, tapping Porta on the shoulder on his way out to say good-bye to them too.

'I suppose,' Lonny said when he and Porta re-joined the table, 'it's too much to ask that you've learned a lesson?'

'Who?' Martin asked. 'Me or him?'

'Either of you.'

Porta shook her head. 'I'm gonna bet on no.'

Kirk smiled. 'I learned that lying to your friends and sneaking around and playing spy works.'

'Hey, yeah.' Martin lifted his glass and toasted Kirk. 'We both got what we wanted by not confronting anyone.'

Kirk lifted his glass, but paused. 'Just so you know, you lied to me, and I lied to you, so…' He waved between them with his free paw. 'We're even?'

'Sure.' The cacomistle smiled.

'Cool.' Kirk toasted, ignoring Lonny's groan, and he and Martin drank together.

# Big Bird

## Frances Pauli

'Status update, Agent Prism. We're listening.'

Prism tapped his tympanic membrane and sub-vocalized deep in his throat. 'We're go for entry, HQ. Perimeter in five. Silent running please.'

'Update us when the disc is in your possession, agent. Good luck.' The voice from the implant cut out.

Prism hunkered beside a rusting dumpster, his scales perfectly matched to the pattern of deep green and red-brown of the metal. His tail curled around the strap of a small tool bag, holding it up near his back where he could tuck it behind his body quickly should someone pass by. Tilting his head to the side, he focused one big eyeball on the building across the street.

He'd gain access through that open second story window. The lower offices were for show anyway. His sources placed the safe, and the stolen disc, on the seventh floor. Business had been closed for six hours, and any staff who meant to vacate the building had already filed out through the twin glass front doors.

His other eye checked the alley behind him, and when nothing moved in either direction, the chameleon began a slow climb up the long wall. He gripped the bricks carefully, rocking forward and back after each step to allow his scales to shift and match the surface. Slow going, certainly, but when Prism held still, he blended. And invisible definitely helped in his line of work.

He climbed, bag tucked to the side so that the hump of his back hid it from the street side. If the last job hadn't gone south so hard, he'd have been in by now. But the last job was a sore subject, and Prism tried to force it from his thoughts. His eyes swiveled, and his mind filled with other places. A beach in Mexico, for one. White sand, hot sun, and all the fried cockroaches he and Bernie could stuff down.

*Except there'd be no Bernie now.*

Prism cursed in the sub-vocal, chameleon growl that could only be heard by other lizards, the device implanted in his tympanum, and a few talented agents who'd picked up the frequency through long training. His old partner had been one of those, but after the last job, Bernie had vanished from the game for good.

*Great job not thinking about it.*

He climbed, shifted color, and stopped when he'd reached a position level with the second story across the street. There, someone had left a window cracked, and Prism fixed an eye on that, brought his tools into reach with his tail, and then used one pinscher-like foot to move aside his lock picks and pistol. Beneath them, he found his grapple gun.

It took both eyes to aim the thing, but when he pulled the trigger, the dart carrying his zip wire imbedded perfectly into the spot he'd targeted. Prism affixed the near end to the bricks beside his head, and then tested the grip by tugging on the strand. When it held, he climbed out onto the wire, hanging below it and gripping with all four feet. His tail rolled up, settling his bag on his belly.

This step, his chromatophores couldn't help with. He'd have to be fast, and he'd have to be lucky, too. He took a deep breath, opened his mouth, and fixed his eyes on the other end of the wire. *Get it just right... Snap and pull...*

His fleshy tongue shot forward, sticking to the zip wire about two thirds down. Not quite enough reach, but the momentum should carry him the rest of the way. Prism jerked, making loose rings of his feet and letting his tongue contract. His body shot forward, riding along the wire in a flash of mottled green, grey, black. The friction burned his toes, but he held on, turned both eyes forward, and slid like a bottle rocket across the gap.

He shot directly into the target building. The impact rattled his bones and forced his feet to fumble for a hold on the smooth concrete. The window. Prism let one eye scan for it. Just a few feet below. He clung to his dart with one foot and reached down for the glass, the sill, the narrow opening.

Catching the edge of the pane, he heaved it up, turned his body into line, and backed down and into the room beyond.

*Perimeter breached.*

He landed in a moderately sized office with a wide desk, a filing cabinet, and too many pictures of the marmot who worked there's family. Prism spent only seconds gazing at the furry faces, but each one registered in his memory like a stored file. Risks. Weaknesses.

If he ever had an office, he'd fill it with photos of strangers.

Prism crept to the door, a wash of dim browns flickering across his body. He listened, tilting his head from one side to the other. The air refreshers rumbled softly overhead. Somewhere distant, an elevator car whined along between the floors. Animals still moved about in the building, closed or not, and he'd have to double up on his stealth tactics.

Prism readjusted his plan. The elevator shaft would have been more covert, but it was deadly dangerous if the cars were still in use. He'd have to utilise the stairwell and pray the guards were lazy.

He cracked the door, scanning the office space outside, then opened it and slid out. The carpet carried a dusky pattern, and the walls were dark wood. Prism adjusted, rocked, and stepped forward one shifting movement at a time.

The hallway was empty, silent. He followed it quickly, found the stairs at the far end, and entered the stairwell without a sound. Greys and ivory. A pattern of shadows and lines. The stairs wound up, one landing at a time. A slim black railing blocked the edge. Prism looked over it, down into the dark pit of two stories. He looked up at the spiral underside of the floors above.

Padding and rocking, he climbed to the seventh floor landing. Once, he froze mid-step when a clattering echo filled the stairwell. Someone below opened a door, shouted, and closed it again. When no other sounds followed, Prism pulled the door wide and entered another hall.

This time, no one had bothered with decor. The grey walls matched the floor, the ceiling. It screamed utility and defense, confirming his intel. The safe was here. The disc was here. Prism lifted his bag over his back and carried it to the door at the end of the hall opposite the elevators.

*Locked and booby trapped. Bingo.*

He blended, pulled his bag closer to the door, and

unzipped it. Keeping one eye trained on the hall behind him, Agent Prism found the tools he needed. He pried open the keypad and short-circuited it. He clipped the alarm wire, and as an extra precaution, programmed in a secure loop to mask his tampering.

When he was satisfied with the job, he opened the door and squeezed into the dark room on the other side. His bag produced a goggle for one eye. Triggering the lights could give him away, but once he'd donned the monocle and set the dial for night vision, he saw little need for it. The room was empty. A square, unadorned floor contained no furniture. The walls were broken only by the safe door directly opposite his position.

Alarm bells went off in his head. He was good, but this was definitely too easy... even for him. Bernie would have seen a trap waiting. He'd have pulled out, tried the other rooms before taking one step forward on that smooth plane of floor.

*But Bernie's dead.*

Caution hadn't spared his partner. It hadn't gotten them safely to retirement. Prism swiveled his gaze over the walls, and then stepped across the room, rocking, listening for the inevitable trap to spring. He reached the safe, however, without dying, and once there, forgot about the danger and turned back to his tools.

The safe was simple. Anything run by a computer chip was a weakness, something to be bypassed, dissected, and cracked. His record on this particular model was 2.32 minutes, but that time, he'd had Bernie on lookout. Both his eyes had been free to focus on the job.

This time it took a full three minutes. Not bad. Certainly nothing to be embarrassed about. Prism checked the edges of the safe door before opening it, and he leaned out to the side in case anything shot out of the square when he did.

Useless precautions. Nothing exploded. No trigger tripped. Prism reached into the safe and extracted the stolen disc. He slipped it into a pocket hidden beneath his arm, another implant, and one that matched his scales perfectly when he was his ordinary color. He reached for his tympanic membrane, but something else caught his eye. Something that flashed green inside the safe, that fluttered when he accidentally exhaled.

He tapped the communications device and reached for the green thing with a free foot. His toes squeezed it, pulled it out for a closer examination even though Prism had known what it was from the first familiar flash. Even though it was an impossible thing. An irresistible trap.

*'We got three weasels with rifles on the rooftop.' Bernie grinned and opened his beak as wide as it would go, wide enough that Prism could have marched right in, if he'd been particularly suicidal. The parrot fluffed his head feathers and snapped his hard mouth closed. 'I'm goin' in.'*

*'I'll cover you.' He'd trained his rifle on the nearest weasel, and held his breath while Bernie's takeoff rattled the scaffolding they'd taken position on. When the parrot's shadow fell across the rooftop, all three weasels looked up. Prism's bullet took the first out, but Bernie's talons grabbed the second. The third got a shot off before Prism's rifle found him. For a breath, he feared for his partner, but Bernie landed, opened that huge beak and grinned back at him.*

*Prism relaxed, shook his head, and waved a signal. Come back and get me. Come back and...*

*The building exploded. Smoke and dust made a blind of the rooftop, erasing Bernie and rattling the scaffolding so that Prism had to cling to it, ride the concussions out. He held on with four feet. Dropped his rifle, and stuck like a tick to the trembling metal.*

*He stuck there until the dust settled, until he'd seen with both eyes that the roof, the weasels, and his partner were gone.*

'Report,' the voice in his ear repeated.

'Target acquired.' Prism turned the feather over and back. He watched the individual strands shimmer. Emerald green with a speck of red just at the tip.

'Well done, Prism. Return at once.'

'Big Bird's here.'

'That's not possible, agent.'

'Then I'm holding an imaginary feather.' Prism ran the surface along his scales. He sniffed it. 'He's here.'

'Big Bird's dead, Prism. You're to report back —'

'No.'

'Agent, you have your orders. Even if he is there, you know as well as we do that it's a trap.'

'And he's the bait.'

'The disc is priority one. You're to return it, now! Get yourself out. If we need to go back in...'

Agent Prism tapped his tympanic membrane and slid the feather into his bag. He closed the safe, retraced his steps to the door and checked the hallway. Empty. Two more doors between this room and the stairwell. Two rooms here and how many stories overhead?

He looked closer. The doors had no keypads, lowering the probability that the rooms held anything significant. They were too small to get Big Bird through, too narrow and too short both. The floor and walls were unbroken slabs, but the ceiling bore a small square opening, halfway down, covered in steel grating.

Prism crept down the hallway until he stood below that. Using his tail for leverage, he stretched tall, reaching with his front feet until he could grasp the edge of the grating. Then, he pressed his nose close to the vent and growled, deep in his throat.

The sound echoed through the metal, reflecting back at him over and over. He listened to it, certain only one other individual in the entire building could hear it. Prism turned his tympanic membrane to the grate. He waited, fully aware every breath he stood here in the open was a risk. Any second, an overly thorough guard might open that stairwell door.

A faint sound filtered back through the vents. Prism's membrane tickled with it. He let out a long breath and dropped to the floor.

Big Bird was in the building.

Prism's heart hammered. His eyes swiveled forward and back. What did it mean? He'd seen the explosion. He'd heard Bernie's last words. 'I'm goin' in.'

A wave of guilt rocked him from side to side. He should have gone back. He'd only assumed nothing could survive that blast, and he'd left his partner behind, possibly wounded, obviously at the mercy of the enemy.

Agent Prism sub-vocalised another growl, a keening rumble sent through the vents as a pale, ineffective apology.

*I'll get you out. I'm coming for you.*

His orders could take a hike. Prism moved with a new purpose. He stepped back to the stairwell, exited the hallway and began to climb. He passed the eighth floor landing, pausing to listen and growl again. He passed the ninth floor, listening, rocking.

Three steps before the tenth, a door below him opened. Stamping feet echoed up the steps. Prism jolted forward, climbing another half flight before he heard the same stutter of sound from above. Animals on the stairs, ahead and behind. He glanced backwards. The tenth floor landing beckoned, but it was too far to risk, the sound of feet on stairs way too close.

He grabbed the railing and pulled himself up and over. The animals below were not in range, but they would be, any second now. Prism slid his body over the edge, reaching for the underside of the stairs with three feet and maintaining a grip on the railing with one. His tail curled, tucked his bag behind him.

The stairs were slick and hard to grab. His scales fluttered, shifting from grey to greyer as the shadows fell across his body. He rocked and stilled, using the pressure of that one foot to wedge himself into position. Mostly out of sight. Mostly invisible.

One eye fixed on the pit below. The other peered sideways toward the stairs and the railing where his foot clung, threatening to tremble and give his position away. The stairwell echoed with the tramping of feet. Three guards appeared below him, sprinting up the steps with their pistols drawn.

This place liked rodents. Agent Prism cataloged the species of the animals below him, noting the weapons and running their specs in his mind. Not that it mattered at this range. He couldn't cling to the stairs and pull a gun from his bag. Any bullet would take him out from that distance.

His pinscher feet slipped against the smooth surface. He could feel his grip going, one fraction of an inch at a time. The rodents ran up another flight, paused so close to him, he could have knocked them over with a flick of his tail. Knocked one over, maybe two. The third would still have time to drill him full of holes.

A shout rang overhead, thrumming through the slick surface he desperately needed to hold onto. Steps rattled his toes. He slid, ever so slightly.

'You find anything?' The big rat leading the lower guards hollered up. His eyes flickered over Prism's position, black orbs in a long face.

'Upper decks are clear.' A deeper voice called down. 'What about you?'

Prism held his breath. He wondered how sharp a rat's eyes were, how good of a nose the guard had. The rat's gaze swept over him again.

'Nothing.' His slim, furred shoulders shrugged. 'Boss says to double the guard on thirteen.'

'Thirteen? Why?' The unseen brute above had a growl in his voice.

'That's orders.'

Behind the rat, the other two guards exchanged a look. They had fatter cheeks, paler fur and wider middles than their leader. If it came to a tail flick, Prism decided to take out the rat first. But he'd have to take them all out, if it came to that. One way or the other. He needed to get to the thirteenth floor before any of them could follow orders.

A move for his bag would give him away, but a few more steps and even a blind rat would be able to make out his foot on the railing.

The guard above cursed, stamped a foot against the stairs and loosened Prism's grip another centimeter. Rat boy took a step, scowling, focusing on the jerk overhead. He'd keep coming, and now was as good a time as any.

Before he fell to his death.

Prism lashed out with his tail, unrolling it as it went and slamming his tool bag into the side of rat guard's head. The guy went down, and his buddies squeaked in alarm. Two guns between them. Prism fixed his eye on the nearest one and opened his mouth. His tongue shot out, latching onto the rodent's pistol as well as his arm. When it contracted, Prism pushed off with three feet, using his grip on the railing to aim his body at guard number three.

They all slammed together. The force of impact — his tongue, his body, and two chubby rodent guards — sent them tumbling toward the tenth floor landing. His body jarred at each step, and his eyes swirled, attempting to pinpoint who was still armed and who was likeliest to make him dead.

His left eye found rat's body, twisted at a less than ideal angle now. That guy wouldn't wake up any time soon... if ever. His other eye caught the two rodents. One lay sprawled beneath the pile, moaning, but the other had reached for something between the mess they'd made of all their limbs and tails.

Prism jerked one foot free. His tail was pinned, but he could turn his head. He struggled with the other three limbs, and shot his tongue smack into the overzealous guard's face, slamming the hamster's head back into the wall with a jerk that hurt all the way back into his throat.

It sent the rodent straight to dreamland though.

Worse than the remaining hamster were the sounds from above. The distinctive ping of a bullet ricocheting off the cement wall drove home an immediate need to move it. Prism planted a foot, hard, on the last conscious guard's chest and heaved with his whole weight, dislodging the tangle of legs and tails so that he could move, but also, exposing more of his body to fire.

Time to skedaddle.

He'd lost the need for stealth now, but he'd also lost his tool bag in the scuttling of bodies down the stair. Another whiz sounded, too close to his head. The hamster idiot whimpered, 'Hold your damn fire.'

Bless him.

Prism swiped his tail above the guy's head to keep him down and found his bag pinned underneath the unconscious rat. He used two feet, keeping one eye on the hamster, and flicking the other between his bag and the stair above. Shadows moved on the wall there, but no one fired.

He tugged on the bag strap, used his tail to keep the hamster pinned, and pulled his tools free. He unzipped the bag, reaching for his pistol. The second hamster groaned, flailing with one arm. He knocked the bag hard and sent it spilling over the stairs. A big green and red feather fluttered out into the open air.

Prism cursed and snatched at his bag.

'Shoot him!' The hamster screamed.

His tools clanged against the stairs. Prism rocked forward and hooked the bag handle with one pinscher. He slipped more than crawled down the flight, grabbing whatever tools he could as he passed and cringing each time a bullet hit the wall.

By the time he reached the landing, he had no option but to duck out into the hallway. Not a second to think of the tools he'd lost, not a moment to check. He couldn't even lock the door from this side, and though the grey hall was blissfully empty, he knew it wouldn't stay that way for more than a breath or two.

Prism sprinted for the elevators. Back to plan A, like it or not. He punched the up arrow and hunkered in front of the doors, using the moment to scan the remaining contents of his bag. Gun, check. All that mattered just then. He plucked the pistol free and aimed it back down the hall.

The doors dinged and slid apart. Prism eyed the car with one eye, empty. He shuffled inside just as the stairwell door opened. One foot punched the number twelve. The other took a wild shot down the hallway just as the car doors slid shut.

They'd expect him to go straight to thirteen. Hell, maybe he should. He still might beat their doubling up and get there first. Somehow, he doubted it though. He watched the floor numbers scroll by, and as eleven went out, slammed the emergency stop button. The car lurched to a halt.

Prism dug through his bag. His grapple gun was gone. Not great. He'd have to get creative on his extraction plan. The extra magazines for his pistol had also fallen out, as had his lock picks. His monocle and the pry bar, however, had settled to the bottom. Prism pulled the latter free and kissed it before setting to work on the doors.

Once he'd pried them open, he faced the shaft wall, bisected by the plane of level twelve. He repacked the remainder of his tools, squeezed his body as flat as it would go, and dragged himself up into the gap. On twelve, the hallway had carpeting. It had no doors near the elevator, and a convenient foyer that covered his movements. He stood, flexed his feet, and reached back into the car, using the pry bar to tap at random buttons.

He pulled it free just as the doors shut. Let them think he was in the shaft. It might keep them busy long enough. Just in case it didn't, he kept his pistol out. His tail threaded through the strap of the bag. He held it aloft, ready to use the thing as a shield or a weapon if necessary.

Prism peered out of the foyer and found another empty hallway. Another series of too small doors, and another stairwell entrance. He should probably check the rooms, but speed was everything now. If Big Bird was on thirteen, he had no time at all to get to him. Sloppy, to leave unchecked doors behind him, but the guard's words drove him into a sprint, just the same.

*Double up on thirteen.*

They didn't want him there, and so, that was exactly where he needed to be. When he reached the door marked, *stairs*, however, he heard steps on the other side. The door knob turned. Prism flattened himself to the side, blended, and aimed his gun.

He fired as the guard stepped out, caught the marmot square in the chest and then used his tongue to drag the guy forward in case there were more behind him. His pistol focused on the opening. His tongue snapped back into his mouth. Nobody else on the stairs. No sound from the stairwell.

Agent Prism rocked once, then scrambled through the doorway and up the stairs as fast as his pinscher feet could carry him. He kept his gun up, climbed with his tail high and his bag ready. At the next landing, he scooted to the wall, pressing flat and using his tail to ease the door open. Holding it with one foot, Prism stuck the tip of his tail out into the hallway. He wiggled it, and when nothing fired at him, slid out and shut the door behind him.

If only he had a way to keep it shut.

The thirteenth floor had no doors between the stairwell and the elevator foyer. The hall took a right turn at the point he'd emerged. At the far end of the latter half Agent Prism found what he sought, a big double door with just enough room to squeeze a large parrot through. There was a keypad of course, and two security cameras mounted near the top of the wall.

He shot both of those, too late, most likely. They'd know he was here, and that meant he had no time to stand around and contemplate things. His tools were gone, and he sprinted toward the door with no plan whatsoever.

He reached it and dropped his bag. He could shoot the pad. Any alarms he set off would make little difference. They knew where he was. But it might not open the doors, and if Prism knew anything, it was that he wanted into the next room. He pulled out the pry bar instead, popped the keypad open and stared at it for half a breath before slamming the end of the bar into the circuits.

Not exactly finesse, but even before the thing stopped spewing sparks, the doors clicked. They gave when he pushed on them, just enough. He used the bar and pried them apart revealing an impossible room.

Carpeting covered every surface, floor, walls, ceiling. It bore a pattern of interlacing lines, splashes of gold and red and deep maroon. His chromatophores tingled just looking at it. It was made for him, that pattern, made to be blended with, and that set off more alarm bells than his decimation of the keypad would have.

A trap designed just for him, with Big Bird as the bait.

Prism reached back into his bag, tucking the pry bar into the bottom and pulling out his monocle. He strapped it over one eye and switched from night vision to infrared. A web of brilliant red lines appeared, dissecting the carpeted room into a glowing maze of death.

Prism locked his free eye on the hall behind him and shifted his body from side to side. He peered into the grid, scanned the far walls, and found a square of red at one end of the room. If he twisted to the side, peeked just as close to the nearest laser as he dared, he could make out the edge of a door.

That red touch pad beckoned, pulsing under the influence of his goggle. He considered the distance, the smooth surface. A bullet might break that plastic, but he doubted it would solve his problem. He could try another way, maybe go out a window and attempt to breach the room from the outside.

His instincts argued there was no time to change the plan. He had run into a corner here, and someone would pin him in place soon. Someone with more guns, and a lot more bullets. He still hesitated at the heat coming off the red lines. He grasped for another way, took a risk and let both eyes scan for anything. Anything else.

What he found only sank him deeper. Across the floor, almost invisible against the carpet, a green feather shimmered. Agent Prism squeezed against the wall, trained his eyes on the red pad and adjusted his position until he found a clear pathway through the lasers, a narrow tunnel of space free from red lines, too small for his body, for any body, but just maybe big enough for a fat, fleshy tongue.

He opened his mouth, closed his eyes, and imagined white sands and fried cockroaches.

'Only for you, Bernie.' Prism aimed, exhaled, and opened his mouth. His tongue shot forward, extending between the lasers, straight as an arrow. It stretched, and yet, fell short of the touchpad by inches. A biting heat flickered across the tip as it fell, and he jerked back, contracting it even as his nerves screamed and burned.

Not quite what he'd planned. He closed his mouth around the pain, swallowed, tasting blood. Too damn close. Just another foot and...

Steps tapped in the hallway. Softly, not quite to the bend in the way yet. Prism lifted his gun, training it on the hall behind him. He leaned forward, pushing his nose right into the room, right up to the nearest laser. He aimed again, both forward and behind, and opened his mouth.

His tongue flew. A snub-nosed revolver appeared around the corner behind him. Prism fired a round at it, cursed, and felt his tongue frying. A slash of fire, a quick pain, and the fleshy tip hit home. The red square flared and died, and the laser lines vanished.

'He's up ahead!'

He ducked into the room, shoving the doors closed behind him. A round bounced off the panel, and another. Prism rocked backwards, blended, and raced for the next gigantic door.

It wasn't locked. That or the laser control had done dual

duty. Either way, it opened when he pulled on the handle. It opened, on the familiar scent of feathers, booze, and a bird who sweat more than he showered.

Prism ducked inside and searched for a way to bar the door. The room was dark, but shadows stood to the sides, suggesting furniture. A mountainous heap in one corner only held his gaze for a second. He could worry about that after. First, he found a chair and dragged it across a floor that complained like the hamsters had, squeaking in protest.

Once that was wedged against the door, Prism whispered to the enormous shadow. 'Bernie?'

'Pete?'

'My god. We thought... I thought you were dead.'

'I am.' The heap shifted. A groan echoed through the room. 'I smell like I am.'

'What's new?' Prism's pulse revved. Alive. He scanned the room with his eyes and then rocked forward. A segment of the far wall was covered in something that rippled in the air currents. 'It's good to smell you again, buddy.'

'You shouldn't have come, Pete.'

'Don't I know it. Gonna have a colossal ass-chewing for disobeying a direct order.' He reached up and snagged an edge of the curtain. It came free with one hard tug, dropping to the floor. The huge window beyond would have filled him with joy if it hadn't been blocked by three solid bars of steel. 'I don't suppose you can fit between these.'

He dropped his bag and began to root through his remaining tools. If he could get even one of the bars out of the way, maybe Bernie could squeeze out. It'd be like old times. Big Bird as the getaway vehicle. They'd make it to that beach yet.

A scraping sound brought his thoughts back to the moment. The chair. The door.

'I mean you *really* shouldn't have come, Pete.'

Agent Prism's heart stalled. He wrapped his toes around the pistol, readied it. 'We got a date with sand, sun, and cockroaches, Big Bird.'

'I hate cockroaches.'

Prism spun around, rolling to one side as he did and bringing the gun up. He trained it on his partner's broad chest, green shimmers flecked with red, a chest that stood between him and the doors. One of Bernie's feet clutched the chair. He'd dragged it free, removed the only thing keeping the rats out.

Or maybe, keeping the rat in.

'Why?' Prism shifted his weight, rocked forward and back. 'What'd they offer you, Bernie?'

'Twice what the feds did.' The colossal, feathered shoulders shrugged. 'Easier money.'

'Working for the enemy.' Prism trained both eyes on the huge bird. Big enough to block the doors, big enough, if it came to that.

'You were all hot and bothered to retire,' Bernie said. 'I'm not ready to leave the game, Pete.'

'So now what? You gonna kill me yourself, buddy?'

'Naw. They want you pretty bad, Pete. My guess is, they won't kill you for awhile.' Bernie's beak clacked shut. He tilted his head to one side, fluffed the feathers on his head, and inhaled. Working up for a big squawk, getting ready to call the rodents down on Prism's head.

'Don't.'

The pistol should have warned him. Bernie would know better than to expect him to miss. Which meant he didn't believe his old partner would pull the trigger at all. It meant, the big parrot was dead wrong. When he opened his beak again, Prism squeezed. The gun fired, a single cracking note, and sent its last round right between the big bird's eyes.

Bernie froze there for a moment, beak wide open, no sound coming out. It wouldn't matter. The rats knew he'd come in here. They'd be at the door now, with only the traitor agent's mighty carcass to keep them out. When the bird finally fell, he landed like a huge overused mattress. His body rippled when it hit the ground, and a cloud of feathers fluttered into the air.

Green and red. Like a holiday.

Prism picked up his bag. He eyeballed the bars on the window, the obvious route out of this joint. Then he shuffled his feet, rocked across the room to his only friend in the world's lifeless body.

'Sorry about this, old pal.' He used one foot to steady the huge head, two to pry open the beak. 'I guess the money wasn't as easy as you thought.'

Agent prism heaved, lined up his tail, and backed in, rocking, flickering, and inhaling as little as possible.

*\*\**

It took the rats an hour and a half to move Big Bird's carcass. They spent a good five minutes shooting out the window first. Shooting at nothing. Afterwards, they'd loaded Bernie into the back of a truck, driven him, rattling and stinking, out into the country to dump.

Agent Prism waited five minutes after the sound of their engines faded to crawl from the parrot's lifeless maw. He'd limped back to the city eventually, mailed the disc to headquarters in a brown paper parcel with no return address. Aside from the data, the package held a small, handwritten note containing only two words. 'I'm out.'

'Can I get you anything else, sir?' A pretty gecko in a flower print sundress leaned over him. She had a nice smile but her green-flecked-with-red scales killed any ideas he might have entertained about flirting.

'Another Mai Tai, please.' Pete stretched out on the lounging pad and let the sun color his scales whatever hue they damn well felt like being. One pinscher plucked at the bowl of fried cockroaches, tossing a handful to his eager tongue.

'On your tab?'

'I'll get it now.' His tail threaded through his bag strap, lifting it into range so that he could reach in and retrieve his wallet.

'That's a lovely bag, sir.' The gecko had huge, amber eyes that looked like gold.

Pete handed her the cash and a substantial tip, and then tucked his wallet away again. Aside from his money, the bag held only sunglasses and a good book. The outside of it shimmered in the sun, each feather stitched to catch the light and reflect like a gem. Green and red.

'So beautiful.'

'Thanks.' He smiled and stared out over the white sands, over the sea and the sun and a bowl of fried cockroaches. 'I got it from a friend.'

# THE OFF AIR AFFAIR
## Huskyteer

The twin-seater droned through the midnight sky. The coyote at the controls glanced from the glowing instrument panel to the blur of the single prop and back, while the ferret beside him stared out into the blackness, watching the Eastern European mountain peaks pass below them.

'A little too close for comfort, don't you think?' he suggested.

'A miss is as good as a mile.'

Through their headphones, an operator tracking their position from far away in New York issued directions. Occasionally, snatches of pop music from a late night Czechoslovakian radio station broke in, and a woman's voice announcing the next tune.

'She sounds nice,' said the coyote.

'Concentrate, please!'

'There. That's our mystery transmitter station.' A red light winked to warn of a high obstruction. Ignoring this danger signal, the coyote pushed the nose forward to take a closer look.

The flash of gunfire from below suggested that their presence was known and unwelcome. The pilot banked steeply, and the plane jerked as something snagged the tail, caught, then snapped free.

Rudderless, their aircraft whipped from side to side. The coyote fought to bring it back under control, sacrificing height and skimming the mountaintops.

'Can we reach the Austrian border?' asked the ferret.

'I think so.' The coyote tapped a dial, and the needle jumped anticlockwise. 'Fuel tank's hit.'

His lips pulled back from his teeth as he hauled on the yoke. The mountains fell away behind them, and they were over flat farmland. The engine began to sputter, and the propeller slowed.

They descended in a gentle glide. The wheels touched grass, bounced, and touched again. The plane zigzagged across the field, heading as if pulled by a string for the single obstruction, a henhouse. They stopped in an explosion of straw, feathers, and startled clucking.

A light went on in the farmhouse and a badger in a nightdress ran out. The meaning of her shouts was clear, if not the words.

The coyote jumped down from the cockpit.

'My apologies, ma'am. My employer will pay for the damage.' He removed his leather gloves and held out his paw for her to shake. Automatically, she took it.

'And just who employs you to fly around crashing into things?' The badger's anger had visibly lessened at the sight of such an attractive pilot, but her fur was still bristling.

'I'm with the United Nations Cooperative Intelligence Agency.'

She took the card he held out to her. 'U.N.C.I.A.'

'That's right. Now, if you need to get hold of me again, you can reach me on that number any time.'

'Any time? Really?' She smoothed down her nightdress.

'Day or night,' he assured her, flashing his teeth in a smile. 'And next time I'm passing, perhaps we can have dinner together. Now, may I use your phone?'

ACT I: 'TOUCHÉ'

The coyote paused outside the television rental shop to check his reflection in the window, adjusted his tie, and walked in.

TV sets large and small displayed the three networks' current offerings in black-and-white or glorious colour: a weather report, a cartoon, and a spy show in which the good guy had been tied up and was awaiting rescue by his partner. The coyote watched the latter for a few seconds, one eyebrow raised.

'They'll put on any old trash these days,' he told the elderly cat behind the counter. She nodded in agreement and pressed a button. A bank of sets on the back wall slid to one side, revealing the open doors of an elevator.

As the coyote stepped through, a ferret in a black polo neck scampered into the shop.

'You're late,' the coyote grinned, and stabbed the DOOR CLOSE button.

'No, I believe...' Contorting his body, the ferret flexed through the doors just as they shut. 'I am precisely on time.'

'Wily Russian.'

'Smart American.'

The elevator opened on a busy reception area. The two agents greeted the squirrel on the front desk, pinned on the badges that would allow them to walk the corridors of U.N.C.I.A. unchallenged, and walked together to the top floor office occupied by Mr Alastair, Head of the North American Section.

'Good morning, Mr Luck, Mr Ilyushin.' The snow leopard smiled and flicked his ears. 'Thank you for your punctuality. Have a seat.'

'Punctuality,' Ilyushin mouthed at Luck, who waved a dismissive hand and checked his watch against the row of clocks on the far wall. Below them lights flashed and spools of tape whirred back and forth. The ferret and coyote exchanged glances and waited for the briefing to begin. Every assignment they were given started in this office. Each one was different, and each dangerous.

'Last night,' Mr Alastair said, 'Radio Bratislava went off the air.'

The agents exchanged glances.

'He did it,' offered the ferret.

'I did not!'

The snow leopard held up a paw.

'The incident may not have been unconnected to your recent activities in Czechoslovakia,' he said, 'but neither of you was directly to blame. There was a break-in at the radio station, and much of their equipment was damaged or stolen. We have one witness: a young disc jockey who had just finished recording the late night show. If we can connect the theft with the transmitter station, and prove that Shrike are involved, we may be a step closer to working out what they're up to.'

'Transmission: Impossible, you might say,' murmured the ferret.

'You might indeed say that, Mr Ilyushin, though I'm not sure why you'd want to. You will both travel to Bratislava--on a commercial flight, this time, which I trust you will find more comfortable--and make contact with our witness.'

'What's his name, sir?' asked the coyote.

'Her name is Danulka Kucera.'

Mr Alastair held out a red folder, and they both made a grab for it. The coyote won and flipped it open.

'Danulka,' he said, rolling the word around his tongue. He studied the black and white photograph: a young dog with perked ears and a curly tail. 'What a ridiculous name to lumber an attractive young lady with.'

'If you say so... Montgomery,' the ferret replied.

'Touché, Nikko. Touché.'

\*\*\*

The transmitter station perched untidily at the summit of the mountain, like a bird's nest bristling with masts and wires. The curve of the upturned parabolic antenna made a vast egg at its centre.

The crow hopped to the window and looked out. A north wind whipped snowflakes across the grey sky, the clouds concealing the lower peaks from view.

'Madam Cornix, if we don't mend those cables, we can't align the satellite properly.' The wolf twisted his paws together, his tail tucked against his legs.

'Then get out there and mend them, Professor. The Volpe twins obtained everything on your list from Radio Bratislava, as well as ensuring the station can't interfere with our transmission.'

The wolf joined her at the window, where the cut cables whipped back and forth in the wind.

'I'm a scientist, not the Wichita Lineman,' he muttered.

'What did you say?'

'I said... I'm not capable of carrying out those repairs. I'd fall, and there's nobody else who can operate the computer.'

'If we're not ready tonight, we'll have to wait for another

opportunity. It will set back Shrike's master plan by months. Our leaders won't be pleased with us, and you know what that means.'

'I know! I know!' wailed the wolf. 'Why are you explaining it all over again? Who do you think is listening?'

'Maybe I just enjoy seeing you squirm.' She fanned a wing and preened the feathers into place. 'I will fix the cables. I'm not earthbound like you. But that means you'll have to tidy up the... other loose end.'

'I don't understand.'

'Radio Bratislava. There was a witness. A young girl. Take care of her.' Madam Cornix made a stabbing motion with her beak.

The wolf tugged unhappily at the lapels of his white coat. 'I'm a scientist,' he said again, 'not a killer.'

'Professor, you work for Shrike. Of course you are a killer. You're just not used to doing it in person. Now get going.'

'The helicopter can't take off in this wind,' said the professor, a trace of hope in his voice. The crow spread her wings.

'Are you trying to lecture me on the principles of *flight*?' she asked, angling her head to watch him with first one eye, then the other.

'No, Madam Cornix.'

'Good.'

A few minutes later a black helicopter took off, swaying as the wind buffeted it.


ACT II: 'I DREAM OF 'I DREAM OF JEANNIE'


The sign on the studio door read RADIO BRATISLAVA. A second, smaller notice, lit by a red lamp burning above it, was in Czechoslovakian.

'What does that say, Nikko?'

''Do not enter when red lamp is lit',' the ferret translated, pushing the door open.

Montgomery followed him in. A technician was wielding a voltmeter over the remains of the equipment, but Montgomery had eyes only for the young dog on her knees in the middle of the floor, clearing the mess with a dustpan and brush. In spite of the dirt on her clothes and fur, the photo in the file had failed to do her justice. She wore headphones and hummed to herself as she worked, oblivious to the noise of her colleague or to the agents' entry.

'Danulka?' Montgomery said. When she didn't respond, he repeated himself, more loudly, then tapped her on the shoulder.

The dog jumped to her feet, the headphones slipping to the floor, and swiped her brush at him. Montgomery, who had evaded many similar attacks in his time, dodged her.

'That's me. Who are you?' Her ears swivelled towards the newcomers and her gaze rested on Nikko, who had positioned himself close to the technician. She brushed herself down and straightened her skirt. The ferret took no notice, focusing his attention on the wolf bent over the console.

'And you are?' he asked.

'From the network. Helping with the repairs,' said the wolf. He glanced from Nikko to Montgomery, and shifted his voltmeter from paw to paw.

'Could I see some ID, please?' Nikko asked.

The wolf froze for a moment, then lunged at Danulka, holding the voltmeter in front of him like a fencer with a sword. Nikko moved faster, intercepting him and twisting his wrist so the meter dropped from his paw. They both crashed to the floor, where they made perfect targets for Miss Kucera's brush.

Nikko squeaked as the weapon glanced off his paw, and the wolf took advantage of the distraction. He leaped up and bolted for the door, slamming it behind him. Montgomery sprang after him, but the wolf had already locked the door from the outside. Montgomery rattled the handle, growling.

Nikko was examining the voltmeter. The metal prongs were discoloured.

'Some sort of toxin,' he said, giving the tip of one prong a cautious sniff. 'I'll call the local office, have this analysed. And give them a description of the wolf.'

'Look, just who are you?' Danulka demanded, waving the brush point blank at Nikko. 'And why was that engineer trying to kill me?'

'You're welcome,' said the ferret, taking a step back.

'We're with the U.N.C.I.A,' Montgomery told her. 'We're... investigators.'

'Could I see some ID, please?'

'You're learning.' He showed her his card. 'Montgomery Luck. And my partner, Nikko Ilyushin.'

Nikko withdrew a packet of chewing-gum from his jacket pocket, extended a single stick in its silver wrapper, and spoke into the device, softly and urgently. Danulka stared at him, her ears cocked. Montgomery smiled at her.

'We used to use cigarette packets,' he said, 'but my partner here is trying to quit.'

'That is a radio? May I see?'

Montgomery moved to block her view of the U.N.C.I.A. communicator. 'I know all this must be a shock, Danulka...'

'Call me Danni,' she told him. 'My friends do. It sounds more American.'

'Oh, you like Americans?' Montgomery's tail swept from side to side.

'How do you feel about Russians?' Nikko added, putting the communicator away.

'I'm not sure yet.'

'Then let me help you make up your mind.'

Montgomery cleared his throat. 'Nikko, stop flirting and break the door down.'

'Why can't you break the door down?' demanded Nikko.

'I have delicate shoulders. And this is a good suit.'

They left the building, Nikko rubbing his shoulder, and walked out into the street. The red roof of Bratislava Castle was just visible above the new concrete high-rise blocks that ringed the city centre.

'We need to talk to you somewhere safe, where we won't be overheard.' Montgomery told the dog, offering his arm. 'A bar, for instance.'

'I know just the place! Come with me.'

The two agents flanked Danni protectively as they mingled with the lunchtime crowd. Neither noticed a pair of foxes stand up from their café table across the road to tail them at a discreet distance.

'This,' said Montgomery, gazing around him with an air of disappointment, 'is not a bar.'

'But a record store is an excellent place to have a conversation without being overheard,' Nikko approved, inspecting a stack of 45s. 'Even if the choice of music isn't spectacular.'

'Shops aren't allowed to sell most American music,' Danni explained. 'Just like we can't play it on the radio. Too subversive.'

Montgomery ducked into a listening booth and put a set of headphones over his large, triangular ears. Holding out a second set, he beckoned Danni.

'You'll love this track,' he promised her, pressing the button that started a record playing so customers could sample it before purchase.

She joined him in the booth. It was a tight squeeze for two, and the coyote made room for her as best he could.

Danni's eyes closed as she tuned in to the song. Montgomery nudged her.

'Maybe we can listen together another time. Right now, we need to talk.'

He turned the volume all the way down. The foam walls of the booth were meant to protect music-lovers from disturbance, but they would also muffle Montgomery's words.

'Shrike tried to kill you earlier,' he said.

'Shrike? That's a kind of bird, isn't it?'

'A bird that stabs its prey to death. Much like that wolf. Shrike is an organisation dedicated to gaining power at any price, and they don't hesitate to dispose of anyone who gets in their way.'

While Danni and Montgomery were talking, Nikko wandered the floor, flicking through the racks of music and examining posters for upcoming concerts. His path appeared random, but he never lost sight of his partner and Danni as he checked the layout of the store from every angle. He noticed the two foxes straight away, although he never looked directly at them. Each wore a grey suit, and they stood out among the mostly young clientele. They were identical in height, colouring, even the way each had brushed a centre parting into his fur. The only difference was that one had brown eyes, the other green.

They were equally *large*.

'Am I supposed to be scared?' Danni's hackles rose.

'You should be. They still scare me, and I've been defeating them for years. But, with your help, Nikko and I will get to the bottom of whatever they're up to.'

Danni grinned. 'I'd much rather talk about your American popular culture. I think about it all the time.'

'You're saying you dream of *I Dream of Jeannie?*'

She laughed. 'Right. But mostly of music. The stuff I'm not allowed to play on my show.'

'Well, I'm no expert, but try me. I bet you like the Monkees.'

Danni nodded. 'And the Animals!'

A shadow fell across the booth as the green-eyed fox stepped in front of it, blocking the entrance.

'What do you think of the birds?' he asked, conversationally.

'The Byrds?' Danni asked.

'The *birds*.' He cracked his knuckles.

'There's a time to every purpose under heaven,' Montgomery said to Danni, 'and it's time for us to go.' He wrapped his arm around her shoulder and tried to shove his way out.

'But the record hasn't finished,' said the fox. He pushed Montgomery back into the booth and twisted the volume knob up. The coyote yelped in agony and threw off his headphones. Catching them, the green-eyed fox looped the cord around Montgomery's neck and began to twist it.

When the two foxes separated, the brown-eyed one had made for Nikko, cutting him off from his partner and Danni. Now Nikko punched him in the stomach. The fox looked down and brushed his shirt, as if to remove a speck of dirt. Then he lifted Nikko by the lapels of his jacket and threw him across the room. The ferret twisted in mid-air--crashed to the floor--scrambled to his feet.

Montgomery broke free of the other fox's grip, shook off the headphone cord and squared up to his opponent. The two danced around each other, looking for an opening. The fox led with a right hook, which the coyote blocked, and followed it up with a straight left, catching Montgomery in the jaw. He staggered back, baring his teeth in a grimace.

Danni looked around for a weapon and grabbed the pile of singles, flinging them into the fight like Frisbees. Montgomery ducked instinctively. The fox, distracted, looked up, giving Montgomery the chance to grab him by the tail.

When his twin ran to help, Montgomery grabbed his tail too, and yanked hard.

'Now that's just cruel,' Nikko observed, raising his voice above two identical yowls of pain.

'I can't hold them for long,' the coyote warned. As if on cue, the green-eyed fox hooked his foot back in a kick, catching Montgomery just below the knee so his leg crumpled under him. Both foxes surged forward, one driving his elbow into Nikko's muzzle, the other catching the ferret when he fell. Holding his body between them, they carried Nikko through the door to the street beyond.

The green-eyed fox looked back over his shoulder and slammed the heavy glass door closed against Montgomery's temple as the coyote gave chase.

A black car waited at the kerb with its engine idling. The two foxes bundled the unconscious ferret into the back of the car and leaped in after him. With a shriek of tyres, it rounded the corner and was gone.

Montgomery put a paw to his head and collapsed on the floor.


ACT III: 'A LONG STRETCH'


'Montgomery? Montgomery!'

The coyote opened one eye. 'Oh. Hello!'

Wincing, he allowed Danni to help him up.

'They've got Nikko! Hurry!' she said, dragging him along by the wrist.

'I was hoping you might be a little less concerned about Nikko, and a little more concerned about me,' he complained as he followed her. The black car was still in sight, just, fighting its way through the busy streets.

'Taxi! Taxi?' Danni waved her paw, but nobody stopped. Montgomery looked around for a suitable vehicle. His gaze flashed up and down the road, stopping at a pig who was parking his motorcycle at the kerb.

'Hi,' he said. 'I need to borrow your bike.'

The pig looked bewildered, and his confusion deepened when Montgomery pushed a wad of American currency into his paw. Before he could speak, the coyote had jumped on the bike and kicked it into action. Danni climbed up behind him and clasped her paws around his waist, her chest against his back. As Montgomery opened the throttle and took off into the traffic, he felt her grip tighten.

'I hope this is a *long* chase,' he muttered.

'Excuse me?' the dog yelled in his ear over the roar of the engine.

'I said hang on!'

He leaned the bike around a corner, striking sparks where the foot pegs scraped along the road. They were gaining on the car as they weaved in and out of the traffic, but now the way was blocked by a bus picking up passengers. A gap no wider than the handlebars remained between the bus and an oncoming truck, and Montgomery slid through it, flattening his ears against the chorus of car horns. Danni gave a small whine, and her knees pressed against the coyote's thighs. He took one paw off the bars to give her a reassuring pat.

They followed the car west along the bank of the Danube. With the white-walled castle in the background, and the mountains beyond, it would have made a pleasant picture if Montgomery had had time to look around.

'I know a shortcut!' Danni yelled into the coyote's ear. 'Go right!'

Danni's shortcut took them into the older part of town, where the streets were narrow and twisting. Montgomery loosened his hold on the bars as they bumped over the cobblestones, and swung left and right as he attempted to overtake a pale blue Skoda whose elderly driver appeared not to notice the bike in her mirrors. He mounted the pavement, squeezing past the tables outside a bar, and dropped back down the kerb to the now empty road. Behind him, two elderly drinkers raised their glasses and roared their approval of the manoeuvre.

He stood up on the pegs to see further, and spotted the black car heading up a side street. Gunning the throttle, he turned into the narrow alley, only to find the car reversing back towards him at speed. Montgomery braked hard, the rear wheel skittering, and tried to haul the bike around, but the car struck it side on. The bike clattered to the ground, sending rider and passenger sprawling. The engine coughed and cut out.

As the car sped backwards Montgomery rolled Danni into his arms, away from the rear wheels. Seeing that he had missed them, the driver accelerated away with a squeal of tyres and a cloud of exhaust smoke.

Montgomery helped Danni to her feet. The bike lay on its side, the back wheel twisted and spinning jerkily. The black car was nowhere to be seen.

'You recognised those foxes, didn't you?' he asked. 'From the break-in.'

'Yes. And now they have your friend.'

'Oh, don't you worry about Nikko,' Montgomery said. 'He can take care of himself.'

***

Nikko lay on a laboratory bench, his wrists and ankles bound tightly to a makeshift system of cranks and pulleys. If he craned his neck, he could see that every wall of the room was lined with humming banks of computers and gleaming electronic equipment. A large window offered a view of the sunset over snow-covered mountains.

'You're an U.N.C.I.A. agent, aren't you?' the wolf demanded. 'Tell me everything you know about us, and where your partner is, and the girl. Please,' he added.

'I don't know what you're talking about,' replied Nikko. 'And, frankly, I do not think that torture is your forte.'

The wolf's lip lifted, showing his teeth, and he pulled a lever. 'We'll see about that,' he said.

Cogs turned, and the ropes holding Nikko tightened. The ferret clenched his paws into fists, but said nothing. The tip of his tail twitched.

A flurry of flapping announced the arrival of the crow, who hopped across the room towards them.

'Well?' she demanded, folding her wings.

The wolf cringed. 'Nothing yet,' he admitted.

'Even though you spent all that time designing a torture table. Amazing.'

She loomed above Nikko, regarding him with first one black eye, then the other, so the ferret saw his face reflected in each.

'Let me show you how it's done, Professor. And you needn't think you're off the hook, either,' she added. 'You could have killed the girl and been long gone before U.N.C.I.A. arrived.'

'I got distracted fixing the equipment.'

'You're a coward who didn't have the guts to do the job he was sent to do. As for those idiot foxes, it shouldn't have taken two of them to capture one ferret. They should have killed all three and got away. They failed, they were no longer necessary, and they have been disposed of.'

She lunged forward, and her beak clicked shut in the fur at Nikko's throat. When she pulled away, white hairs were clinging to it.

'Where's the girl? Where has your partner taken her?'

'To dinner and a dance, knowing him.'

She struck his muzzle with her beak, but using the side, not the stabbing point. Nikko closed his eyes and hissed through his teeth.

'The sooner you tell us what we want to know,' she said, 'the sooner you will be allowed to die.'

'That doesn't sound like a very good deal to me.'

'By the time I'm finished with you, you will be begging for death.'

Nikko arched his neck to look around. 'Quite the interesting setup you have here,' he said. 'What exactly are you hatching? A nuclear missile?'

The wolf's ears perked and his tail gave an excited swish. 'As a matter of fact, it's...'

A harsh squawk from Madam Cornix cut him off. The crow's chest puffed out, and she preened her flight feathers.

'You'll find out soon enough,' she said. She hopped to the

window, so that Nikko had to squint to make her out in the glare of sun on snow. 'Professor, please continue.'

The wolf returned to the controls of the rack. Nikko tensed.

'Oh, I know you've been trying to buy time while you wait for your friend to rescue you,' said the crow. Her nostrils flared. 'But he'll never make it. In fact, with the full coop-eration you are just about to give me, he will be found and killed.'

'I wasn't planning to cooperate,' Nikko said. He smiled up at her, managing to look relaxed in spite of his bonds.

'He's a... difficult subject,' explained the wolf.

'Why? Look at him-- he's all soft and fluffy. He should be easy.' Her beak hovered over Nikko's throat, then his heart.

'I'm a scientist, not a torturer.'

'Think of it as an experiment. What is the most efficient way to extract information from the specimen?'

'Have you ever tried torturing a ferret?' asked the professor.

To demonstrate, he placed his paw on a lever and clicked it up a couple of notches. Nikko's torso stretched easily to accommodate the pull of the machine. The professor spun the wheel hard to the left so Nikko's legs now pointed in the opposite direction to his upper body, but he did not appear at all discomfited by the situation.

'They're just too flexible,' the wolf said sadly.

'Then think of some other way! You keep saying you're a scientist--don't you have drugs? Scalpels? Acid?'

'I'm a *computer* scientist,' the wolf protested.

Madam Cornix rotated her head and fixed him in the glare of one glittering eye. He trembled.

'Maybe you have a soldering iron?' offered Nikko.


ACT IV: 'It's For The Birds'


'Slow down. You might slip and fall,' panted Montgomery. 'At least, one of us might,' he added to himself.

Danni, bounding ahead up the narrow, treacherous trail, turned to grin back at him.

'Silly! I know these mountains--I grew up in them. My family are shepherds, but I wanted to come down and work in the big city. You might say I'm the black sheep of the family!' She grinned, showing her pink tongue. 'American joke. Did it work?'

'Very good,' Monty told her. 'Nikko's been trying for years and he hasn't mastered the American joke yet.'

The trail grew steeper, and they climbed in silence. The transmitter station sat far above them, wedged in the peak. Montgomery let his muzzle hang open, and rolled up his shirtsleeves, while the fuzzy-coated dog appeared untroubled by the heat of the day or the physical effort of the climb.

'Break?' Montgomery asked at last. They sat down in the shade of an overhanging rock, where patches of snow still lay. Montgomery scooped up a pawful to cool his tongue.

'If you're thirsty, try sucking a pebble.' Danni picked one up from the path and tossed it to him. The coyote caught it between two claws.

'Is there anything you don't know?' he marvelled.

'What's happening in *Peyton Place*?' said Danni hopefully.

'Sorry. I don't watch a lot of television.'

'Then what do you *do* in the evenings?'

Montgomery was spared having to answer this by a noise above them. Two armed figures dressed in grey jumpsuits dropped from a ledge to land on the path in front of them. One was a tubby marmot whose rifle was almost as tall as he was.

The other was a black sheep.

Danni looked at Montgomery, who shook his head. 'Don't say it.'

The sheep gestured with a hoof. 'Your gun, please. And no tricks.'

Montgomery reached inside his jacket for his pistol, and passed it over.

'What a comedown for a sheepdog,' whispered Danni, as the sheep herded her along at the point of his rifle.

If the climb had been hard before, it was much more difficult with their paws held above their heads, but dropping them earned a jab in the ribs from a rifle muzzle.

'Wooly bully,' muttered Montgomery, staggering so he fell

against Danni.

'Question,' she whispered. 'If you had a gun all along, why didn't you shoot the foxes?'

'Doing that sort of thing in the street tends to frighten people.'

'*Silence!*'

At last, they reached the transmitter station. The marmot tapped a code into the keypad by the door, which slid open to admit them, and they walked along grey corridors to what Montgomery guessed was the nerve centre of the station. The fake technician from the radio station was inspecting the readings on a row of dials, watched by a crow who stood a head taller than he did.

'Nice of you to show up, Montgomery,' said Nikko, still stretched out on the bench, as his partner was pushed through the door.

'Lying down on the job again, I see.'

'Nikko! Are you all right?' Danni asked as the sheep prodded her into the room.

'Oh, Montgomery, what did you have to bring her for? We were supposed to be protecting her!'

'You've met her. You think I was offered the opportunity to leave her behind?'

'Silence!' Spreading her wings to their full extent, the great crow seemed to fill the room. Danni tucked her curly tail between her legs, and even Montgomery took a step backwards.

'Tie them up,' she told their captors. 'They can all witness the beginning of the new age!'

'Yes, Madam Cornix.' The marmot pushed Montgomery down into an office chair and tied his paws behind him, while the sheep did the same to Danni. He passed Montgomery's pistol to the crow, who examined it.

'Ah, the specially designed and produced U.N.C.I.A. gun. Ideal for undercover agents.' She placed the pistol on a shelf. 'Now get out!' she ordered, and the two guards trotted obediently away.

'And what new age, exactly, is beginning?' Montgomery asked, as the sound of their footsteps faded.

'In just a few minutes, the main American and Russian

satellites will pass close to one another in orbit, directly above this station. Using a powerful beam, we will gain control of every radio and television station, every international phone call, every air and sea navigation system. Imagine what that means for security forces, unable to coordinate. For the navigation of ships and planes. For isolated communities, stranded without the means to call for help.'

'It will be a disaster.' Nikko squirmed in his bonds.

'Not for us, mammal. Remember, every bird's brain contains an inbuilt, accurate navigation system. And with the power of flight, we can get wherever we need to, fast.'

Madam Cornix paced, her claws clacking on the concrete floor.

'By the time the satellites can be destroyed and replacements sent into space, it will be too late. This world will belong to its true rulers--the birds!'

The wolf cleared his throat. 'Madam Cornix? It's time.' He placed his paw on the red switch.

Madam Cornix pushed him to one side. Holding out one wing, she extended a primary feather.

'This is a historic moment,' she said, 'and *I* am going to throw the switch.'

She threw the switch.

***

'TEN,' boomed a recorded voice. Lights flashed on control panels, and an electronic hum filled the air. The wolf darted from one terminal to the next, checking readouts and making adjustments. Printers whirred as needles recorded information on graph paper in jagged peaks. Inch by inch, Montgomery began to roll his office chair across the floor, closer to Danni.

'NINE.'

Danni was staring at a battery pack that had been plugged into the computer console. 'That's mine,' she growled. 'You people stole my equipment and shut down my radio show.'

When Madam Cornix and the wolf followed her pointing finger, Montgomery bumped the back of his chair up against the young DJ's and fumbled with the knots that secured her paws.

'EIGHT.'

Madam Cornix's wing flicked open like a knife, knocking Montgomery back so his chair spun away on its castors. It hit a row of switches, and a light changed from green to amber.

'Careful!' The wolf shoved Montgomery's chair aside and examined the control panel, watched intently by the crow.

Contorting his slim body, Nikko wriggled his wrists and ankles free of their ties, slid down from the table and sidled across the room to take Montgomery's pistol from its resting-place.

'SEVEN.'

'Stand together, please. Up against the wall.' Wolf and crow obeyed him.

'You could have done that any time, couldn't you?' Montgomery asked out of the side of his muzzle.

'Just waiting for the right moment,' Nikko confirmed.

'Well, hurry up and untie us. This game of musical chairs is making me dizzy.'

'SIX.'

'Montgomery, cover them. Danni, tie them up.'

Nikko thrust the pistol into his partner's paw and ran to one of the consoles lining the walls. Scanning the screen, he began typing instructions and hitting buttons.

'Does he know what he's doing?' Danni hissed to Montgomery.

'I'm not sure,' the coyote replied. 'Do you?'

'I grew up in the mountains. I know knots.'

As she reached out to bind Madam Cornix's wings, the crow folded them around her, trapping the dog against her chest. Using Danni as a shield, she hopped up on to the windowsill.

'FIVE.'

'You think you've won, but you can't stop the countdown!' she cawed. 'And you can't catch a bird!'

She struck at the window with her beak. The glass shattered, and she spread her wings, poised for flight. Silhouetted by the rising moon as it shone through her outstretched feathers, the Shrike leader made a black, menacing shape that seemed to fill the room.

Montgomery fired.

'FOUR.'

Madam Cornix fell from her perch and flapped on the floor in a circle, unable to rise. Her beak gaped pink in a grimace of agony.

'My wing! You've broken my wing! Now I'm no better than you mammals!'

'THREE.'

With a howl, the wolf threw himself at Nikko and closed his paws round the ferret's throat, squeezing hard. Montgomery, on the other side of the room, aimed his pistol but was unable to get a clear shot.

Nikko writhed in the wolf's grip, still striking keys.

'TWO.'

Danni punched the wolf in the jaw, and he crumpled.

'Thank you,' Nikko said, pouncing on the terminal and typing at a rapid rate. 'Impressive.'

'I come from a long line of shepherds,' she told him. 'It's not the first time someone in my family has had to deal with a predatory canine.'

'Remind me never to make a move on a shepherd,' Montgomery requested.

'ONE.'

Settling in a chair and placing a set of headphones over her ears, Danni joined Nikko at his work, turning his keyboard solo into a duet.

'Hey. What do you think you're doing?' asked the ferret, barely glancing up.

'Helping,' she said brightly. 'I'm not just a disc jockey--I do know a little about radio engineering, too.'

'ZERO.'

The room was bathed in a red light. Electricity crackled, and Nikko was thrown back from the console. Danni rushed to help him up. Outside, the dish antenna turned on its axis, transmitting its message to the circling satellites.

'Are you all right, Nikko?' Montgomery asked.

'A little charred around the edges, perhaps.' Nikko brushed at the fur on his head and arms, which was sticking up the wrong way, and stared out of the window at the antenna.

'We failed,' he said, flatly. 'They've won. Chaos

everywhere.'

'Not Kaos,' Montgomery corrected. 'Shrike.'

'On the contrary.' Danni beamed. 'I managed to reprogram the system.'

Montgomery looked at the computer banks, humming with power as lights blinked on and off, and the ticker tape spewing reams of incomprehensible data.

'How?' he asked.

'How do you think I know so much about Western television? Intercepting, amplifying and garbling signals is a little skill I have. I couldn't prevent Shrike's transmission from reaching the satellites, but I mixed it up a little. Right now, households across the USA are being treated to an evening of Soviet television broadcasts, while the USSR enjoys your finest American commercials and game shows.'

Nikko allowed one of his dazzling smiles to grace the room.

'It will be a most important and interesting exchange of culture between the great world powers,' he said.

***

The cabinet radio, record player and television was the largest and most expensive piece of furniture in Danni's apartment. Montgomery placed a 45 on the turntable and clicked the autostart. They might be out of immediate danger, but a good spy never risked being overheard. Besides, it was a good tune.

'When all this is finally cleared up, Danni, I'll send you the entire Billboard Hot 100,' he promised.

'It's a kind thought, Montgomery, but possession of such items could get Danni into very big trouble with the authorities,' Nikko pointed out.

'Not if she's working in our New York office, as part of the Communications division,' said Mr Alastair.

Danni's tail wagged so fast it blurred. She turned to the snow leopard, who had made himself comfortable in an armchair.

'New York?' she asked. 'Really?'

'Really,' purred Mr Alastair. 'Your expertise will be invaluable to us at headquarters. And, of course, as an U.N.C.I.A.

employee you will be free to return and see your family whenever you wish.'

'In the meantime, perhaps you would like to show me some of Bratislava's night spots? I'm sure you have some wonderful restaurants. And cosy little bars. Intimate, you might say.'

'Or you could show me some of the more cultured attractions?' suggested Nikko. 'The theatre? The opera? All on U.N.C.I.A.'s dime, obviously.'

Mr Alastair's tail tip twitched, but he did not protest.

'With a whole evening of American television to watch?' Danni's tail wagged even faster. 'I don't think so!'

Coyote and ferret looked at each other.

'Well,' said Montgomery. 'I can't remember the last time I spent a nice, quiet evening watching television. How about you, Nikko?'

'No, me neither.'

'Please, stay.' Danni patted the couch to either side of her, and the two agents sat down. 'I wonder what's on tonight?'

'*The Mister Ed Sullivan Show*, I think,' said Mr Alastair. 'What? Not everyone leads the exciting social life you two gentlemen do.'

'Oh, good, you're staying too. Quite the party.' Montgomery raised an eyebrow at Nikko.

'Naturally, Mr Luck.'

Curling his tail around him, the head of U.N.C.I.A. North America rested his chin on his paws and stared intently at the tiny screen.

# Game of Shadows

## HJ Pang

Zimmer was a promising wolf agent, and the section's favourite to being promoted to Head of Special Operations. However, being passed over in favour of an older and pain-in-the-tail senior for every year for five years running had proven to be more than he could bear. The many bullet holes in Schultz said that much. Wolves were supposed to be the most loyal of agents, but there were always exceptions to the rule. Everyone wanted to be the Alpha, what with a pack hierarchy and all.

A nasty business it was, but men like Zimmer were put on earth to do such work. I was brought in from Retrieval Ops. This investigation called for nothing but the best, and with their golden boy on the run, the job fell to me.

Retrieval Ops was a relatively new section. Rogue agents used to get their comeuppance from agents of their own section. However, the bonds and favours that may have been formed with their former colleagues often proved problematic in securing their capture. Although Retrieval Ops worked for the Agency, the fact that we were private contractors meant that we did not have to wade through the bureaucratic nightmare of the Agency, answering only to the Director and Schultz. This gave us the benefit of the doubt when hunting double-crossers; it was only through the recommendation of the late Schultz that we had our jobs. From intercepted work emails and cafeteria talk, I gathered that a number of the staff had complained that with no defections since our formation two years ago, the millions spent on our section could have been instead channelled towards operational funding.

Personally, I think they're just jealous we're better equipped than they are. And much better paid, of course. Besides, you don't pay the cops only when the crooks appear.

Each organisation wasn't a true brotherhood in itself, be it a corporation or agency. They all had their own credos and secrets, even within respective departments. No one outside it was to be trusted, and it wasn't easy getting them to cooperate in my investigation. I had worked with militaries in the past, and trust me when I say it was far more challenging working with an intelligence agency. Everyone played their own game in the clandestine, and the fact that I was both from Retrieval Ops and a contractor didn't improve matters. That, and the fact that I'm a tanuki. With the reputation raccoons have, some people just didn't understand that we aren't the one and the same, appearances aside.

I worked with Laja on this operation. Having known each other since we were cubs, our many successful ops gave the fox and I a good working relationship in the field. In the game of shadows, everyone had to be able to count on one another. How we managed to confirm the facts of Schultz's murder along with the retrieval details of Agent Zimmer was a miracle on its own, but the intel we cross-referenced from several surveillance analysts suggested he had yet to leave the country. The fact that the killing happened in one of the most secure buildings in the country suggested Zimmer held his impunity in high esteem, but surely an agent of his salt would have found some way to disappear by now.

*** 

It was a well-known fact that rogue agents (among others) turn to the criminal underworld as a means for escape and procurement. The perceived anonymity it held was all but a myth, for how could those who thrived on deception not betray members of its fold, if only to better line their pockets? Money flowed like lifeblood, even more so in the criminal grapevine, and it didn't take long for us to find out where Zimmer had gone. Cost a pretty penny straight out of the section fund, too, not counting the escrow fee. Let's just say it was far too big to count as "Incidental Expenses".

It was unusual for one to head directly to an airport after committing a capital crime, but some agents think they're untouchable. Being able to hide in plain sight in all manner of operations throughout the globe gives a sense of bravado even I experience from time to time. Zimmer had checked into a lounge at a small private airport under an alias, replacing the few guards with Mafia enforcers that answered to him. But no airport was completely secure, not if anyone works there. Does anyone ever notice how many staff in the office came and went without anyone noticing? Routine is after all the enemy of security.

So it wasn't difficult for us to check ourselves in as additional hired help from the Rising Phoenix Brotherhood. I swear, the organised gangs should really use more catchy acronyms for their gangs, it might help with their marketing strategy. Three uneasy conversations and exchanges of gang signs later, I found myself but five metres away from where our mark waited. Only the reinforced concrete wall of the waiting room stood between him and us.

The old bluff-your-way-in method never failed. Only this time it did. Directional charges on the other side of the wall blew me and Laja away in a shower of concrete and rebar.

I was so stunned that I didn't register what happened until we were surrounded. I say 'I', because Laja lay motionless next to me, a piece of rebar lodged in his chest. Balaclava-clad assault teams and the gangsters replacing airport security encircled us. One of them had relieved me of my customised .45 as I collected my thoughts. As the dust cleared, who else but Zimmer should be standing before us, hands outstretched to his sides with his bush of a tail flapping behind him. Wolves were a proud species, but Zimmer had to be the worst. I mean, what kind of guy does dramatic poses right after icing someone?

'Suzuki, I presume.' said Zimmer. His smile extended all the way to his ears and fangs.

I blinked behind my facial markings. 'We've met. I interviewed you right after your last op.'

An assault trooper bashed me in the chest with his rifle butt and I choked. 'You hold too much importance of your section's role,' Zimmer continued, stepping around me as he assessed his handiwork. 'Did you really believe that I, Zimmer of Highnorth, would ever commit an unsanctioned killing against a member of my own organisation? Did you think I would throw away everything in the name of Loyalty and Country, if only to slake my anger at not having been promoted?'

'Hell if I know. Stranger things have happened.' I replied.

'Oh, but you've yet to hear the best of it,' said Zimmer as he bent over me. 'You think you understand the world of shadows like we do. But do you think that the success of the Agency is dependent only on hard work and dedication?' The wolf paused. 'All that is nothing without the training and technology to make them more than they can be. Training and equipment that could have been paid for by all that money tied up in your section! Do you know how hard the budget cuts in the last two years hit us? Of course not! Because you were too busy enjoying those millions allocated to you! A department that exists not to serve, but to question our loyalty!' He spat.

I could see where this was going, but I had to be sure. 'So you did kill Schultz.'

'You're looking at the new Head of Special Operations.' smirked Zimmer.

'Who can only be appointed by the Director himself,' I raised my eyebrows. 'So old Rusok realizes he can cut one department, and at the same time, promote a prospective agent. That's as far out as budget cuts go.'

'Government money belongs to the Agency, not to the likes of you,' snarled Zimmer. 'Do you know why it was so easy for you to track me down? The Agency wanted you to find me. They all know what it means with you and Laja gone. No more loyal agents waiting for false hopes of promotion, just so that two puffed-up schoolboys can steal their jobs,' He stood up. 'Men, take this shit away. I'll make sure you all get a bonus.' Zimmer put his finger to his earpiece as the guards lifted and dragged me and Laja away, the gangsters following close behind.

As I was jostled away through the dark service corridors that led to a convenient disposal hatch, I smiled a little smile. For in the Game of Shadows, nothing was ever as it seems. The only thing that counted was who you knew, and how well you greased their paws.

I had paid the gangsters trailing close behind my captors pretty well. Even before I heard the click of guns being readied, I knew I would have my revenge… and that of Laja's.

# The Winged Fox

## K. R. Green

Sonata eyed up the man who'd come through the village gates, her pointed ears twitching at the sound of the metal gate falling shut. He brought with him a fox-like creature she'd never before seen in the flesh, but she recognised it from one of her drawing books. Its wings were tucked back for now, but she made out brown and black feathers atop his rusty orange fur.

The man himself looked human: although a thick brown beard covered a large part of his face, he had no fur to show. The Enfield trotted alongside him, its ears prickling up like hers.

When he came to a pause outside her tent, she pulled herself to her feet, stretching out her front paws alongside the table top, flexing her front claws briefly. The sun glistened off her golden-orange fur, and she let out a brief purr at the resolved tension in her shoulder. Time to figure this pair out. Strangers were not unwelcome, but they were rare.

'Hello?' The man had a thick accent through that facial hair, but Sonata's roommate turned from her armchair where she read a book, and stood to greet the man. The yurt she and Lilith shared was not large, nor overly-cramped, but with him at the doorway, and Lilith crossing the room, it left little room for anyone else, despite his size. He was barely taller than Lilith, and Sonata decided to remain up on the furniture for now. Let them discuss his business here, human to human, as it were.

Instead, Sonata moved her gaze over the Enfield; a fox in every way but for the brown and black feathers adorning his shoulder blades. There was a small ruffle, but he did not extend them. Still, from the books she'd seen, they'd be around half its length again, either side.

Her roommate smiled, moving to the entrance-way. 'I'm Lilith. What are your names?'

'I'm Kyle, and this is Pele.'

Lilith crouched to greet the Enfield, but looked back up at the man. 'What brings you here?'

'We're seeking treasure, travelling the whole forest, trying to see the world before I turn thirty.'

Lilith stood up. 'Treasure?'

'Well. Fungi, rare herbs, flowers... Things the clans value.' He ran his left hand through his hair. 'Anything that will enable us to barter for supplies.'

Sonata narrowed her eyes, already replaying the man's reasons. What brought him to a little clan here then, if he didn't have things to barter?

Lilith put her hand on his shoulder, directing him across the courtyard. 'Let me lead you to the Tavern, and maybe someone here can recommend some local spaces to check out for your foraging.'

Sonata waited, watching the interaction, and following the newcomers' move towards the tavern. Time to report them in.

She leapt down, slinking out through the back entrance and headed up to Magma's hut. She snuck inside, and having paused to sense for others, shifted back into her human form.

Magma sat on a little cushioned bench, smoking a cigarette. The woman smiled; her red hair cut short above her ears, which flickered much like an animal's, despite her human appearance.

'He has arrived, although brings a human with him.'

That made Magma pause, holding her cigarette away from her mouth for a few moments. 'A human?'

'The man claimed to be seeking rare flowers and fungi to trade with the clans. The Enfield did not speak, and Lilith was guiding him to the Tavern. I thought I should let you know.'

'Yes, thank you Sonata. Let me know as things evolve.'

Sonata shifted back into her feline form, moving back across the clan towards the tavern on her way home. She spied the Enfield in the corner; the man drinking a pint of something. Lilith was not there, so she returned home, slipping under the yurt wall into her bedroom.

Here, she shifted back to her normal form, and took a

shower; washing the grass and dirt from her blonde hair. By the time she'd dried off and found some fleece pyjamas, Lilith had come to bed.

Sonata hung up her towel on the bathroom hook and climbed into her bedding pack. 'How did it go?'

'He's an interesting one. I couldn't read his creature. Did you recognise it?'

'Yes. It's an Enfield, essentially a winged fox.'

'What did Magma say?'

Sonata sighed, lying back against her cushions. 'Just to keep her updated. Did you discover anything useful?'

It was Lilith's turn to roll onto her back. 'Well, he seemed genuine, but that almost makes the Enfield less trustworthy in my eyes.'

'He's staying though, right?'

'Yes. For tonight at least; at the Tavern. We should go around tomorrow; see if we can gather any more information on the fox.'

'I wish someone here could actually communicate with them. Surely a canine shifter would be able to have a brief discussion, at least.'

'Perhaps. But Magma employed us, so... we better rest up and get her some results. However we have to.' And with that, Lilith rolled over to turn out the solar-powered lamp, and settled down beside her to sleep.

*** *

Pele was resting in front of the fire of the Tavern sitting room, snoozing in the sun. Sonata sat across from the sofas over by the bar, watching the fox snore. Why would an Enfield turn up here, at this time? It was never a coincidence, but the timing of this was too close to the equinox celebrations. They had to be working for the Wolves.

Lilith was chatting up Kyle, showing him some of the local foraging trails: one of the least valuable routes of course, but still one that would allow her a space to get to know him.

One of Pele's eyes watched her, although his muzzle rested on his paws like any canine. She felt the gaze, and found herself glaring back.

Time to make a move, one way or the other.

Sonata padded across the space, not looking away from that gaze. 'Do you speak feline?'

The Enfield tilted his head to one side, and made a low whine. That wasn't the best start. Should she risk it? She paused, churning the ideas of her options. *Are you a shifter?*

Well, if he was, she'd just outed herself.

*You have mind-speak.*

Ah. Well that was helpful. She knew that much about him, then. *Not fluent, but some, with effort.* Interestingly, his physical body did not move as he responded to her mental questions. *How fluent are you? I know shifters can... use it.* She was careful to limit her wording.

Pele shut his eyes. *I don't need to think about it, I just always could. My species can.*

*Your species, as in shifters?*

The canine almost seemed to sigh, a slight tilt of the jaw and a roll of the eyes. It was a surprisingly human gesture for a creature that claimed not to shift. *We're called Enfields. I know this is a feline colony and I am not welcome here. I appreciate that I am an outsider. But I have a human to keep safe, and he stumbled up this trail. So please, I'd really like to get some rest.* He sighed through his nose, a physical sound rather than mental one. She still didn't know if he was the shifter.

But she took the hint, not wanting to shut down her one opportunity to learn in the first conversation. *Apologies for keeping you up. Do come by my tent if you need anything.*

She headed up to Magma's hut, glancing back only once to see that he still watched her.

That was fine. She'd made the first connection, and she was leaving him to consider it. Now, she had a job to do. And a library to explore.

She remained in her feline form until she had travelled well behind the closed doors of the resource centre, and only shifted one she was into the library itself. It wasn't as well ordered as it had been when they first set up camp, but it was the only resource she had.

So what had she learned? Enfields, as a species, appeared able to use mind-speak. That was worth knowing. He'd understood her, so it was both a positive: being able to communicate quietly, but also meant he'd be able to hear the conversations of shifters.

The perfect cover for a spy.

But then, why hadn't he ignored her? Unless she was his target, why engage in the conversation. Her mind raced through the possibilities. Maybe he wasn't the true agent: perhaps rather a tool for the man. Or was he just trying to give her a little honesty so she wouldn't question him so much.

And she knew what Magma would say. It was Sonata's job to weed out those seeking to uncover their clan's secrets. Whatever the cost.

Her hands moved along the spines of their books; seeking anything that may give her information about Enfields, mind-speak in general or the relationships of attuned creatures in mythology. Where else could she look for information about winged foxes, after all?

Although she searched a couple of books, most were unhelpful: vague mentions, fanciful stories woven for children, with magic and mystery. But nothing concrete to help her search.

She stalked across the clan paths, slipping under the wall of her bedroom, and collapsed into bed still in her feline form.

Lilith was already in bed, and she snuggled up against her fleecy pyjamas.

*I was getting worried.*

*Sorry, I lost track of the time.* Then she remembered that Pele would be able to hear them, and took a moment to enjoy the warmth of her fur, before shifting back and whispering. 'The Enfield can understand mind-speak.'

Lilith met her gaze evenly. 'An Enfield can probably hear whispers too, but okay.'

She had a point. Sonata sighed, grabbing her fleece and lying back on the pillow. 'How was your day?'

'I think he's genuinely here as he claims. We may just wish to offer him supplies and hope they move on. I found nothing incongruent in his explanations.'

'Did he say why he had a Myth with him?'

'He said Pele had got caught in a trap he had set, and felt he couldn't kill such a creature. But when he let it go free,

Pele hunted out a rabbit and brought it back for him. As far as I can tell, he believes he's got himself a pet dog.'

Sonata sighed, thinking back over Pele's explanation.

It couldn't be a co-incidence. She didn't believe in them.

\*\*\*

Kyle was at their door early the next morning, so Sonata set off to the inn in her human form; careful to smile and nod at people as she went. Some were already awake, but others snoozed in their yurts, their snores heard even over the bird-song. How the creatures hadn't fled this place with Malas shaking the very earth with his night-time roars, she didn't know. Still, he was a wonderful man aside from his blocked nose and throat.

Sam was already up, tending to the herb garden, and she grinned his way before heading through the door to the inn.

'Morning, Kel.'

'Morning Sonnie. You helping out again today?'

'Sure thing. How many you got for me?'

'To be honest, just the one today. New guy's room needs a clean. He's already left, so I'd start there. Room seven.'

She grabbed the wooden box from under the counter, complete with rags for cleaning and clean bedding that would have been folded last night.

She grabbed the key for number seven from the drawer and headed up the steps, her ears already prickled for sounds. If Pele was there, she'd struggle to find out very much, but the guise of cleaning gave her ample opportunities as long as he remained in their space. She knocked briefly, then unlocked the door.

She let the door fall shut behind her, and began by opening one of the curtains partially. The light didn't tell her much: it looked as ordinary as any human room might when someone visited. She began by clearing the used water tankard, switching it out for a clean one from her box.

Having checked the bathroom, and looking under the bed when reaching for the corner of the bedclothes, she felt satisfied. Pele was not here. She moved quickly, taking both a cleaning rag and new pillow case as she wandered the area:

able to cover should he return at short notice.

But it all seemed normal. Nothing out of place from anything she'd searched before. But on the floor under the bed, beside the bedtime table, lay a weird trinket: a bit like a pendant with lights. It was something from the new world: technology she'd heard about in training but never seen before. She didn't touch it, but moved the bed slightly to cast light on it. She'd need to sketch it in detail for Magma to make any kind of recognition.

She hurried to return the room to normal, clearing it as quickly but also thoroughly so no questions would be raised, and had to stifle a sigh as she locked the door back outside. Taking some steadying breaths, she steeled herself for the exit. This was what she'd been trained for.

'All done, Sam. You okay if I pop home for a few; I meant to grab something for Magma and I've left it.'

He grinned from his spot by the sink, wiping a goblet dry on a cloth. 'Wouldn't wanna upset her. I can do without you today, really. Head off now.'

Sonata laughed, already heading out the door. That had been… interesting, at least. Still, she couldn't get too caught up. She replayed the shape of the trinket over and over, and only froze when she stepped through the open yurt flap to see Pele at the doorway to her and Lilith's bedroom.

Shit.

She clenched her teeth together, thoughts racing to keep her voice calm.

She spoke out loud, uncertain if he would know her human form. 'Can I help you?' Apparently she needed to keep her wits about her with this one.

Pele turned to face her, winged fluttering a little on his back. She watched him, waiting for a next move. But he just watched her. No mind-speak. No recognition. Just like a dog.

'You shouldn't be in here unattended. Are you hungry?'

She walked over to the cupboard, fishing out a strip of dried cured meat. She offered it to him, pacing it close to the external doorway; hoping to move him from her bedroom. She didn't think she had anything that may be recognisable as incriminating, but the fact he was snooping made her nervous.

But he didn't follow her to the meat. He didn't move at all.

What would a human's next move usually be? Did she dare confront him? But if he did harm her, it would definitely allow them to kick the man out. Perhaps that would be best.

She stepped towards the Enfield. 'What are you looking for? Maybe I can help.'

In response, Pele took another step into her bedroom, and Sonata hissed. She hadn't meant to, but instincts were there for a reason. 'Please leave, if you understand me. You are not welcome in my bedroom. We all need a place that feels safe, dog. Including me.'

Pele's ears prickled, flitting one way then another, until he slunk past her, head down but tail still up. He was not leaving willingly, nor out of fear. Sonata felt her ears twist, her feline soul acting through even her human body.

She followed him out, watching him return to the inn; not letting her eyes off him until he the door of the inn shut behind him. But now she didn't want to leave for Magma's meeting.

Scanning the room, both for sights and smells, he clearly hadn't made it as far as the bedroom, but had explored the open plan living space. Still. She saw nothing particularly out of place, and nothing which would cause her alarm for him to have seen. The book of mythical drawings was open to the Enfield page, but it just described the looks with a couple of black and white sketches; so again, nothing she would worry over.

But something had brought him in. Either their conversation before, or something already planned. She had to speak with Magma about the trinket, let alone this. But Magma would not leave her home on a day like this. It was too close to the ceremony.

Sonata sat on the bedding roll in her bedroom, feeling a little vulnerable without knowing really why. She could smell that he hadn't come in here. But he had intended to. Without even thinking, she took off her shoes and clambered under the covers, eyelids barely staying open.

Her last thought was of needing to tell Lilith.

\*\*\*

Her ears carried watery sounds to her, faded noise of movement, quiet chatter, but nothing concrete. In time though, the sounds got louder, came closer, and she felt the air of bodies moving around her. Smelled the scents of people from the clan. When her eyes opened though, she could only see light. No shapes, no colour.

Panic bubbled in her throat, and she tried to move her arms, to lift her hands to his face, but she couldn't feel them.

Someone spoke, the words garbled at first, although her brain slowly untangled them. 'Sonata. It's Lilith. Can you hear me?'

But she couldn't move her lips, couldn't see anything. She wanted to thrash, wanted to fight, to force her body into action: but she couldn't feel anything. 'If you can hear me, try opening your eyes.'

Her heart skipped a beat; a thundering thud against her chest. She had, hadn't she?

Then she found her mouth, and a quiet hiss sung out beneath the chatter. Well, it was a start.

'She hissed. That means she's at least alive.'

Wow, what had happened to lead to that kind of comment? Had she died? She tried to think back, but her memories were fuzzy. She'd just gone to bed, hadn't she?

Then she found her eyes, and realised her eyelids were stuck shut. She tried to blink, desperate to prove to herself she had sight. But when one lid did open, she screamed; a hoarse, painful outburst as the light burned against her retina.

That brought her head and neck to consciousness, as she shook her head to one side, trying to protect her eyes from the blinding bright light.

A new voice came through; one she didn't recognise easily. 'Light sensitive, can we move these lights a bit for her?'

Was that... Kyle? What was he doing giving directions?

But the space around her went dark, she felt the movement of people around her, and when she next opened her eyes, she could make out the outline of those around her.

Lilith leaned forward when Sonata moved her head, smiling down at her. Sonata tried to smile back, although she wasn't very sure her face was responding.

'You should start to feel better now, the antidote is working. Can you tell me what happened?'

Again, Sonata's mouth wouldn't move.

She would have eyed up Kyle, if she knew which body outline belonged to him. *Lilith?*

*I hear you.*

*Is it safe to… do this?*

*Just tell me what you remember.*

The paranoia of being over-heard swept through her. All the training they had endured to ensure the safety of the clan, and the control of any information fell short of hr ability to discern who was around her. But Lilith was also trained, and she trusted her partner.

*I found the Enfield in our yurt, but he left and I then felt tired and decided to lie down.*

*Do you remember eating or drinking anything?*

It was odd. Even in mind-speak, Lilith had a lilt of her accent which always made Sonata feel at ease. *I didn't. I just came back because I felt tired, and then was to go to Magma.*

*She's here.*

*Where are we?*

*You're still in bed. Magma, myself, Sam and Kyle are tending to you. We think there was a poison somewhere.*

*Kyle knew about it?*

*Kyle has some training in shamanism. When he said he sought treasure in the plants, he knows his healing herbs.*

She paused, taking a while to process the full meaning of Lilith's information. *So what now?*

*Now you rest, and I update Magma.*

*Can you tell her Kyle had a trinket in his room, under the bed. Like a necklace, but it created its own light, like a candle. I didn't touch it, but I wonder if that's why I felt tired.*

There was a pause. Lilith was likely processing the information, either looking to Magma or at Kyle. *I'll tell Magma.*

*Thanks.*

*Love you.*

*You too.*

***

When Sonata woke again, she was alone with Lilith in their bedroom. Whoever else had been here, the room smelled of oddly-mixed scents. She could tell Magma had visited, the stale cigarette smell over-powering practically any other herbs Kyle may have used to reverse her affliction. Her partner slept beside her, wheezing quietly. Sonata smiled, slipping an arm around Lilith, and just enjoying the peace. But she could no longer sleep.

And despite the slither of guilt, she stroked Lilith's shoulder. 'Morning.'

The moment Lilith's eyes opened and focused on her, she saw the smile in them. 'You're awake.'

'Yes. Can you fill me in?'

Lilith's arm came around Sonata's waist. 'Well, you're no longer working. Magma insisted you take a break to recover, especially as you were injured on the job.'

'And the newbies?' She still wasn't sure who could overhear them.

'Magma is continuing the investigation herself. She has offered her own space for Kyle and Pele to stay, away from the clans members; under the guise of their own protection since most of the villagers assume they harmed you.'

Sonata blinked, not sure she understood. 'So what happens now?'

Lilith smiled, stroking her cheek. 'You rest.'

'And then?' Now she recognised the smile: that knowing smile that Sonata wasn't going to like the answer.

'She's taken over, you're off the case, so you're free.'

'Free to wonder who the hell nearly killed me, based on your phrasing.'

Lilith's face went red. 'I was scared, Sonata.'

Shame tightened across her chest. 'I'm sorry Lilith. I still don't really know what to think or how to respond. I've worked for Magma for years, and nothing's beaten me like this.'

They hugged tighter, Sonata feeling stable in Lilith's arms. 'I can't just give up.'

'I know, darling. You don't know how.' Lilith sighed, her breath warm on Sonata's neck. 'Just be careful, okay? I can't lose you.'

Sonata felt the pressure behind the words, and nodded, unable to respond out loud for fear of lying.

'Is it not suspicious; that Kyle knew how to cure me?'

'He used very general healing herbs: lavender and lemon-balm to minimise infection and sage to reduce inflammation. He treated symptoms topically, not any specific medical diagnosis. Else he likely wouldn't need to barter for a living.'

Sonata leaned her head back, desperate to relieve the crunch of pressure in her muscles. 'And how can we be sure that isn't a cover story?'

But Lilith was already rolling over, facing her back to Sonata. 'You're alive because of him. I think it only fair to give him the benefit of the doubt.'

It made sense, but she couldn't just let it go that easily.

Everything happened for a reason.

***

Sonata slunk into Magma's hut in her feline form: ginger fur brushing against the dirt along the windowsill. Magma had one of the two wooden structures in this glade, but as the headquarters for all information gathering, it was crucial to keep the data safe.

She could smell the Enfield, but most strongly, she smelled sage. A cleansing herb, used for purification and truth. Even the stale cigarette smoke was muffled beneath it. Magma was sat in her study, and Sonata noted the lack of surprise in her face when she hopped up to the stool beside her, and shifted.

'Tell me what you know.'

Magma was not one to do as requested, but Sonata was beyond the state of politeness. Her life had been at risk, for this mission. She intended to seek out the answers that would explain it.

She expected a fight, but Magma merely looked over her thin-rimmed spectacles and sighed. 'The device you found was recovered. We have no clear understanding of it, and Kyle has professed to knowing nothing of it except that the Enfield brought it to him. It does not seem to harm him, but we have quarantined it. Just in case.'

It didn't make sense. 'Yet they have remained here?'

'Yes. We have no proof to accuse, especially after Kyle helped aid your recovery. The more we discuss his journey here, the less willing he sounds in anything that the Enfield has done.'

'So you think Pele has done something?'

'I cannot say, but it appears Kyle has not.'

Sonata shut her eyes, squeezing the lids tight for a few moments. 'Very well. But what is Pele after? The ceremony cannot be of benefit to the canines.'

'Information is often valuable enough, Sonata. You know that.'

'Then why take me out?'

'That, I do not know, child. But your job now is to rest: to let the dust settle, so that Pele may relax his guard.'

Heat flared across her face and chest. She had done what she was told every step of the way. And look where it had got her. 'You charged me with seeking out secrets, no matter the cost. I've paid my dues. Why shut me out now? Do you really think he may become sympathetic to our ways?'

'I believe Kyle to be of great influence, however subconscious. We must not act too hastily, else each visitor brings a fresh threat. Understanding the full motive is of far greater value if we are to survive the uprising.'

Sonata looked out through the doorway towards the library. They did not have enough information to move forward. Not yet. In some ways, the enemy could become the greatest source of knowledge. A weapon to tip the odds. She could hardly argue with that logic.

'And who will see to his safety?'

'Lilith has agreed to keep Kyle close. And I am tending to Pele's needs. So I don't want you meddling, do I make myself clear?'

Magma's eyes flashed briefly, and even her feline self shrunk back under the gaze of a tiger. Spymaster or not, she was not to be disobeyed.

Sonata left Magma's hut in her human form; the plain black cloak she'd put on that morning swishing a little around her knees. If she was off the case and forbidden to meddle, she'd just have to see to her own mission.

Smiling back at the clan, she headed into the forest, and

up towards the snow-topped mountain where the Wolves
roamed free.

# Le Chat Et La Souris
## Tom Mullins

### 1943

Harry's slender, clawed hand jumped around the piece of scrap paper, scribbling down the words that squawked from the headset he held awkwardly to his large ear. A curl of smoke rose from the cigarette clenched in his teeth, sketching a soft wave in the air before him. The words he dictated appeared to be nonsense, random. But he already guessed what their true meaning might be. Harry had started to recognise the patterns and could translate parts of the literary mess without first checking. This made him both proud and concerned. It meant they would need to change the cipher very soon. If he could figure it out, then the Germans wouldn't be far behind. For a moment the sound wavered and the radio lights dimmed. But Harry gave it a quick smack with his tail and it sprang back to life, the voice continuing uninterrupted. Thanks to his sensitive ears, Harry didn't miss a word.

The rats were bred to win the war. Using a stolen German formula, the rodents were designed to mutate into savage creatures of brutal combat, stronger and faster than any human soldier, and viciously loyal to the British Empire. Imagine the scientists' disappointment when the rats, while definitely smart and fast, would shy away from any sort of combat or conflict, and would much prefer to tinker with an old jeep engine while listening to the wireless.

Harry Brown was one such rat.

The radio's message ended. Harry opened a tiny codebook and translated the absurd poem into information. It was very much a similar message to the last few days. Nothing to report. Hold position. An inspirational quote from Churchill, and one even more so from de Gaulle.

*Vive la résistance! Vive la France!*

Harry took a long drag on his cigarette and sighed, filling the cramped room with smoke.

A hatch opened above him, letting in light and letting out the wisps of burnt tobacco.

'I told you not to smoke down here,' a woman said in French. She wiped her hands on the front of the apron that covered her blue dress, then climbed down the wooden ladder into the small hidey-hole. The sturdy woman's face was lined from a life of smiles and frowns. Although these days, a frown was more likely.

'I can't exactly smoke out there, can I, Damiane?' he said, placing the cigarette next to an empty mug. Harry's French was nearly perfect, but his British accent slathered every word. He waved the paper at Damiane. 'The latest news from England.'

Damiane took the paper and ran her eyes over it. 'Not the most exciting news, but it will still give the people hope. I'll have Lucien do up copies tonight.'

'You should have a chat with Lucien. He's got the bloody Nazis breathing down his neck, making him print their awful propaganda, and quite frankly he's turning into a nervous wreck. He looks like he hasn't had a decent night's sleep in over a year.'

'Lucien knows the risks and knows how important his work is to the resistance, and the people.'

Harry leaned back in his chair and shrugged at her. 'He doesn't share your bull-headed courage, Damiane. He spends every minute of every day looking over his shoulder, and it's driving him mad. He's your brother, Damiane, and he's all you've got left. Give him a break.'

Damiane stared at the paper as if it craved her attention. Without looking at Harry, she said, 'Lucien will print these up tonight.'

Harry let out a huff and shook his head.

'And then he can have a break,' she added, pointing a finger at the rat. 'The people will have to find their own hope for a while.'

'That's my girl,' said Harry, giving her a grin. 'You should take some time off too, and stop trying to save France single-handedly.' He picked up his cigarette again, but Damiane snatched it from his paw.

'Somebody has to.' She sucked on the cigarette and then let out a long sigh, her shoulders visibly relaxing. At that moment, the radio sprang into life.

'What on earth?' Harry used his tail to snatch up the headphones while he scrambled for another sheet of paper. His paw held a pencil poised over the paper, but he wrote nothing, instead listening intently to the message.

'Who is it? What do they want?' Damiane hissed at him, but he just gave her a short, sharp shush. Barely twenty seconds later, the radio fell silent. Harry carefully placed the headphones down.

'Well?'

Harry looked up at Damiane, ears tilted back in mild surprise. 'It seems that we are getting a visitor. Someone by the name of "The Cat".'

'The Cat? Who are they? What do they want?'

'They're a spy, apparently. And they have a very important message to give to us.'

*** 

Dusk was normally a beautiful time of day in the little town of Carrefour. The sun would always begin to sink behind the old church on the hill, letting darkness gently settle among the brick buildings and cobbled streets, while the sky remained a pale blue. At five o'clock the lamps would be lit, bathing many doorways and awnings in a warm, orange light.

These days, however, several unsightly additions smothered the view like a persistent damp cloud, turning even the inviting glow of the lamps into a dim, cold glow.

Lucien spotted several of these unsightly additions as he came stepping down the street, arms full of paper. He swore and turned to walk the other way, hoping they had not recognised him.

'Lucien! So good to see you this night.' The voice spoke French, but its owner was not. Jackboots, polished black to a fine sheen, clipped against the street. Smart trousers were tucked neatly into the knee-high leather. The black uniform was pressed with an almost unnatural severity, so much so that the various adornments clung to the material without causing a single crease or wrinkle. The most striking emblem was, of course, the bright red armband sporting an all too familiar symbol in the centre.

There was no escape now. Lucien's balding head started to sweat. He turned around clutching his stack of freshly printed papers, and did his best to smile in the face of vileness.

'Captain Brandt. I'm surprised to see you away from the château this time of night.'

'It is such a lovely evening, I thought I would go for a walk.' Captain Brandt was a thin man and nearly an entire foot taller than Lucien. He was young for an officer, but not unusually so, and could be considered rather handsome despite his prominent brow (not to mention his political alignment). He also smiled a lot. It was a broad, movie-star smile, and Lucien found it extremely unsettling. At least the two armed soldiers flanking Brandt remained stone faced and professionally dour.

'In fact, I came searching specifically for you, to ask a favour.'

This, Lucien found even more unsettling.

'I have a printing job for you. I was going to offer to supply some of the paper and ink, but it seems,' he paused and glanced pointedly at the stack of paper, 'that you have plenty already. How surprising.'

Lucien tried to fumble out an excuse, for the supplies, to leave, anything. But he got as far as stuttering out various noises when Brandt plucked one of the flyers from the pile. Lucien's eyes bulged as the Nazi silently read the document.

'How very, very interesting,' Brandt murmured.

Lucien couldn't breathe.

'Artichoke stew... Artichoke gruel...' He turned to one of his soldiers and read directly from the paper. '"A delicious milkless, eggless, and butterless cake." I thought French cuisine was supposed to be impressive.' He laughed lightly at the soldier, who was allowed a brief chuckle but otherwise did not move.

'It is hard to cook our impressive cuisine when we have no food to cook with.' The words escaped Lucien before he could bite back his tongue. He sucked in a small breath as if it would reverse his outburst.

Brandt glared at Lucien, all signs of casual friendliness erased. But after a beat his face softened again. He gave the flyer back and clapped Lucien on the shoulder. He either didn't notice the man recoil at his touch or simply ignored it.

'The rationing has taken its toll on all of us. But I promise, when the Führer liberates this country there will be meat and cheese and cake, and plenty of it to share and feast.'

'Of course, Captain,' Lucien said, staring at the Nazi's boots.

'Anyway, I have a job for you.' He snapped his fingers, and one of the soldiers produced a piece of paper and handed it to Lucien. 'Have four hundred of these printed and delivered by tomorrow and I might be able to slip you and your sister a potato or two into your rations.'

'Yes, Captain. Thank you, Captain.'

'Wonderful. I must be off now. Good evening, Lucien.' Brandt turned and headed down the street, the two soldiers following closely behind.

'Uhh, Captain! You were going to lend me some paper?'

'You appear to fully stocked already,' Brandt called out, barely turning around.

Lucien let out a sigh. 'Of course.'

He lifted the German notice and read it with tired eyes, shaking his head. It offered a reward for information of, or the capture of local resistance fighters.

Of course.

*** 

'Oh please, Sir. You simply must let me through. It's my Papa, it's nearly his birthday and Mother fears he doesn't have long for this world what with the war and all, and I simply must see him. I don't think I could I forgive myself if he passed without me telling him just how much I love him.'

The German soldier cleared his throat and nodded for a few seconds, mentally translating the seemingly never ending string of French inside his own head, while trying not to think about how pretty the French girl before him was, with her brown curls and button nose and quaint little bicycle.

He coughed and said in very poor French, 'I understand. We are checking your papers. Please be patient.' He motioned to his fellow soldier, who examined the young woman's documents slowly and thoroughly.

'Oh thank you so much for understanding. I can't imagine how difficult it must be, keeping the peace with everything going on, but I know that you try your best, and it can't be easy protecting us from the horrible English.'

The soldier coughed again, and glanced at his partner who only seemed to be catching every other word of the girl's outbursts. Finally the partner held up the papers and said something in German. The soldier nodded, took the documents and handed them back to the girl.

'Everything is in order. You may proceed.'

She clutched the papers to her chest as if they were a treasured memory. 'You have no idea how happy you have made me!' Before the soldier could react, she leant forward and pecked a kiss on his cheek.

He stood rigid and cleared his throat while his cheeks turned beet red. His partner raised an eyebrow and muffled a snigger.

The girl pulled two apples from the bicycle's front basket and handed one each to the soldiers. 'Here. A gift for you kindness. But I must leave you now. Au revoir!' She mounted the bicycle and peddled away, brown hair painted gold in the afternoon sun, waving and smiling at the Germans.

They watched the pretty lady for a few seconds, then one turned to the other and held up his apple.

'Where did she get these from?' he asked in German.

His partner shrugged. 'Who cares? It's a free apple. Enjoy it while you can, it might be ages before you get your hands on another one.' He bit into the fruit and munched on it.

The first soldier looked from the apple to the disappearing girl, then shined the fruit on the front of his uniform, and took a bite.

The woman on the bicycle flew down the path with the dirt road bumping along swiftly below her. Her smile had vanished and her face had darkened. After a quick glance behind her to ensure she was well out of earshot, she spat on the ground as if expelling a bitter flavour.

'*Putain Nazis!*'

***

Harry lay in his tiny, jumbled together cot, staring up at the ceiling. Or rather, the underside of the floorboards. His tail slowly wriggled around beneath him to the beat of his own thoughts. He'd hardly had the chance to leave the tiny, secret room in the time that he'd been here. How could he? He certainly couldn't just walk around the town and try to blend in, no matter how good his French was. He was a rat, which was odd enough for this world, but all rats were British. Specifically engineered by English scientists for the war effort. He may as well have been a walking Union Jack.

He sighed and reached up to scratch his ear. He was generally quite comfortable with small, enclosed spaces. Most rats were; it suited their nature. But being cooped up in this hidey-hole was starting to become unbearable. He wanted to go out, and enjoy a drink, some music, and the company of someone that wasn't just a disembodied voice on the radio.

He wanted to go home.

Harry turned over onto his side and stared at the radio. He listened to its silence.

He would tell Damiane tonight. It was time for him to return to England. They'd successfully smuggled several British pilots across the border to Switzerland. One more lost soul shouldn't be a problem for Damiane. Harry just hoped she would understand.

He suddenly smelled someone enter the bakery upstairs. The smell easily cut through the scent of stale flour. He only knew of one man who could smell this nervous.

'Lucien!'

Harry sat bolt upright when he heard Damiane scream her brother's name. He didn't want to eavesdrop, but his keen hearing made it practically impossible not to.

'You were supposed to print out the newsletter last night!' Harry could practically smell poor Lucien shrink away from his sister. 'What the hell is this?'

'I'm sorry. It's Brandt, he ordered me to print out those notices.'

'Oh? You take orders from Nazis now?'

'He would have arrested me if I had refused. What would you have had me do?'

Harry heard the stomping of boots above him.

'You should have told him to stuff this piece of paper right up his-'

Harry suddenly popped his head up through the bakery's trap door, drawing the attention of both siblings. 'I couldn't help but overhear your little family spat,' he said, interrupting Damiane's ranting. 'And frankly, if you're not careful, then the entire town will hear it as well.'

Damiane glared from Harry to Lucien, but then took a deep breath. 'Lucien. Why did you deliver Nazi propaganda instead of the newsletter?' She spoke calmly, but the steel in her eyes remained.

'I told you. That damn Nazi, Brandt. You honestly expected me to throw it back in his face? I would have been shot.'

Seeing the fire return to Damiane's face, Harry crawled up from the hatch and stood between them. 'Let's all just calm down a bit. What's done is done. It doesn't sound like Lucien had a lot of options, to be honest.' It wasn't easy, trying to act as a mediator when you were a good foot shorter than everyone else. 'What exactly is this notice you were forced to print?' asked Harry. Damiane handed the rat the flyer, who quickly scanned it. 'Well this isn't so bad. I quite like artichoke stew.'

'It's on the other side, Harry,' Damiane muttered.

Harry flipped over the paper. 'Oh my God!' He almost flinched away from the offending words. He read from it aloud. '"Any households harbouring resistance terrorists will be shot. Any persons colluding with resistance terrorists will be shot..."' he quoted just a few choice sections of the flyer. '"Anyone who can offer information on any resistance activity will be greatly rewarded." Blimey, Lucien, I don't blame you. If an armed Kraut had handed me this and told me to jump, I bloody well would have fallen in line as well.'

Damiane let out a noise of disgust.

'Oh, cut him some slack. We can't resist if we're all dead.'

'Please, Damiane. I have Brandt breathing down my neck every other day, sending soldiers to my press to print this order and that order... What if they find one of our flyers? Mine is the only press for miles, he'll know it was me!' A moment of silence followed. 'We've lost nearly everything in this war. Everyone. I can't lose you as well.'

Damiane paused, the hardness gone from her eyes. She opened her mouth to say something, but instead there came a knock at the door. The siblings both turned to look. Harry was back down his trap door as quick as a flash and Lucien covered it with a moth eaten rug. Damiane opened the bakery door just a crack, making the bell above it jingle. A young woman with a bicycle stood at the threshold, framed in a halo of light from the setting sun. She smiled at Damiane, apparently waiting for something.

'We're closed,' Damiane said simply and started to close the door. But the young woman's hand shot out and caught it.

'But I need to get my passport stamped in blue,' she said, low but clear.

When Damiane heard the familiar phrase, she let the door creak open again. 'Then I shall stamp it twice with green ink,' Damiane replied, completing the code. 'Come in, quickly.' When the young woman was inside, Damiane quickly scanned the street but saw no one. The door closed and locked with a click.

'You must be Damiane Larousse,' said the young woman, removing her coat and tossing it over the seat of her bicycle which she leant against the wall. 'It's an honour to meet you. What you've managed to do for the people here is extraordinary.'

'I just do what I must.' Damiane waved away the compliment. 'But you must be "The Cat?" They wouldn't tell us your real name.'

She chuckled. 'Yes, they wanted to protect my identity over radio transmissions. My name is Marianne Rousseau. And I'm here to meet "The Mouse." It's all rather dramatic really,' she added with a smile.

'Excuse me, but I appear to be missing something,' Lucien

butted in. He turned to his sister. 'Who exactly is this woman?'

'Lucien! Don't be so damn rude.'

'No, no,' said Marianne. 'I am forgetting my manners. I'm Marianne, from the Paris resistance. You must be Lucien Larousse?' She held out her hand. Lucien didn't take it.

'How do you know my full name?' he said. The muscles in his face trembled, as if marionette strings pulled randomly at his cheeks, lips, nose, and brow.

Marianne slowly lowered her hand. 'I was briefed before coming here. I have a very important mission to complete and-'

'My God, who else knows?' Lucien dragged his fingers through his thin hair.

'There is no need to worry,' said Marianne. 'It's need-to-know information. Only a few people in Paris-'

'Paris is crawling with Nazis!' Lucien squealed.

'Lucien, pull yourself together,' Damiane ordered. But Lucien shook his head and started pacing around the bakery.

'No. No no no. I can't do this anymore. My name is out there. *Our* names are out there!' He gestured wildly to his sister. 'Brandt has me printing our own execution notices, and now we are harbouring spies?' He took a second to breathe and calm himself, then clutched his hands together, begging. 'Damiane, please. I hate the Nazis as much as you, but I want us to survive this war, not fight it. I want us to rebuild what we had so we can honour everyone we've lost.'

'Lucien,' Damiane said softly. 'If we want to survive, then we have to fight.'

Lucien started to back away, shaking his head. 'No, I can't. I just...' The words vanished from his lips, his face pulled taut in a panic. Then he turned and disappeared into the street, leaving the door wide open behind him. Damiane scanned the street but saw no one. She sighed and closed the door.

'You should go after him. He's upset, he might do something stupid,' Marianne said, crossing her arms over her chest. Her friendly smile had been replaced with a grimace.

But Damiane shook her head. 'He's not the type. He just needs some sleep. He'll be fine in the morning.'

'Very well,' said Marianne, dismissing the issue with a brush of her hand, although her frown remained. 'My mission needs to be completed as quickly as possible. The less distractions the better. I need a coded radio message sent. As I said, I've been ordered to meet someone named "The Mouse". A radio operator, I believe. They told me you could find him.'

Damiane couldn't help but chuckle. 'Yes, I know how to find him. In fact, he's probably listening right now. Aren't you Harry?'

The rug jumped up as if possessed, flung back by the opening trap door.

'"The Mouse,"' said Harry, exaggerating the French syllables to make the words seem as if they were drizzled in treacle. His thin elbows rested on the floorboards of the bakery, the rest of his body still down in the secret room, so only his head, shoulders and arms were visible. 'I like it. Very poetic. Rolls off the tongue wonderfully.'

'Marianne, meet Harry Brown.' Damiane gestured to the rat, who pulled himself out of the hole.

'Lovely to meet you, Marianne.' Harry held out a paw in greeting. Marianne did not take it. Instead she stared at it, unsmiling. Harry dropped his arm down and let out a sigh at the unfortunately familiar behaviour.

'This is a rat,' Marianne said to Damiane.

'Very observant,' Harry muttered.

'Yes, Harry is a rat. He is also an excellent radio operator,' Damiane snapped.

'How can you trust something that isn't human?'

The glare Damiane shot at Marianne was icy, aggressively so, and it left a crack in the younger woman's demeanour.

'I... I can't just trust someone sight unseen,' Marianne managed to stammer out.

'Trust? You were practically licking Damiane's boots the moment you walked through the door. But you can't trust me because why? I've got a tail and big ears?'

'I've heard the stories of you English mutant creatures,' Marianne spat out. 'Scared, crafty, sneaky. You were basically bred to be cowards.'

'We were bred to be savages. I'm quite pleased with how

we actually turned out.'

'Enough!' Damiane rounded on Marianne, a pointed finger threatening to stab the spy's chest. 'You're being a stupid girl. You would jeopardise your mission over some bizarre prejudice?'

Marianne sucked in air through her nose and breathed it out as violently as she could.

'Fine.' Her arms folded across her chest and her mouth pursed into a thin line. 'How did an English rat end up in the French countryside?' It was more of an accusation than a question, but Harry decided to play along.

'I'm a flight mechanic. Our supply plane got shot down, but me and the pilot managed to get out before anything too untoward happened. We slipped past some Nazis, then ran into some Maquis who smuggled us safely to Damiane's lovely bakery. From here my pilot headed for Switzerland. I was supposed to go with him, but the radio here was all busted so I thought I'd help out and fix it up. That was about three months ago. I've been manning the radio ever since.'

'Your French is suspiciously good for a rat.'

'You should hear my German.' He said with a bitter smile. '*Es ist fast so gut wie mein Französisch.*'

'*Dein akzent ist schrecklich,*' Marianne shot back at him, crossing her arms.

'Enough games, both of you,' said Damiane. She turned to Marianne. 'You have information you need sent?'

Marianne reached into her coat and tore at the stitching. From inside the lining she pulled several sheets of paper that she handed to Damiane. Damiane immediately handed them to Harry.

'I worked as a translator for the German command in Paris. I've been collecting secrets and information for nearly two years. Most of it I had to hoard, it was too risky to try to smuggle out. I couldn't afford to raise any suspicions. But when I saw this, I knew it was time to finally flee.'

'What is it?' Damiane asked.

'Rockets,' said Harry. He stared at the paper and swallowed. 'Very long range rockets.'

'Long enough to strike at England from the mainland. Or anywhere else they wanted. These weapons will win the

Nazis the war.'

Damiane leaned against the countertop and let out a string of profanities.

'This information is amazing. Schematics, locations, targets, timetables...' Harry's voice faltered. 'Oh my God. These launch times are only days away.'

'This is why I was ordered to find you. They couldn't risk sending it from Paris. It would be intercepted and decoded by the Germans before the Allies could prepare an airstrike. They'd just move the rockets to a new location.'

'We're close enough to the border that if the cretins holed up in the Chateau did pick up our transmission, it would take them a while to get it back to German command. Not to mention they'd have a lot of fun trying to get through one my ciphers,' Harry said, stroking his whiskers with a slender finger.

'Well then, Harry. It's time to get to work,' said Damiane.

'What, now? I mean, right now this instant?'

'Of course.'

Harry grinned and threw Damiane a quick salute. 'Yes, Ma'am!' The rat practically dived down into his hidey-hole, preparing paper and pencil before Damiane and Marianne could even climb down the ladder. By the time they were looking over his shoulder, he was already halfway done scrawling out the Nazi launch information in code.

'I'll give it to them a bit at a time, in different ciphers,' he explained, still scribbling.

Behind him, Marianne stood with her arms folded, trying to glean any other hidden information in the rat's writing. Damiane caught her staring, and gave the younger woman a glare of her own.

Harry dropped the pencil and reached for the microphone and headset, holding the latter to his round ear.

'Alright, loves. Let's save the world.' Harry hit a series of switches on the old radio. It blinked into life. The life and lights wavered. Then crackled. Then sparked. And then went out with a pathetic whine.

All three stared at the suddenly inert, not to mention crucial, radio.

'Oh bugger,' said Harry.

Orange light began to fade from the dirt path, slowly receding away from Lucien's brusque footfalls and replaced by the blue sheen of dusk.

Sweat beaded on the top of his balding head. His hands trembled, clenching into fists over and over again. His eyes stared at the ground directly in front of him.

Suddenly he stopped, for the first time since storming out of Damiane's bakery. He looked up and around him, at the trees that slowly melted into a short fence line. He recognised the back of one of the village farms and wondered how long he had been walking.

In the distance he could see the stone form of the Carrefour Château. It was half hidden by trees, but Lucien could still see the outside walls had been draped with that awful, awful flag. He spat into the dirt at the sight of it.

His thoughts turned to Damiane. She was his last living relative. Everyone else had been lost to this damn war. When would she realise that she would soon be lost as well? He tried to picture their future, a life beyond the war. But it was too hard. He just couldn't see it.

Lucien let out a muted sob.

A crinkle caught his attention. Nailed to a tree by a fence post was a piece of paper. He tugged it from the nail and stared. It was one of the notices he'd been forced to print. A reward for resistance information. His eyes filled with tears, but instead of a cry Lucien let out a snarl, and he mashed the paper into a ball.

But then he stopped. He took a breath. He opened the notice and re-read its creased message. Then his gaze drifted back up to the occupied Château.

Maybe there was a way to save them both.

\*\*\*

The radio fizzed and popped. Harry swore.

'It's no use,' he said, putting down the pliers and soldering iron. 'I can't fix this, not without proper parts.'

'Now what the hell do we do? We can't just go out and buy the parts.' Damiane rubbed her forehead with her fingers.

'We could try to get them smuggled in?' Harry offered.

'Don't be stupid, we'd have to leave town to make contact with another resistance cell. That would take days. Weeks even!' Marianne hissed. 'I have to warn the Allies about the rockets now!'

'It was just a suggestion,' Harry said, raising his paws. 'I'm trying to be helpful.'

Marianne crossed her arms. 'I'm not sure that you are, rat. Maybe you've sabotaged this radio on purpose, hmm?'

'For God's sake!' Harry shot up from his stool and stood in front of Marianne, his open paws beating against the air. 'What do I have to do to make your realise that I'm on your side?'

Marianne opened her mouth to retort, but Damiane stepped in between them.

'Shut up, both of you! We have a mission to complete. And frankly, I think the future of this country is somewhat more important than your incessant bickering!' She looked between the two youngsters, glaring at each of them in turn like a disapproving mother. Both Harry and Marianne turned their faces sheepishly away. Damiane took a breath and continued. 'Now. The priority is the information. If we can't get it out over the radio, and we can't fix the radio, then we deliver it to the Allies in person. We can get you,' she said, pointing to Marianne, 'over the border to Switzerland in just over twenty-four hours. But we will need to leave now. Gather your things, and any supplies you can find.'

Marianne nodded and climbed up out of the hidey-hole. Harry turned to Damiane, scratching behind his ear.

'Um, Damiane, I... This has been some of the best work I could have done for this whole bloody war, but...' Harry stuttered and his tail drooped. But the older woman gave him a smile and pat on the shoulder.

'I understand my friend. You've been a wonderful part of our team. But you have a home to go back to. There is no shame in that.'

Harry broke into a wide smile and his tail waved back into life. 'I guess I'd better pack.' Harry's collection of belongings was meagre, and easily fit into a small, leather knapsack. He scurried about and collected anything useful for the journey ahead, as well as several loaves of bread that he'd manage to secret away for this very occasion.

'Made with actual ingredients,' he said to Marianne with a grin, holding up the bread.

'I'm sure they are horribly stale.' Her tone was almost as dry as the bread.

*** 

Damiane pulled on a thick coat and a backpack stuffed with only the most essential of supplies. The journey for her would be quick and lean. Leaving the bakery empty for too long would most definitely arouse suspicion. And she couldn't risk leaving a message for Lucien either. He would just have to do without her for a couple of days.

'It's nearly nightfall. Are you both ready?' said Damiane. The others nodded in response. 'Excellent. When we leave the town, we'll need to head south for an hour or so to avoid any-'

A loud knock at the door silenced her. All three turned and stared. The knock came again.

'We're closed!' Damiane called out.

'We would like to have a word with you, please!' The voice had a very definite German accent. Harry's tail went as stiff as a pipe.

'I said we're closed!' Damiane barked. She motioned at the other two, who ducked behind a long empty counter. 'We have no more flour and no more bread to sell. Go away!'

The doorknob rattled and twisted.

Damiane marched towards the door and ripped it open, causing the young German soldier to jump back in alarm.

'Are you deaf?' she whispered loudly at him. But when Damiane saw the scene in the street before her she shrank back in a growing panic.

'What are you doing here?' Damiane demanded.

Inside the bakery, Harry and Marianne hid beneath the counter.

'What on earth is going on out there?' Marianne whispered. The voices that seeped through the walls from outside were muffled. Harry pressed an ear up against the chipped plaster.

'Can you hear?' she asked urgently.

Harry shushed her and concentrated. As he listened, his tail swished against the floor, growing faster and faster. Marianne eyed the squirming appendage as if it were a snake.

'It sounds like... Oh no.' He shook his head. 'You poor, scared bastard.'

'Good evening, Damiane,' Captain Brandt called out with a smile. His black coat wavered in the soft breeze. Fifteen soldiers stood around him, rifles in hand. Standing next to the Captain, wringing his hands and sweating, was Lucien.

'Lucien? What is this?' Damiane muttered.

'Your brother and I have had a most interesting conversation,' said Brandt. He waved his hand around casually, as if discussing the odd weather they'd had. 'And it seems this little resistance cell has been hiding under my nose this entire time. And! As an even better prize, I am told there is a wanted Allied spy hiding here as well.'

Damiane took a shaky step back. She fixed her wide eyes on her brother and slowly shook her head back and forth. 'Lucien. What have you done?'

'I'm sorry, Damiane! But this is the only way. If we go quietly then we'll be looked after. We can still survive this!'

'You stupid fool. This is not about us. This is about the freedom of all of France. Of the world!' She turned and marched back inside the bakery.

'Damiane, wait!'

But the heavy door slammed shut.

Brandt huffed and tilted his head towards the hunched

Frenchman. 'I knew your sister was hard-headed, but I didn't think she was a complete fool.' Then he shouted out to the building in front of him. 'Damiane! You, and whoever else you have hiding in your little bread shop, will surrender yourselves to me. You will find me most amiable if you come peacefully.'

There were several seconds of silence. Brandt frowned.

'If you refuse to cooperate, however,' he muttered, then barked an order in German. A pair of soldiers rushed forward carrying a large metal drum. They started to pour its contents against the front walls of the bakery. The stink of petrol filled the air. 'It would be a shame to damage such a beautiful, old building,' he called.

Lucien turned to Brandt. 'You promised you wouldn't hurt her!'

'I promised that I would not kill her. Otherwise I simply would have shot down the door. If she is smart then she will not be harmed. This is simply to encourage her. Now be quiet, little man.' Brandt adjusted his gloves and waited until the last of the petrol was splashed against the old bakery.

'You have until the count of five!' Brandt called out. 'If you fail to show yourself at that point, then I will burn this building to the ground. One!'

The soldiers moved away from the bakery, clear of the spilled fuel.

'Two!'

At a single nod from Brandt, one of his men lit an oil soaked torch and held it aloft and at the ready.

'Three!'

He stared at the bakery, but saw no movement inside. The only sound was the soft crackling of the torch.

'Four!'

Lucien turned again to Brandt, his sweaty hands wringing themselves in front of him. 'Please! Captain! She won't listen. Damiane never listens. Not to our Father and not even to me.'

Brandt sighed. 'Then what use are you?' The Nazi pulled his pistol from his holster and fired. The crack of the gun and the following thud echoed around the street.

'Five!'

Harry's vision, like most rats, was not as good as a human's, but he could smell Damiane's anger as easily as fire smoke. He watched her cautiously as she slid a metal bar across the door.

'Damiane, it's not his fault. He's just doing-' the rat tried to say.

'Be quiet.' Damiane didn't look at Harry. 'He's doing what he thinks is best for us. He's a fool.'

'Damn right he's a fool!' said Marianne, pointing a finger at the older woman. 'He's ruined this entire operation. You are supposed to be in charge of this... this warren, but you can't even control one scared, pathetic man!'

'Shut up!' Damiane yelled. 'Lucien has done something very stupid, but he is still my little brother and he is scared. Now give me time to think so I can get us all out of this mess.'

'Um, we may not have that much time,' said Harry, his thin snout raised into the air. 'I can smell petrol.'

'They're going to burn us out!' Marianne snarled. From outside, they could hear someone counting. And then, a gunshot. It rang through the bakery, freezing them into a momentary silence.

Harry could smell something terrible, a scent he'd become much too familiar with over the years. Even through the loud stink of the petrol he could smell burnt gunpowder and blood. He closed his eyes and shivered as he imagined the face of the body that the stench belonged to. He threw a cautious glance at Damiane. She stood dead still, eyes fixed on the floor, heat slowly rising from her.

'Damiane...' It was Marianne who spoke. She had dared a glance out of the bakery window. 'I'm so sorry.'

Damiane suddenly marched forward, wrenched opened the trap door and jumped down into Harry's hidey-hole.

'Wait! Damiane, what are you doing? We need to get out of here.' Harry scrambled after her, pausing only for the briefest of moments to sniff the air. 'They've lit the fires. We need to get out, now!'

'You will escape through the back window and into the alley. Stay in the shadows. Reach the tree line.' She picked up a small crowbar and jammed it between some wooden floorboards. 'Head south for an hour, then keep going east until you get to Switzerland. Don't get caught.' As she spoke, Damiane yanked away the wood slats, and pulled a metal box out of the hole.

'What? No! I don't know how to get to Switzerland. I'm a rat. I can't just go flouncing around the French countryside. How am I supposed to protect Marianne?' Harry watched her open the box. Inside was a pistol, a machine gun, an armful of ammunition, and three German stick grenades. He stared open mouthed at the secret stash, before finally saying, 'And what the bloody hell do you think you're going to do with all that?'

'I'm going to avenge my brother, and kill as many of those Nazi bastards as I can.' Damiane hauled the box up, straining with its weight, but years of hauling sacks of flour and grain had taught her body strength and endurance. She tossed it up onto the bakery floor with a grunt then climbed up after it.

Harry, yet again, scrambled after the dangerously focused woman. Smoke billowed in under the door and through gaps in the windows.

Marianne looked ready to punch someone. She marched up to Damiane, fists balled up tightly. 'We are all going to burn alive if we don't do something!' She wasn't wrong. They could all feel the heat, hear the cracking of the fire outside.

'You will get out while I draw their fire,' Damiane said, loading the machine gun.

'Damiane, you can't,' said Harry.

'I can.'

'No. You can't. Because you need to get Marianne across the border.'

'You will do just fine, Harry,' Damiane said, sternly.

Harry snatched the gun out of Damiane's hands and slammed it against the table. He looked her straight in the eye. 'What is the mission priority?'

Damiane said nothing, just stared back at the rat.

'I said, what is the mission priority?'

Damiane looked away. 'The information,' she said softly.

'Which means that Marianne's safety across the border must be guaranteed. And you know the way better than anyone. You know how to keep her safe.' Harry gently took her hand in his paws. 'There will be time to mourn Lucien later. But right now, this is not about us. This is about the freedom of all of France. Of the world.'

Hearing her own words echoed back, Damiane couldn't help but flinch.

'Damn you, Harry. You crafty rat. So be it. We go together.' Damiane slung the machine gun over her shoulder, and stuffed the grenades into her belt.

Marianne picked up the pistol and ran to the back window, and muttered 'finally,' to herself. She smashed the glass with the gun just as the front door of the old bakery went up in flames and began to splinter. Quickly pushing out all of the broken shards, Marianne climbed out with relative ease. Damiane needed a little assistance to climb through, and then Harry slipped out after her.

The alley surrounding them was dark and filled with smoke. Harry had to cover his nose with his paw. Sweat dripped from the humans' noses, and they could all hear the flames roar behind them as it spread through the building.

Marianne snuck forward, leading the others, but then stopped, placed a finger to her lips and pointed forward. Two German soldiers stood just outside of the alley's exit.

'Probably more beyond them,' she whispered.

Damiane tightened her grip around the machine gun and opened her mouth to say something, but Harry jumped in before she could make a sound.

'I'll distract them. I'm faster than most humans, I can draw them away from here.'

Damiane gave him a pained look. 'Harry, no, you have to get home. Let me go.'

But Harry just chuckled and shook his head. 'Brains will win this war.' He pointed at both humans. 'Brains and bravery. I don't have a lot of either. Natural cowards, us rats.' He winked at Marianne whose eyes darted away.

Damiane nodded and clasped him by the shoulder. 'Thank you, my friend. And good luck.'

'Stay safe, both of you.' Harry started to move past them, then turned back to Damiane. 'Um, I'm going to need that,' he said pointing at the machine gun, then the grenades. 'And those.'

With the grenades tucked into his trousers and the gun slung around his thin shoulders, he turned again towards the exit of the alley.

'Wait,' Marianne said suddenly. There was a softness in her eyes that Harry had not seen before. It lasted only a moment before her steel returned. She gave him a terse nod and said, 'Don't let us down.'

'Tally-ho,' he whispered, and then lobbed a grenade out of the alley.

A moment of surprised curiosity passed over the Nazis' faces, followed immediately by a moment of panicked fear as they dived away. Their shouts and screams were drowned out by the explosion. When the dust cleared a few seconds later, Harry sprinted forward and leapt over a body. He spied two more soldiers standing fifty feet away, staring in shock at their fallen comrades.

'Come and get me, you sausage-sucking muppets!' Harry screamed out in English. He fired the machine gun, blasting up the cobbled street at the Nazi's feet in a quick burst. Then he turned and ran, cursing himself for his terrible aim. Behind him, he could hear the two Nazis shout and the pelting of their boots. Well, they certainly sounded distracted. He desperately wanted to turn and make sure that Marianne and Damiane had escaped from the alley, but doing that would be a very stupid move, for all of them. So instead he kept running, around the short row of buildings that sat next to the bakery, over a small wall, and onto the main street. He skidded to halt as the terrible scene opened up before him. The bakery was an inferno. Standing smugly outside, the light of the flames flickering against his face, was a Nazi captain and his fifteen soldiers. In a crumpled heap was the unmistakable form of Lucien, a small puddle of blood outlining his still head.

Harry only had a few seconds to take it all in, when bullets started whizzing past his head. The two Nazis had caught up with him, shouting warnings and alerts in their native tongue. He dived behind a fruit truck and returned fire. Bullets tore through the two pursuing soldiers' uniforms in a spray of red.

'What in God's name is that?' someone screamed in German. With shaking paws, and smoke curling from the barrel of his gun, Harry turned to see Captain Brandt pointing at him with an open mouth of disgust. 'An English mutant! Kill it! Now!'

Harry let out a squeak as fifteen gun barrels were suddenly pointed in his direction. Faster than any man could, he yanked a grenade from his belt, pulled hard on the string and tossed it into the squad of Nazis. He didn't stick around to see what happened. Harry dashed from behind the fruit truck and pelted full speed up the street. Among the shouts came an explosion, followed by screams. After that, more gunshots. He fired the machine gun blindly behind him, but after a few seconds it let out only a series of sharp clicks.

Harry hunkered down as he ran and started to zig-zag around the street. There was a hollow thump, and a searing, burning pain in his leg. He pitched forward onto the cobblestones, and a chill ran up his spine as his leg started to go numb. Harry let out a cry and felt hot blood rush over him. It felt as though his bone has exploded within his own flesh. But the rat gritted his teeth and pushed himself up, managing to hobble forward despite the excruciating pain. The empty machine gun suddenly felt as though it had doubled in weight, so he threw it aside.

Harry managed a few more paces, but another searing hole blasted through his left side. He let out a scream and toppled over, tail thrashing in pain. Harry lay motionless on the ground, sucking in as much air as his could, his body too heavy to move. He felt paralysed.

A black, leather boot dug under his shoulder and flipped Harry onto his back. He stared up into the scowling face of Captain Brandt. Several soldiers surrounded them, training their sights on the rat.

Brandt examined Harry like a stinking, dissected animal. 'So this is what the British created? What a foul creature.'

'We are better humans than you will ever be,' Harry spat out in German. His teeth were stained red with his own blood.

Brandt looked almost offended at being spoken to by the rat. 'You will die like the beast you are.' He pulled out his pistol and pointed it at Harry's head. But he paused when the rat started to chuckle. It was a wet, guttural noise.

'We will both die like beasts.' Harry pulled his tail from underneath him. It was curled around his final grenade. The string hung limp from the end of the stick.

Brandt gasped and recoiled.

The grenade exploded.

***

The breath of the two women spread out in front of them like fog, before quickly dissipating. Damiane stopped and turned, leaning against a tree. Marianne joined her. The woods around them were dark and thick, but they could easily see the orange glow that burned like a beacon behind them. It nearly lit up the entire town, but the glow was not as powerful as it had been minutes before. The fire had consumed the building and was burning itself out. Soon, it would crumble into ash and embers.

A chill rushed through her. She had nowhere to go now. Her family and home were gone. Destroyed.

Marianne seemed to notice her gaze. The younger woman placed a gentle had on Damiane's shoulder.

'Are you okay?'

Damiane nodded at Marianne.

'Do you think Harry got away?'

'I can only hope. He was a good man,' said Damiane, her voice wavering. She had lost more than just one good man tonight. A sob fought to get past her throat.

'Damiane,' Marianne whispered gently.

Damiane turned and saw in Marianne a face full of fear and concern. But in her eyes, she saw strength and a fire that burned brighter than any old bakery could.

'I will be fine. I just... I just need something to fight.' Damiane started trudging her way through the woods once more, with Marianne following behind. She would rest later, when the fight was won. And only when the fight was won.

# BIOGRAPHIES

Politiets Efterretningstjeneste
International Cooperation Dept.
   Subject: Biographical Information
   Please find included, as requested, all information regarding one Dan Leinir Turthra Jensen as can be disclosed under current cooperation agreements.
   Name: **Dan Leinir Turthra Jensen**, commonly known as Leinir (lay-neer)
   Born: ████████ June, 1980
   Gender: ████████
   Citizenship: Denmark
   Last known residence: ████████, England
   Spouse: English citizen by the name ████████, partnership ceremony conducted at the furry convention ████████ in May 2012
   Occupation: Software Developer with the free software company ████████, previously with ████████, working primarily within the KDE free software community.
   Known hobbies: Writing, cooking, costuming, the furry subculture
   General:
   We recommend particular attention is paid to the involvement of this person in the overlap between the furry subculture and writing communities. It is the understanding of the service that certain speculative science elements can be found within the writing, some of which is commonly known as "science fiction", while other parts under the genre of "social realism" is to be considered similarly subversive. Should investigation be conducted in such a nature that direct involvement with the person is undertaken, then it should be emphasised that the aforementioned hobby of cooking should be considered generally non-lethal to infiltrators and even occasionally and potentially pleasant.
   Warning:
   The involvement in socialising, costumed or otherwise,

within the furry subculture should be considered less innocuous than other such situations. Direct contact with this element should be considered a potential contaminant to any investigator. Experience has shown that upon contact, agents might find themselves involved in such nonconformist activities as dancing, hugging and otherwise socialising. Going native is a distinct risk, and contact should be made under extreme caution.

**C. A. Yates** – the fiendishly veiled pseudonym of Chloë Yates – graduated top in her class at the Howard Marks Menagerie of Abstract Espionage in 1947. Specialising in infiltrating Post-Nazi Scientific Research laboratories she, as part of an initiative now considered legend, headed the team responsible for the successful liberation of the Bubaline Obstinacy from the clutches of the infamous madman Professor Venedictos Von Holinshed in 1967. Unable to prevent the mad scientist's escape, however, Yates felt compelled to finish the job and, alas, her determination turned into a lifelong obsession. Driven mad by her failure, although some say Von Holinshed's disappearance during the Intergalactic Scourge of the Sororal League in the 1980s – disguised as a series of Jeff Goldblum movies to protect the innocent – should have been the end of it, Yates's career culminated catastrophically in the total decimation of the vegetarian frozen food compartment of a Lidl in Crewe. Witnesses reported seeing a white haired woman screaming "AND YOUR LITTLE DOG TOO, YOU WEASEL BASTARD" at the Brussels sprouts while trying to fit as many vegan Magnums down her pants as she could.

Yates now lives in the Swiss Alps, a patient at the überpleasant, maximum-security psychiatric facility known as Die Boobie-Luke. She spends her days crocheting effigies of Von Holinshed and singing to the moon.

You can find her online at her website www.chloeyates.com and wandering vaguely through twitter as @shloobee

**Madison Keller** is the author of the epic fantasy Flower's Fang series of young adult fantasy novels, the humorous fantasy Dragonsbane Saganovella series, as well as numerous short stories. Madison originally hails from the great state of Utah, but for the last eight years they have made the Pacific Northwest their home. When not writing Madison enjoys bicycle riding, sewing, and playing Dungeons and Dragons with their pals. They live in Oregon with their partner and their pack of adorable Chihuahua mixes.

Goodreads - https://www.goodreads.com/author/show/8095301.Madison_Keller

Twitter - @maddiekellerr

Website – http://flowersfang.com


**K.C. Shaw** is a fantasy writer who lives in East Tennessee. She also produces and hosts Strange Animals Podcast. Her latest novel, Skytown, is available from Fox Spirit Books.


Alias: **Miles Reaver**

Status: Clean

Last Known Location: Norfolk, UK

Case History: First published work in Dogs of War 2: Aftermath, operation title: 'Going Home'.

Published works to follow are; 'Black As Midnight, Red As Blood', 'Stud Club' and 'Blue' appearing in THP's Breeds anthologies.

His upcoming story 'Red Skies' is soon to be published in THP's Purrgatorio anthology.

Background information: Immense coffee lover, often quoted as saying 'No such thing as a too strong cup of coffee'.

Although Miles considers himself a Noir writer, he has been seen dabbing into the horror genre as of late and has plans to do so in the future. His most active period is during the cover of night. In his spare time he enjoys reading Detective novels, drinking coffee and rewatching his favorite crime series.

Contact can be established on his twitter feed at
@MilesReaver

**Jan Siegel** was twenty-four when pulled out of the slush
pile at Faber for the prestigious Introduction series. Faber
wanted her to be a 'literary' writer but she was keen to write
popular fiction and has published in several genres, under
several different names, with several major publishers (eg
Hamish Hamilton, Viking Penguin, Little Brown, Century
Arrow, Harper Collins). She prefers SF and fantasy realism
and has won/been nominated for awards and received wide
critical acclaim in all genres. Her fantasy is often bracketed
with Philip Pullman and J. K. Rowling and her SF has been
compared to Stanislaw Lem. As Jemma Harvey, her excur-
sions into romcom (more com than rom) led her to be picked
by Heat magazine for their Top Ten Summer Reads. She also
writes poetry, usually incorporated into her novels, and is
currently involved in a major project to promote great poets.

**Will Macmillan Jones** is a poet, novelist and oral storyteller
who lives in Wales, a lovely green verdant land with a rich
cultural heritage. He does his best to support this heritage
by drinking the local beer and shouting loud encouragement
whenever International Rugby is on the TV. When not writing, he is usually lost with the help of a satnav on top of a
large hill in the middle of nowhere looking for dragons. He
hasn't found one yet, but insists that it is only a matter of
time.

He writes Dark Fantasy, fantasy he fantasises is funny,
Space Opera and books for children. Some of his pieces have
won awards but he doesn't like to talk about that as it draws
attention to the fact that other pieces haven't.

www.willmacmillanjones.com

**Amanda McLachlan** lives on a wind-blasted hill in Somerset.
From spring to autumn she cares for orphaned wild animals,

and in winter she hibernates.

If you take the first letter of every word on the seventh line of all of the prime numbered pages in **Neil Williamson**'s short story collection, Secret Language, and parse them through a Rubinoff one-time cypher, you will be rewarded with a bonus story that hints at Neil's secret identity. Or you can believe Neil's cover story as a renowned testudinologist, massive spy fiction nerd and veteran of the brutal Siberian training school known as the Glasgow SF Writers' Circle.

**Kyell Gold** is the public alias of a covert operative fox who has been studying the human world for many years. He has passed the time in between reports back to The Den by writing stories and has won Ursa Major Awards, Rainbow Awards, Coyotl Awards, and Leo Awards for his fiction. To better study furry writers, he helped start RAWR, the first residential workshop for furry writing, and has taught there for three years. You can find more about his declassified work at http://www.kyellgold.comor follow his public identity on Twitter at @Kyellgold. Other fox operatives: you know how to reach him

Special Agent **Frances Pauli**/Code name Mamma Bear.

Responsible for forty seven successful missions with only three known casualties:  her sanity, her thyroid, and her waistline.  Frances works undercover as a frazzled, middle-aged housewife with a pension for crochet and furry animals. Her favorite weapons are: Stealth Science Fiction, Free-fall Fantasy, and a Non-lethal dose of Romance.

Last recorded insertion point: http://francespauli.com

SHRIKE DOSSIER - TOP SECRET - EYES ONLY
CODE NAME: **Huskyteer**.
LOCATION: Based in London, UK. Frequently sent on

missions within Europe.

CASE HISTORY: Became an active agent in 2012, disseminating short stories and even poetry through known furry publishers including Sofawolf Press and FurPlanet Productions. Has been awarded two Ursa Majors and two Cóyotls for her fieldcraft.

HOBBIES: Motorcycling, karate, saving the world.

DISTINGUISHING MARKS: Glasses, terrible jokes, looks good in hats.

FAVOURITE FICTIONAL SPY: Maxwell Smart, Agent 86 for Control.

REMARKS: Weird and extremely dangerous. Do not approach unless equipped with gin, biscuits, a tiny adorable dog and/or a really good pun.


Spies thrive on lies and deceit, and writers are no different. Most of us lead double lives, especially furries, who must lead two lives as fursona and human. **H.J Pang** has been writing (and spying) since he studied in Polytechnic, working on novels long before he realized short stories were a thing. He believes short stories are no less important than novels, and gives readers a good glimpse into the life of its characters. A life they would rather keep in the shadows.

Despite the immense heat and random climatic changes, H.J still resides in Singapore, where he finds inspiration in real and fictitious situations. He hopes no one is spying on his private and online life, but that is really too much to hope for.

He can be prodded at https://twitter.com/hjpang3


**K.R. Green** writes stories about sorcery, dragons, falconry, and resilience. She lives with her husband and two cats in Hampshire, drinking herbal tea, reading, and gazing up at the stars. With a background in mental health and degrees in Psychology & Neuroscience, her creative ideas are built on the foundation of human nature, even if they show up as a talking fox.

When she isn't painting pictures with words, she supports families for the local council by day, and mentors curious creatives to follow their inner fire by night, without the self-doubt, anxiety and exhaustion. You can find her writing blog at www.krgreen.co.uk and connect on Instagram at @MapYourPotential.


**Tom Mullins** was born in England in 1988, brought up in Australia, and has the inconsistent accent to prove it. He is a librarian at a Queensland university where he assists law students with referencing software and improving research skills, yet he still struggles with PowerPoint. Tom lives with his amazing partner in Brisbane, Australia, a city with summers so humid you could swim through them. When not working or writing, Tom loves playing Dungeons and Dragons, board games and video games, and has recently developed a love for classic and cult movies that he's never seen before. His archnemesis is.

**Thank you for buying this Fox Spirit Book. We hope you enjoyed it.**

Fox Spirit believes that day to day life lacks a few things. We need the fantastic, the magical, the mischievous and even a touch of the horrific to stave off the banal and humdrum. Let the skulk bring you stories full of wonder and mischief delivered with a sharp bite.
Join the Skulk at foxspirit.co.uk

Lightning Source UK Ltd.
Milton Keynes UK
UKHW010701010219
336544UK00010BB/608/P